"YOUR F

DETECTIVE BEAUMONT."

That stopped me cold. "Dead?" I repeated. "How? Drowned?"

Deputy Mike Hanson shook his head. "Nope."

"What, then?" I demanded, feeling a clammy sinking in my gut. "You can tell me. I'm a homicide cop."

"Not here you're not," Hanson replied decisively. He didn't add that here in this god-forsaken corner of Nowhere, Arizona, I was just another one of the suspects.

"Deputy Hanson," I said quietly, "you should probably know that my departmental issue .38 is locked in the glove-box of my car."

The startled look on Deputy Hanson's face confirmed my worst suspicions. Joey Rothman hadn't drowned. Somebody had plugged him. And I knew with dead certainty that the murder weapon had to be my very own Smith and Wesson.

J.A. JANCE

MINOR IN POSSESSION

A J.P. BEAUMONT MYSTERY

AVON BOOKS  NEW YORK

This is a work of fiction. Names, characters, places, and incidents either are the product of the author's imagination or are used fictitiously. Any resemblance to actual events, locales, organizations, or persons, living or dead, is entirely coincidental and beyond the intent of either the author or the publisher.

AVON BOOKS, INC.
1350 Avenue of the Americas
New York, New York 10019

Copyright © 1990 by J.A. Jance
Inside cover author photo by Jerry Bauer
Published by arrangement with the author
Visit our website at http://www.AvonBooks.com
Library of Congress Catalog Card Number: 89-91871
ISBN: 0-380-75546-7

First Avon Books Printing: April 1990

AVON TRADEMARK REG. U.S. PAT. OFF. AND IN OTHER COUNTRIES, MARCA REGISTRADA, HECHO EN U.S.A.

Printed in the U.S.A.

WCD 20 19 18 17 16 15 14

To Dick and Cynthia,
with whom we share
far more than an anniversary
and
To St. Thomas,
who brought the words home to us

MINOR IN POSSESSION

CHAPTER
1

It was ten to eleven, almost time for lights-out. Mad as hell and far too wound up to sleep, I lay in the October chilled darkness of my authentically rustic cabin listening to a new squall of rain drum a wild tattoo on the noisy tin roof. Sunny Arizona my ass!

Sunny Arizona. That's what my attorney, Ralph Ames, had told me when he was extolling the virtues of Ironwood Ranch, a posh drug and alcohol rehab establishment that had risen from the ashes of a failed dude ranch outside a small, godforsaken town called Wickenburg in the wilds of central Arizona.

I, Detective J. P. Beaumont, a Washington boy born and bred, had never set foot in the state of Arizona until the day I came to Ironwood Ranch. Driving north from Phoenix's urban sprawl in my rented Grand AM and passing through a forest of grotesque three-and five-armed cactus, I felt like the Alaska Airlines MD-80 had taken a wrong turn and dumped me on some alien planet. I was overwhelmed as much by the empty desolation of the desert as by my reason for being there. And that was *before* I got a look at Ironwood Ranch itself, before it had rained for three solid days and nights, and before I had met my roommate—Joseph (Joey) Rothman. The little shit.

I was lying there on the bed, leaning against my lumpy wagon-wheel-motif headboard, and waiting for Joey to come home for the night so I could pin his ears to the back of his head. My whole body ached to get with the program.

Roommate selection in rehab places is pretty much like that in jails or families—you're stuck with whatever you get for the duration. The luck of the draw had deposited me in a drafty cabin along with an arrogant nineteen-year-old punk whose attorney had plea-bargained a drunk-driving offense down to a minor-in-possession charge. According to the plea agreement, Rothman's MIP would be worked off by a six-week stay at Ironwood Ranch with the entire hefty fee payable by the carrier of Joey's daddy's health insurance.

I didn't know any of that in the beginning. What I will say is that our introductory conversation didn't exactly get us off to a flying start. Fresh out of the detox wing and still relatively shaky, I was busy unpacking my lone suitcase and trying to settle in when a young man bounded into the cabin, shedding a wet bathing suit as he went and leaving it in a puddle in the middle of the worn hardwood floor. (Ironwood Ranch's pool, stables, tennis courts, and shuffleboard courts are all holdovers from the old golden days of dude ranching, while the five-man hot tub is an upscale concession calculated to keep the place current with prevailing social practices.)

"I'm your roommate, Joseph Rothman," he announced casually. "Joey for short." He stood in the middle of the room, pulling on first a pair of boxer shorts and then a heavy terry-cloth robe. "You must be the cop," he added, disappearing into the bathroom.

His parting remark left me with a sudden lurch in my gut regarding Ironwood Ranch's ongoing commitment to patient confidentiality.

"That's right," I replied.

A moment later he reappeared carrying a comb—my tapered barber comb. I regarded his presuming to use my property as a fundamental breach of roommate etiquette. It also violated one of my mother's fundamental edicts about never sharing combs or brushes with anybody. When I reached out to take it from him, he blithely handed it over, feigning surprise, as though he had picked it up by accident and failed to notice that it wasn't his.

"Sorry about that," he said. "I musta left mine up in the dressing room. What's your name?"

"Beaumont," I answered. "J. P. Beaumont. People call me Beau."

Joseph Rothman was a little less than six feet tall, with the tanned good looks and sun-bleached blond hair of a well-heeled California surfer. Expansive shoulders and a muscled chest topped the narrow waist and hips of a dedicated body builder. My first impression was that he was probably in his mid-twenties. Later I was shocked to discover that he was still one month shy of his twentieth birthday.

"Where from?" he asked, settling easily onto one of the two monkishly narrow beds that stood against opposite walls. The action spared me having to ask him which bed was mine.

The frankly appraising look he turned on me was equal parts derision and curiosity, as though I were some kind of laughable old relic that had turned up on a dusty museum shelf. Nothing in either his question or his attitude inspired me to volunteer any extra information.

"Seattle," I said tersely.

The grunted one-word answer kept a lid on a growing urge to explain that I was a homicide cop who had been busting punks like him since well before he was born. Instead, I concentrated all my attention on sorting a tangle of hastily packed socks into matching pairs. Almost. I ended up with two extras, one blue and one black, that didn't match anything.

Joey Rothman leaned against the wall, still watching me and making me painfully aware of the slight but uncontrollable trembling in my hands. The detox nurse had told me the shakes might last for several more days. I held onto the edge of the drawer, hoping the involuntary quiver wasn't too noticeable.

"What are you in for, booze or drugs?" he asked.

"Booze," I answered carefully. "What about you?"

Joey Rothman gave me an insolent, half-assed grin—a braggart's grin. "Me," he said. "Man, I do it all."

Right that minute, I could cheerfully have murdered Ralph Ames for convincing me to check into Ironwood Ranch in the first place. He was the one who had forced me to take my doctor's diagnosis of liver damage seriously.

But at that precise moment, with Joey Rothman sitting there on the edge of his bed smirking at me, for two lousy cents I would have shit-canned the whole idea, signed myself right back out, gotten into that little rented Grand AM down in the parking lot, and driven off into the sunset. Unfortunately, I'm a stubborn man. I pride myself in never starting something unless I plan to finish it. No matter what. Including having to put up with nosy punk kids.

Slowly I closed both the drawer and the empty suitcase. With the case in hand, I turned away from the dresser expecting to meet Joey Rothman's gaze. To my relief I found that he had dismissed me and was totally absorbed in examining the flat plane of his belly, a portion of his anatomy which he regarded with obvious relish.

"Did you know they've got a weight room and hot tub out by the tennis courts?" he asked.

"So I've heard," I replied without enthusiasm.

Exercise of any kind isn't a great turn-on for me, and as far as hot tubs go, I prefer the privacy of the upholstered two-seater in the bathroom of my penthouse condominium at Belltown Terrace in Seattle.

I went to the room's single closet and boosted my empty suitcase up onto the unoccupied half of the top shelf. Shoving my quivering hands deep in my pockets, I returned to my own single-level bunk bed and perched on the edge of the thin mattress with its squeaky layer of springs.

"What do you do?" I asked.

"As little as possible, and that's the truth." He gave a short laugh. "It's not bad," he added.

"What's not bad?"

"This place. Food's pretty good, considering, and the trim you can get around here is awesome."

"Trim?" I asked stupidly, thinking he must be talking about either weight lifting or haircuts.

"You know, dude, women. I mean, there's so much free stuff floating around here loose that they ought to rename the place Mustang Ranch II. You do know about Mustang Ranch, don't you?"

Of course I knew about Mustang Ranch. Who the hell didn't? No heterosexual male over the age of puberty hasn't heard about Nevada's most infamous brothel, but I resented Rothman's youthful condescension and I bridled at the thought of being demoted back into the ranks of high school locker room sexploit bullshit. We weren't dealing with a generation gap here. This was a genuine, full-blown generation void.

"I understand they charge," I responded dryly, but my sarcasm flew right over Joey Rothman's head.

"Like I said," he continued, "it's awesome. All you have to do is be up for it, if you know what I mean."

He grinned again, and gave me a sly man-to-man wink. And that was the second time that afternoon that I wanted to murder Ralph Ames.

That opening conversation had taken place three and a half weeks earlier. I had spent one frustrating session with Louise Crenshaw, Ironwood Ranch's no-nonsense Director of Client Affairs, pleading with her to let me move to another cabin and/or trade roommates with somebody else, but she had been adamant.

"Absolutely not. Learning to get along with all kinds of people without chemical assistance is a very important part of your recovery," she had told me icily, and that was that. No plea bargains accepted, at least not for me.

Since then, I had gotten along with Joey Rothman mostly by avoiding him, except when absolutely necessary at mealtimes or during the required group grope sessions. I heard some rumors to the effect that he had been dealing drugs both before and during his enforced stay at Ironwood Ranch, but I didn't pay that much attention one way or the other. It was, after all, none of my business.

Joey obligingly spent very little time in our cabin. When he did happen to be there, usually before meals, he spent his time absorbed in writing in a cloth-covered notebook. I assumed he was keeping a journal, one I figured reeked with post-pubescent sexual conquests. I much preferred him confining those overblown locker room exploits to the privacy of his diary rather than discussing them with me. In the evenings he was almost always out, tiptoeing into our cabin long after lights-out each night like some randy caterwauling tomcat.

A fifteen-year-old girl named Michelle had come into treatment at about the same time I did, on the same day in fact. I had thought for a while that Joey was actually sweet on her, if someone as screwed up as he was ever got sweet on anybody, but tonight I had been forced to revise that assessment.

And that revision was precisely why I was waiting up for him. It was the middle of my fourth week of treatment, Family Week, as they call it at Ironwood Ranch. It's the one week out of six when a client's family members are invited to come stay for five days to tell what they know about the client's past behavior and to make a stab at beginning their own recovery.

My own family, such as it is—two nearly grown children and my ex-wife Karen—were all three in attendance. As a consequence, you could say that my stress levels were up. Off the charts is more like it. In the ten years since our divorce, it was the first time I had seen Karen face-to-face.

The counselors at Ironwood Ranch must be some kind of salesmen. They had somehow managed to convince her that it was not only her duty but also in her own best interests to leave her new husband at home in Cucamonga, California, attending to the accounting needs of a chicken-ranching conglomerate, and come to Arizona along with Kelly and Scott to help confront me with all my sins remembered.

Earlier that afternoon, during a stormy group session, Karen had detailed to my chemically dependent peers and their visiting family members all the relevant gory details (at least the details she felt were relevant) about how too much work and too much MacNaughton's on my part had caused her to fall in love with another man and to have to get a divorce.

I had spent a miserable two hours in what we clients—there are no patients at Ironwood Ranch, only clients—refer to as the hot-seat. I had to sit there silently, with no opportunity for reply or rebuttal, and endure an emotional bloodletting, listening to a familiar litany of holiday meals missed or ruined, of things left undone that should have been done, of people I loved who had felt neglected and cheated because I had been too busy doing and being what I thought I was supposed to do and be.

After dinner I was still licking my emotional wounds. Karen and I were sitting on a couch in front of the roaring fire in the main hall, talking quietly, and doing a relatively rational postmortem on our marriage. Our son Scott, a serious-minded sophomore at Stanford, had gone back to the motel to study, and daughter Kelly had left the dinner table saying she was going off to the rec center with some of the younger people to play a game of Ping-Pong.

Things were going fairly well until I caught a glimpse of Joey Rothman standing on the patio outside the window. He had paused there while he planted a lingering kiss on the face of whoever happened to be with him. Only when he hurried away and left her standing alone did I realize that the kissee was none other than my own daughter Kelly—my seventeen-year-old daughter Kelly.

Trim indeed!

I went outside looking for him right then, ready to tear him limb from limb in typically fatherly fashion. Naturally Joey Rothman was nowhere to be found, and naturally Kelly and I got in a big beef about the incident that escalated into Karen and me being drawn into a verbal shouting match as well. Louise Crenshaw had wandered past the melee and had given me a look of unqualified disapproval. Karen and Kelly left in a huff a few minutes later, and I went back to the cabin to smolder and wait.

Eleven o'clock came and went but still no Joey Rothman. That was all right. I was prepared to wait however long it took. Half an hour later, the rain died down. In the sudden quiet I heard approaching footsteps. They seemed to be coming down the path from the main hall. Joey's and my cabin was the last one at the very end of the path. As the footsteps came past the final pair of neighboring cabins, I was sure my time had come.

Joey's usual pattern was to sneak into the cabin barefoot, carrying his shoes like some errant husband, and to get into bed without turning on the light. Tonight I planned a slight variation on that theme. I was just sitting up and groping for the switch on the bedside lamp when the cabin door crashed open, sending the doorknob banging into the wall behind it. Before I could find the lamp's switch, the overhead chandelier with its eight-bulbed wagon wheel flashed on in my face.

"You son of a bitch," I began as I scrambled to put both feet on the floor. Halfway out of bed I stopped, looked again, and froze where I was.

The panting man standing in the open doorway with his eyes bulging and his face a mask of undiluted fury wasn't Joey Rothman at all.

CHAPTER
2

"**W**here the hell is he?" the man demanded savagely.

"Where is who?"

"Don't play games. Rothman, that's who!"

I recognized the man instantly as the father of Michelle, the mousey fifteen-year-old druggie. Because we had been admitted at approximately the same time, it was Michelle's family week as well as mine. I remembered the man from the family group sessions, an integral part of treatment, which are counselor-moderated discussions involving both clients and family members. I recalled that Guy Owens worked as some kind of honcho, a high-ranking officer, at one of the military installations in Arizona. His name surfaced, but the rest of the family details escaped me. During Group that week I had been far too engrossed in my own family's difficulties to pay much attention to anybody else's.

"Tell me where he is," Owens growled.

He must have figured I was personally concealing Joey Rothman from him. He took another

menacing step into the room. Half sitting half lying on the bed, I was in no position to defend
myself against attack if he chose to come after me
with physical force.

"He's out," I said curtly, "and if you're coming
in, do you mind shutting the door behind you?
It's cold as blue blazes."

The timely invocation of good manners has
stopped more than one unwelcome intruder in his
tracks. Guy Owens was no exception. He paused
uncertainly, glancing from me back over his
shoulder toward the open door.

"What's the matter?" I continued, pressing the
slight advantage. "Were you born in a barn?"

Without a word Guy Owens returned to the
door and slammed it shut. The action gave me just
enough time to get both feet firmly on the floor
before he swung back around and hurried over to
the open bathroom door. He went so far as to
walk inside and pull back the shower curtain.

"He's not in there, either," I said. "What are
you doing here? What do you want?"

"I want Rothman," he snapped. "And when I
find him, I'm going to tear his balls off and stuff
them down his throat."

Too bad I hadn't thought of that myself.
"Sounds like a great idea," I said cheerfully, "but
you'll have to take a number and get in line. Mind
switching off the light? It's after eleven. If the
night nurse sees it, she'll come riding down here
on her broom and kick ass."

Guy Owens frowned. "You want me to turn off

the light and sit here waiting for him in the dark?"

I shrugged. "Why not? That's what I'm doing. Two's company, right? Pull up a chair."

Without further discussion, Owens did as he was told. He grabbed the wooden chair away from Joey's narrow student-style desk and pulled it along behind him as he returned to the light switch beside the door. In a moment the room was once more plunged into murky darkness. I heard him drop onto the chair with a heavy sigh.

"What do you want him for?" I asked.

There was a long stony silence in the cabin. It lasted so long that I began to wonder if maybe I had only imagined asking the question rather than really saying it aloud. Guy Owens' answer, when it came, was little more than a strangled croak.

"She's pregnant, goddamnit! Fifteen years old and pregnant. That worthless little fucker knocked her up! I'm going to kill him."

Michelle Owens wasn't my daughter, thank God, and as far as I knew, Kelly wasn't pregnant, but I knew exactly how Guy Owens felt.

"That settles it," I said. "As soon as he shows up, you get first crack at him."

There was another pause, a little shorter this time. When he spoke again, the mildly jesting tone of my comment seemed to have defused the atmosphere enough to convince Guy Owens that we were both on the same side. He was a burdened man desperate to unload on someone, even a relative stranger. I was it. Possibly sitting there in that darkened room made it easier for him to open up.

"Misha takes after her mother," he said forlornly. "Whenever Fran got pregnant, she was always sick as a dog from the very first day. Her morning sickness lasted for a full three months all four times. I could almost set my watch by it. I should have figured it out myself when she looked so terrible all week, but I didn't.

"At lunch today one of the nurses took me aside and told me she had noticed that Misha was losing weight. She was afraid there might be some serious physical problem. The nurse set up an appointment with a G.P. in Wickenburg so I could take her there this afternoon right after Group. He called me with the results just a little while ago. 'There's nothing wrong with your daughter,' that asshole tells me. 'She's pregnant, that's all.' "

He paused, waiting for me to say something, but I couldn't think of a damn thing. I was too busy being grateful as hell that Michelle was his daughter instead of mine.

"Pregnant, that's all," he repeated bleakly. "Jesus!"

We sat there again until the silence was as thick as the darkness. Eventually, Owens heaved his ghostly figure out of the chair and stumbled to the window where he stood staring back up the path, his arrow-straight silhouette backlit by cloud-shrouded moonlight.

"Why isn't he here?" he asked plaintively.

The menace had leaked out of his voice as anger-fueled adrenaline dissipated. "I thought everybody was supposed to be back in their cabins by lights-out. That's what the damn brochure says. You know, that full color one full of happy horseshit they send out to all the families."

"That may be the official rule, but Joey Rothman doesn't much concern himself with the rules," I offered quietly. "Anybody's rules."

We were silent again until once more Owens felt compelled to speak, his voice husky with suppressed emotion. "It must have happened right after she got here. The doctor says she's about three weeks along, and she's only been here four weeks."

"I know."

I remembered all too clearly my own first two fitful nights in the detox wing. The endless nighttime hours had been haunted by the distressing sound of Michelle Owens in the room just up the hall where she whimpered endlessly into her pillow. I hadn't felt terribly sorry for her at the time. I had been too busy feeling sorry for myself. I did now.

"Your daughter and I were in the detox wing at the same time," I said.

In the darkness I saw the whitish blob that was Guy Owens' face turn from the window to face me. "That's right," he said, "you're the one who's a cop, aren't you? Misha mentioned you in one of her letters. She never talked about Rothman, though, not once."

"You're sure it was Joey?"

"After I talked to the doctor, I went to her cabin and demanded that she tell me. I just came from there."

"And what did she say?"

"What the hell do you think she said? That it was him—Rothman. She said she was sure he'd marry her. Like hell!" Owens' hard-edged outburst ended with a snort. I couldn't tell if the sound was part of a laugh or a sob, and I had the good grace not to ask.

For another several minutes we stayed as we were, him standing by the window staring out and me sitting on the edge of the bed, each lost in our own thoughts.

"What are you pissed at him about?" Owens asked finally, as though it had just then penetrated that Joey Rothman was on my shit list too.

"The same reason you are," I replied evenly. "He was nosing around my daughter after dinner tonight. I'm waiting up to let him know she's off limits."

"You mean beat hell out of him, don't you?"

"If that's what it takes. Some people learn slower than others. With some it takes remedial training."

"And Misha thinks that sorry jerk is going to marry her? For Chrissake, how dumb can she be?"

"She's how old? Fifteen? How smart were you at fifteen?"

"Smarter than that," he snapped. "You can damn well count on that."

He turned back to the window and looked out.

"Wait a minute. There's a light on in one of the other cabins."

I scrambled out of bed, hurried over to the window myself, and looked up the path. A moment later the first light went out only to be followed by the light coming on in the cabin next door.

"Oh, oh," I said. "You'd better get the hell out of here fast. Lucy Washington must be doing a bed check. It'll be bad enough if she comes in here and finds out Joey's gone. If she also finds an unauthorized visitor . . ."

Owens didn't need a second urging. He was already pushing the chair back across the room.

"I'll go," he whispered urgently, "but do me a favor. When that SOB comes in, don't tell him I was here. I want to blindside that little cocksucker."

"Believe me," I told him, "I wouldn't want to spoil your surprise."

Guy Owens left then, quickly, disappearing around the far side of the cabin away from the path. I heard him strike off up the hill, crashing blindly toward the tennis courts. I hoped Santa Lucia, Ironwood Ranch's tough-talking night nurse, was still far enough away that she wouldn't be able to hear him.

Fumbling with buttons and zipper, I stripped out of my clothes, shoved them in a wad under the bed, and slipped between my mangled covers. By the time the door opened and the overhead light was switched on, I was ready with an Emmy Award-winning performance of someone being rudely awakened out of a sound sleep.

"Okay, Mr. Beaumont. Where's Mr. Rothman?"

I've no idea how she got her nickname. That story had become lost in Ironwood Ranch's group memory. Her real name was Lucy Washington, and as near as I could tell, this huge, implacable black woman wasn't particularly saintly. She was also totally devoid of anything resembling a sense of humor.

I blinked my eyes several times, holding both hands over my face to shield my eyes from the glare. "You mean he's not here?" I asked innocently.

"You know damn good and well he's not here. Look for yourself. Does that bed look like it's been slept in? So where is he?"

"Believe me, Mrs. Washington, I have no idea. If I did, you can bet I'd be the first to tell you."

"Mr. Beaumont, I've been hearing all kinds of wild rumors about your roomie Mr. Rothman tonight, tales about him being out and around and doing things he shouldn't be doing. You wouldn't know anything about that, now would you?"

"Not a thing," I said.

Lucy Washington stared at me impassively. She didn't believe me, not for a moment, but at least she didn't call me a liar to my face.

"I see," she said finally, giving up. "I tell you what. When he shows up, you let him know he'd better drag his white ass down to the office and see me. On the double. Understand?"

"Got it," I said.

She switched off the light, turned, and stepped outside, banging the door shut behind her. I waited long enough for her to be well away from the cabin before I got up and looked out the window. I could see the wobbling beam of the flashlight as she trudged back up the hill toward the main ranch house.

"Damn," I said, under my breath.

I knew my not blowing the whistle on Joey's truancies would be yet another black mark that would go against J. P. Beaumont in the annals of Ironwood Ranch, and that my transgression, however minor, would be duly reported to Louise Crenshaw, the final arbiter of client affairs.

Louise Crenshaw had made it clear during my admission interview that since I hadn't come in as a destitute, homeless bum, I hadn't yet hit bottom in her book. As a consequence, I was nowhere near ready to get better. She missed no opportunity to throw juicy tidbits about my alleged misdeeds to the group, items she regarded as ongoing proof of my lack of serious intent as far as recovery was concerned. This incident would provide more grist for her mill, and it gave me one more bone to pick with Joey Rothman, once I managed to lay hands on him.

I stood there in my skivvies and tried to calculate my cabin's Grand-Central-Station potential for the remainder of the night. I figured chances were pretty close to one hundred percent that when Joey Rothman came to the surface, he would return home with Ironwood Ranch's version of a police escort. Without turning the light back on, I dragged my clothes out from under the bed and got dressed. Then, wrapping two blankets around me, I bundled up in the cabin's only comfortable chair and settled down to wait. I wanted him to *know* that I was waiting up for him, and I didn't think it would take long.

But that's where I was wrong. I woke up cold as hell and with a stiff neck and both feet sound asleep at four o'clock in the morning. Joey Rothman's bed was still empty. It was raining again, and the cabin was downright frigid. The heating system for each cabin consisted of an old-fashioned, wall-mounted gas heater that required a match each time it needed to be lit.

When the circulation returned to my feet, I hobbled over to my desk in the dark, still wary that turning on the light would summon Santa Lucia's immediate return. I pulled open the drawer and groped blindly inside, expecting to lay hands on one of several books of matches I had left in the front right-hand corner of the drawer. They weren't there. Throwing caution to the winds, I turned on the desk lamp.

As soon as I did, I could see that someone had hastily rummaged through the drawer. I'm not so fastidious that I know where each and every item is in a drawer, but I certainly knew the general layout, and the items in the drawer were definitely not as I'd left them. With a growing annoyance, I pulled the drawer wide open and examined it closely.

It's always tough to discover what isn't there. The things that *are* there are perfectly obvious. What's missing is a lot harder to see. It took several minutes, but finally I figured it out.

My keys. That's what was gone, the keys to the rented Grand AM. Unlike some other treatment centers I've heard about, Ironwood Ranch prides itself on the fact that people come there and stay voluntarily. Instead of daily bed checks, we had intermittent ones. At patient check-in we were allowed the privilege of keeping our keys and personal property under what Louise Crenshaw described as Ironwood Ranch's atypical honor system.

Which is fine as long as you're dealing with honorable people, which Joey Rothman obviously was not. I knew damn good and well he had taken my keys and probably the car as well. I had visions of him smashing up the rental car, turning it over in a ditch somewhere. On my nickel. With Alamo Rent A Car and American Express taking the damage out of my personal hide since Joey Rothman was anything but an authorized driver. The only way to prevent that was to get on the horn right then and report the vehicle as stolen.

Curfew or no, I pulled on my jacket and headed for the main building. Almost there, I decided to take a detour to the parking lot to see if the car might possibly have been returned in one piece. And sure enough, there it was, still in the same parking place where I had left it originally, but not in quite the same position. It was parked at an odd angle. Despite the chill, slanting rain, I walked around the car twice, examining it in the pale light of the parking lot's mercury-vapor lamps. As far as I could see, it didn't have a mark on it.

Stopping by the driver's door, I noticed it was unlocked. I opened the door and slid onto the seat. The keys with the rental company's cardboard tag still attached were in the ignition. Breathing a sigh of relief, I grabbed them and stuffed them in my pocket.

So Joey had taken the car out for a joyride, but it didn't look as though he'd done any damage. I wondered where he'd taken it. A glance at the mileage on the odometer told me nothing, because I didn't remember how many miles had been on the car when I picked it up in Phoenix.

I was about to back out of the car when I remembered the rental agreement. It would have the mileage on it. I had tossed that in the glove box along with my holster and my .38 before I ever left the airport. The Smith and Wesson is just like my gold card—I don't leave home without it, and I hadn't wanted to turn it over to someone else when I checked into Ironwood Ranch. Instead I had left it in the locked glove box of a locked car—which is fine as long as nobody else has the key.

Now, stretching full length across the seat, I dug the keys back out of my pocket and unlocked the glove compartment door. It fell open at once and the tiny light inside switched on.

I had put the gun in first and the rental agreement second, so the agreement should have been right on top. It wasn't. The gun was.

At first I didn't think that much about it. I pulled the Smith and Wesson out, intending to put it on the seat beside me long enough to retrieve the rental agreement, but as I brought it past my face, I smelled the unmistakably pungent odor of burnt gunpowder. The gun had been fired, recently. Sometime within the past few hours.

"What the hell has that goddamned fool been up to now?" I said aloud to myself. I swung out the cylinder and checked it. Two rounds had been fired.

Shaken, I put the gun back where I'd found it and relocked both the glove box and the car, then I went looking for Lucy Washington.

If Joey Rothman thought I wasn't going to report his car prowl to the proper authorities, he had another think coming.

CHAPTER
3

Louise Crenshaw wore sobriety like the full armor of Christ. Her nails ended in long sharpened talons polished to a brilliant magenta. She consistently wore the kinds of dress-for-success costumes that would have been far more appropriate for hawking securities on Wall Street than they were for riding roughshod over a herd of hapless recovering drunks. Rumor had it that she had come to Ironwood Ranch as one of the first full-time counselors, married her boss Calvin Crenshaw without much difficulty, and immediately assumed the throne.

The lady's age was difficult to determine. Her skin had that transparently fragile and stretched look that comes from having had more than one meaningful encounter with a plastic surgeon. Even the most skillful face-lift technique hadn't entirely erased the road-map ravages caused by years of hard drinking and chain smoking.

Her husband, Cal, was a pudgy dough-boy of a man whose group-session drunkalogue chronicled years of failure at everything from running

27

an auto dealership to selling computerized office products. He had finally sobered up and was wanting to help others do the same when his mother died leaving him sole owner of the aging Ironwood Ranch. Cal had decided to turn his inheritance into a treatment center. To hear him tell it, he was well on his way to screwing that up as well when Louise came along at just the right time and saved his bacon.

Cal himself seemed content to hover vaguely in the background while his front-office wife appeared to be everywhere at once—overseeing admissions, dropping in and out of group-session discussions, personally directing everything from how the laundry was run to what went on in the kitchen.

Louise was a formidable woman, particularly when crossed, but I was provoked enough myself that morning that I was actually relishing the approaching confrontation when I heard her high heels beating an angry staccato down the tiled hallway toward the office where I waited.

"How dare you!" she demanded shrilly as she strode into the office and slammed the door behind her. I may have been spoiling for a fight, but she was the one who set the tone of our meeting.

"How dare I what?" I asked, striking a deliberately provoking, nonchalant pose.

Louise Crenshaw bristled, infuriated that much more by my offhand attitude. Setting her mouth in a thin, grim line, she stepped around to the other side of a plain oak desk and sat down facing me. She was making a supreme effort to control herself, but the results weren't entirely successful. I noticed that her brightly tipped fingers closed tightly over the ends of the chair armrests even as she leaned back to regard me with a studied look of arch contempt.

"You're a bully, Mr. Beaumont, and you know it. How dare you browbeat Lucy Washington into letting you call the sheriff's department?"

The previous night's lack of sleep hadn't left me feeling particularly charitable toward anyone, most especially Louise Crenshaw. During our verbal battle over whether or not to report the car incident, Lucy Washington had invoked Louise's name over and over. According to Santa Lucia, Mrs. Crenshaw had decreed an unwritten but nonetheless inviolable rule that she and only she was to notify the authorities of any irregularities involving Ironwood Ranch and its residents. But at four-thirty that morning the Crenshaw answering machine had been the only one in the household taking phone calls.

I had finally overruled Lucy Washington's objections by simply picking up the telephone and making the forbidden call myself.

"Let me point out that my car had been stolen, Mrs. Crenshaw. Why the hell shouldn't I report it?"

"Oh, come now, Mr. Beaumont. Stolen? Aren't we being a bit melodramatic? Joyriding is more like it. After all, I understand the car is safely back in the parking lot this morning. I believe it was already there by the time you made your forcible phone call to Deputy Hanson up in Yarnell. Isn't it far more likely that Joey just borrowed it?"

My temper flared not only at her tone but also at her holier-than-thou attitude. "No, he didn't borrow it," I replied shortly, "because the word 'borrow' implies my giving permission, which I most certainly did not. He took the keys out of my desk without asking. I don't know where he went with it, but according to the rental agreement, it's been driven several hundred miles since I picked it up at the airport. I drove straight here. That couldn't be more than seventy-five miles at the outside."

She frowned. "Your family is here this week. Isn't it possible one of them used the car?"

"They came in their own cars," I replied. "And I haven't been anywhere near the Grand AM since I checked in other than to walk by it in the lot on my way to Group."

The magenta nails moved swiftly from the armrest to the desktop, where she tapped them thoughtfully.

Sitting there eyeball to eyeball with Louise Crenshaw, I somehow failed to mention the .38, and not because it slipped my mind, either. At the moment the fact that Joey Rothman had fired my Smith and Wesson worried me a whole lot more than the idea of his taking the car, but what was the point of bringing it up? I figured there'd be enough hell to pay if and when Madame Crenshaw discovered that the gun existed at all. In the meantime, what she didn't know didn't hurt her.

"Speaking of Deputy Hanson, where the hell is he?" I grumbled. "He told me he'd be here between six-thirty and seven, and it's already after seven. How far are we from Yarnell anyway?"

Louise sat up in her chair, rested her elbows on the desk, folded her hands together, leaned her chin on them, and smiled an icy smile.

"I called Mike's office this morning as soon as I learned what was going on. It seemed to me that the situation didn't merit his making a special trip."

"Are you telling me you told him not to come?" I sputtered.

Louise gave me another chilly, condescending sneer. "If you'll just allow me to finish, Mr. Beaumont. I told Mike I didn't think it was necessary for him to make a special trip down here just for this, but he said he was coming to Wickenburg anyway. In fact, he would have been here by now, but the dispatcher said there's been another incident of some kind, an emergency situation downriver a mile or so. He'll stop by here when he's finished with that."

We sat there for some time glaring at one another. Louise Crenshaw was somebody who thrived on playing power games with other people's lives. Not only playing, but playing and winning. I've no doubt she was personally effective in treating some of the patients who came through Ironwood Ranch, but for those who crossed her, for those who didn't take her word for the gospel and who fought back, she was a bitch on wheels.

Finally, conceding at last that I wasn't going to break the long silence, Louise crossed her arms. "So where is he?" she asked.

"Who, the deputy? You tell me."

"I don't mean the deputy. Where's Joey Rothman?"

"Beats hell out of me. By this time, he's probably sound asleep in his own little beddy-bye. I'm not in the habit of policing his nighttime forays."

"He's not there. Cal just went up to check." She paused and cocked her head to one side. "What do you mean 'nighttime forays'? You said before that there are several hundred unaccounted miles on your car. Are you saying he's done this before, been out past curfew and left the premises?"

"Joey Rothman is *always* out after curfew," I said, taking real pleasure in the two small blotches of color that suddenly appeared on Louise Crenshaw's pallid cheeks. "Maybe you should tell Cal to try looking in Michelle Owens' cabin," I suggested helpfully.

She sat bolt-upright in her chair then with both hands clenched around the edge of her desk. "What do you know about that?" she demanded.

I shrugged. "You know. The usual gossip—that Michelle Owens is knocked up and that Joey's the soon-to-be-daddy."

She paled at that and sat up straighter. "That's not exactly gossip. That's inside knowledge. The results of Michelle's pregnancy test weren't known until late last night. How did you find out?"

"Word gets around," I said, shrugging noncommittally.

"You're not going to tell me where you heard it?"

I didn't see any reason to drag Guy Owens into the discussion. Worrying about his daughter, he already had enough on his mind. "No," I replied, standing up. "Is that all?"

"It isn't all," Louise Crenshaw returned sharply. "Not by any stretch of the imagination. If Joey Rothman has been out of his cabin past curfew every single night, why haven't you reported it before this?"

"In case you haven't noticed, being your brother's keeper went out with Cain and Abel."

"Mr. Beaumont, Joey Rothman is here for treatment."

"So am I, lady," I pointed out. "My treatment and nobody else's. I'm not paying good money to come here and baby-sit some young punk who's walking around with his brains in his balls, someone who told me Ironwood Ranch should be renamed Mustang Ranch II, if you get my meaning, Mrs. Crenshaw."

She met my gaze with a brittle stare. "That will be all, Mr. Beaumont."

"You're damned right that's all, because I'm tired and hungry. I'm going to go have breakfast. When the deputy gets here, call me." With that, I stalked out of the office, leaving Louise Crenshaw sitting alone at her desk in isolated splendor.

As I walked toward the dining room and smelled the enticing odors coming from the kitchen, I realized just how hungry I was. Good food is a major part of Ironwood Ranch's treatment program. The idea is that addicts shove all kinds of unhealthy substances into their bodies while neglecting most other forms of nourishment. I had expected the normal tasteless institutional fare, but the cook, a short but exceedingly wide and usually smiling Mexican lady named Dolores Rojas, wasn't the normal institutional cook.

Dolores and her husband, a bowlegged cowboy named Shorty, had been at Ironwood Ranch for twenty years. Her domain was the kitchen, while he ran the stables. Her responsibility was to feed everybody, while his job was as general handyman in addition to looking after the small string of saddle horses that were still used for occasional client trail rides and outings. On the side he boarded and trained a small number of privately owned animals. Dolores and Shorty lived in a modest but immaculate trailer parked down the hill near the stable.

Breakfast wasn't actually served until eight, but I had fallen into the habit of coming down earlier than that for a jolt of Dolores' eye-opening coffee. I would stand there on the sidelines and watch her unhurried but purposeful mealtime preparations. It was through these early morning chats with Dolores Rojas that I had learned scraps of

Ironwood Ranch history that weren't necessarily part of the group treatment catechism. In addition, I had picked up some invaluable firsthand knowledge about Mexican cooking.

When I got there that morning, Dolores was busily patting white dough into paper-thin tortillas which she baked quickly on something that looked like an inverted metal disc—maybe part of an old-fashioned plough—which had been placed over one of the gas burners of the immense, old-fashioned stove. Dolores Rojas prided herself in serving only freshly made tortillas.

"What's for breakfast this morning?" I asked, taking my cup of coffee and sidling up to the serving window.

"Chorizo and eggs," she answered.

Prior to Dolores my knowledge of Mexican food had been strictly limited to what was available at a place in Seattle called Mama's Mexican Kitchen and those south-of-the-border aberrations served by various fast-food chains. Dolores dipped out a spoonful of something that resembled reddish-colored scrambled eggs, put it in one of the still-warm tortillas, wrapped it expertly into a burrito, and passed it to me.

"Sausage," she said. "Hot sausage and eggs."

The spicy, eye-watering mixture wrapped in the tortilla bore little resemblance to the sausage and eggs my mother used to make, but it was nonetheless delicious.

"Wonderful," I said, chewing.

Dolores nodded in satisfaction. "Good. Now get out of here and let me finish."

I took the hint, my coffee, and the remainder of my burrito and went over to stand by the window. The rain had let up, at least for the time being. People were beginning to venture out of their cabins and meander up to the main hall although I noticed a group of several people head off in the opposite direction.

Soon Ed Sample, an attorney from Phoenix, joined me by the window. "What's going on down there?" I asked.

"River's up," he said, sipping his own coffee. "Unusual for this time of year, but then so are the rains."

"You mean there's actually water in the river?"

When I first arrived at Wickenburg, I had crossed the bridge over the Hassayampa River on my way to Ironwood Ranch. I recalled seeing an official-looking sign that proclaimed NO FISHING FROM BRIDGE although no water had been visible in the dry, sandy bed. With the onset of the rains, however, a sluggish, muddy stream had appeared.

"Somebody said it's about eight feet deep right now."

"Eight feet?" I repeated, astonished. "Where'd it all come from?"

"Drainage from up in the mountains. As much has soaked into the ground as it can handle. The rest is runoff. From what Shorty Rojas said, it could go over the banks sometime today. By the time all the water drains out of the high country, we could have a real serious problem down here."

"Great," I said. "That's all we need."

Ed Sample looked at me appraisingly. "You ever see a flash flood in the desert, Beau?"

I shook my head.

"Every year or so we get a carload of tourists washed away. They see what they think is a few inches of water in a dip and they end up being washed downstream by a wall of water."

"You mean those DO NOT ENTER WHEN FLOODED signs are serious? They're not some kind of joke?"

"Not at all," he replied.

That gave me something to think about. Maybe the NO FISHING sign wasn't a joke either.

People were beginning to carry filled plates away from Dolores' serving line. I refilled my coffee cup, set it at an empty table near the window, and went to collect my own plate. In addition to the chorizo, eggs, and tortillas, there was also a selection of fresh fruit. Despite my earlier sampler burrito, I was still hungry. I carried my food-laden plate back to the table.

I had barely sat down when Michelle Owens edged into the chair next to me. She looked wan and sallow. Instead of a plate, she carried a cup of hot water and a fistful of saltine crackers. I've been a father, and I know the drill. Saltine crackers are the order of the day for someone suffering from morning sickness. Once more I was supremely grateful that this pale-faced young woman and all of her problems were none of my concern.

"Where's Joey?" Michelle whispered. Evidently her choosing the seat next to mine was no accident.

I glanced at her. Michelle Owens was plain, amazingly plain, hardly the type of girl to appeal to someone with Joey Rothman's flashy sense of panache. Her hair, a dismal, cheerless brown, had a slight tendency to curl at the ends, but there had been no effort made to style it attractively. Her eyes were red and swollen. She wasn't wearing any makeup, and her naturally pale complexion had a grayish tinge to it, probably as a direct result of continuing bouts of morning sickness. She still wore braces. Pregnant and still in braces. No wonder her father was pissed.

"Where is he?" she asked again, more urgently this time. "I went by the cabin to see him, but he wasn't there."

"I'm sorry, Michelle, but I can't help you," I answered kindly. "As far as I know, he never came home at all last night."

Her lower lip trembled and she ducked her head while two fat tears spilled out of the corner of her eye and dribbled down her cheek. "What if my father . . ." she began, then stopped.

"What if your father what?" I asked.

She shook her head. "Never mind. It isn't important."

Just then one of the counselors, a lame-brain named Burton Joe, brought his plate to our table.

He sat down across from Michelle and smiled at her beatifically.

"And how are we this morning?" he asked. It was the medical rather than the royal we, insinuating and saccharine. "Feeling better?"

Michelle Owens kept her eyes lowered and didn't answer. I was outraged. Surely the Ironwood Ranch rumor mill was fully operational, particularly among the counselors. There was no reason to give Burton Joe the benefit of the doubt. He knew good and well whereof he spoke.

"Leave her alone," I snapped. "She's just fine."

I looked around, vainly hoping that Guy Owens would show up and come to his daughter's rescue, but family members weren't encouraged to arrive until a few minutes before the morning counseling sessions began at nine o'clock.

"My, my, we certainly are touchy this morning, aren't we."

"Yes," I replied tersely. "We certainly are. I didn't have much sleep last night and neither did Michelle here, so why don't you bug off and leave us alone."

Burton opened his mouth to say something in return, but just then several more people joined us at our table. They had been part of the expedition that had gone down to see the river, and they were busy speculating about how deep the water was and whether or not we'd have to evacuate some of the cabins if the water came up over the banks.

Under the cover of the table, Michelle Owens

reached for my hand and squeezed it. "Thank you," she whispered.

Her gratitude at my small kindness was disconcerting. A forkful of egg and chorizo turned to dry pebbles in my mouth. I was no longer hungry.

"Want to go look at the river?" I asked.

She nodded wordlessly and rose to go, waiting for me beside the door while I took my plate back to the window to be rinsed.

We didn't speak at all as we walked down the muddy path to the Hassayampa. Somehow I got the feeling that there was something Michelle wanted to say to me, but every time she got close to doing it, she drew back, and I didn't force the issue. I couldn't think of any reason for her to confide in me with her problems, and I wasn't about to pry. She seemed to find a certain amount of comfort just being in my presence, and I was content to let it go at that.

When we got to the bank, the river was every bit as spectacular as the other clients had said it was. Off and on during the previous month, I had taken occasional walks along the sandy riverbed without seeing a trace of water, but now four days of rain had transformed it into a rushing, muddy torrent, running from bank to bank, seven or eight feet deep and at least a quarter of a mile wide. I never knew the desert *had* that much water in it.

Keeping well away from the bank, we stood there for some time watching in dumbstruck silence before Shorty Rojas joined us, shading his eyes against a sudden burst of sunlight as he stared across the raging flood.

"What do you think?" I asked. "Is this as high as it goes?"

He shook his head. "I hear it's still raining up in the mountains," he answered, "and the guy on the radio said it's running about seventy-four thousand cubic feet per second. They're calling it a hundred-year flood."

Michelle Owens looked alarmed. "What does that mean?"

"A flood this bad only happens on an average of every hundred years or so," I explained.

Shorty nodded. "That's what they say," he observed laconically, "but this here's the third one I've seen, so their hundred-year call ain't exactly scientific. I may have to move them horses up to a higher corral." He turned and walked away.

Eventually Michelle and I headed back as well. It was eight-thirty. People would be filtering into the various group-session rooms for the short, early morning mixed group with both clients and family members present. We had just passed Joey's and my cabin when I saw a patrol car go jouncing up the dirt road past the tennis courts. The lights were on. So was the siren.

It almost made me laugh aloud. An hour and a half late and the damn deputy shows up in response to my car prowl call with his lights flashing and siren blaring.

And to think Louise Crenshaw had called me melodramatic.

CHAPTER
4

I went on into the ranch house and hung around by the coffee table in the dining room, expecting at any moment to be summoned into Louise Crenshaw's presence to meet with the deputy, but that didn't happen. The deputy disappeared into thin air. Nobody bothered to come looking for me.

Karen and the kids showed up a few minutes later. Kelly still wasn't speaking to me, which didn't exactly make me feel terrific. She had her mother relay a message to ask me where Joey Rothman was, and I passed along the information that I didn't have the foggiest idea and couldn't care less. On that happy note we all filed into the portable, a semi-permanent, classroom-sized building which was the site of my group's mixed session.

I dreaded the morning's opening Round Robin when the counselors went around the room, calling on each person individually and inquiring after everybody's current state of mind. It was an exercise intended to bring out into the open whatever murky feelings might have surfaced overnight since the last session. During the course of family week, Round Robins often resulted in emotional fire storms.

One thing I had already learned from my three and a half weeks of treatment was that everybody involved, family members and addicts alike, had long since learned to function by putting on as normal an outward appearance as possible while keeping their real feelings buried far beneath the surface. In chemically dependent families, nobody dares say what they really think or feel for fear the entire house of cards will come tumbling down around their ears.

Living through Round Robins, "touching base exercises" as they called them in the Ironwood Ranch lexicon, is often a scary, treacherous process.

That particular morning it was especially so, and not just for me. I glanced around the room. Naturally, Joey Rothman was nowhere in evidence. Kelly, sullen and pouting, sat with her arms crossed staring moodily at the floor. Just because she wasn't speaking *to* me didn't mean she would have any compunction about letting loose with a full pyroclastic blast in front of the whole group. That unpleasant prospect made me more than a little nervous.

Directly across the open circle from Kelly sat Michelle Owens, still pale, red-eyed, and miserable. On Michelle's other side sat Guy Owens, tight-lipped and explosive, wound tight as a drum and waiting expectantly. Still searching for Joey, he eagerly scanned each new face every time the door opened and closed. I idly wondered if that little twerp of a Burton Joe and his female counterpart would be tough enough to handle the ensuing donnybrook if Joey Rothman was dumb enough to turn up in Group that morning. There were enough people present that Rothman probably wouldn't get hurt too badly, but Guy Owens would scare the living shit out of him. Of that, I was certain.

So while part of me looked forward to the coming confrontation, relishing it, another part of me empathized with Michelle Owens and wondered what would happen to her if her father lit into Rothman and beat the crap out of him. I also worried how Michelle would take it if Kelly happened to mention that her quarrel with me was also about Joey Rothman, the father of Michelle's unborn child. So sitting in that room waiting for things to happen was very much like sitting on a keg of dynamite.

But somewhere along the way, a little of the dynamite was unexpectedly defused. Before the session officially got under way, Nina Davis, Louise Crenshaw's personal secretary, hurried up to where Michelle and Guy Owens were sitting, said something to them in urgent undertones, and led them from the room. As the door closed behind them, I let out an audible sigh of relief. Unfortunately, Burton Joe heard it. As soon as the Round Robin started, he called on me. First.

"I heard you mention at breakfast that you

hadn't slept well last night, Beau. Is there any specific problem you'd like to discuss with the group?"

Like hell I was going to discuss it with the whole group. "Not really," I replied as nonchalantly as possible. "I was waiting up to talk with Joey, but he never came in."

Kelly swung her head around and stared at me in disbelief. "Why don't you tell them the truth, Daddy?" she blurted passionately. "Why don't you tell them that you were mad at Joey because he's a really awesome guy? You caught us kissing and jumped to all kinds of terrible conclusions. You acted like I was a stupid two-year-old or something. I've never been so embarrassed in my whole life." With that, she burst into tears.

Her frontal attack left me with no line of retreat. Everyone looked at me. Glared is more like it. I felt like I was totally alone, standing naked at center stage under the glare of an immense spotlight with every flaw and defect fully exposed. I waited, hoping a hole would open in the floor and swallow me, but just when I was at my lowest ebb, help came from a totally unexpected quarter.

Scott, sitting on the other side of Kelly, leaned back in his chair far enough to catch my eye behind the back of his sister's head. He winked at me as if to say "It's okay, Pop. I've seen these kinds of fireworks before. Hang on; it'll pass."

For the first time in years, I could feel that ineffable bond of kinship flowing back and forth between my son and me. It lanced across the room like a ray of brilliant sunshine, giving me something to cling to, putting a lump in my throat.

"Is that true, Beau?" Burton Joe asked.

That blinding sense of renewed connection with Scott left me too choked up to answer. I nodded helplessly. Misreading the cause of my emotional turmoil, Burton Joe nodded too, an understanding, encouraging nod. As far as he was concerned, my uncontrolled show of emotion demonstrated a sudden breakthrough in treatment.

"Just go with it," Burton Joe said solicitously. "Let it flow."

Other words of reassurance and support came from around the circle. Ed Sample, sitting next to me, gave the top of my thigh a comforting, open-handed whack. I couldn't explain to any of them what had really happened. Talking about it would have trivialized it somehow, when all I really wanted to do was grab Scott in my arms and crush him against my chest. But that didn't happen, either.

The outside door opened. Everyone shifted slightly in their seats, disturbed by the sudden intrusion into the privacy of the session. This time, instead of Nina or Louise Crenshaw, Calvin Crenshaw himself stood in the doorway.

"Sorry to disturb you, Burton," he said slowly, "but I need to speak to Mr. Beaumont."

Burton Joe nodded. "All right," he said. "You can go, Beau."

We were all used to Louise popping in and out, but for Calvin Crenshaw to interrupt a group was unusual to begin with. Beyond that, and despite an apparent effort to maintain control, it was clear to me that something was dreadfully wrong. Calvin Crenshaw's complexion was generally on the florid side. Now his skin was livid—his cheeks a pasty shade of gray and his full lips white instead of pink.

I got up quickly and followed him from the room. I waited until he had closed the door to the portable before I spoke.

"What's wrong?" I asked.

Before the session started, I had been ready to tear into the deputy for putting me off, for not calling me in to talk to him as soon as he arrived at Ironwood Ranch, but the emotional rollercoaster of the past few minutes had left me hollow and drained. I didn't want to fight anymore, but I did want to know what was going on. Calvin didn't answer right away. He seemed to be having some difficulty in making his lips work.

"Where's the deputy?" I asked. "I know he showed up, but I still haven't seen him."

"Up there," Calvin croaked, waving his hand vaguely in the direction of the path that detoured around the ranch house and led up to the parking lot. He swallowed then, as if recovering control of his voice. "Where are your car keys, Mr. Beaumont?" he asked.

"Excuse me?"

"Your car keys. Where are they?"

Something about the way he spoke, the timbre of his voice as he asked the question, put my interior warning system on yellow alert. "Why do you want to know?"

"Just tell me."

"They're not in my desk," I said, stalling for time, hoping for a hint of what was really behind the question.

Through the four weeks Calvin Crenshaw had come across as a fairly easygoing guy. He seemed content to linger in the background while Louise hogged center stage. Not everybody would have caught the slight grimace of impatience that flashed across his face in reaction to my answer. I could see in his face that Calvin Crenshaw already *knew* that the keys to the rented Grand AM weren't in my desk. Someone had already looked.

"What were you doing in my room?" I demanded.

Calvin turned to walk away, but not before I caught the giveaway blink of his eye that told me I was right. There was something else there as well, a hardened line of resistance that I had never seen before. He started up the path, but I strode after him and caught him by the arm.

"Look, Calvin, I asked you a question."

"Go talk to the deputy," he replied. "He's waiting for you in the parking lot. I hope you have the keys with you."

Saying that, he shook off my restraining hand and hurried away. For a moment I stood there watching him go, then I did as I was told, heading up to the parking lot with the car keys in my pocket. Unwilling to give Joey Rothman another chance at making a damn fool out of me, I had carried them with me when I left the cabin.

Once I reached the parking lot I saw a lanky man wearing a khaki uniform and a wide-brimmed hat standing next to my rental.

"You Detective Beaumont?" he asked as I approached.

I nodded. No one at Ironwood Ranch had called me Detective since my arrival four weeks before. For reasons of personal privacy, I had played down the police officer part of my life as much as possible. As I came closer I noticed that the leather snap on his holster had been loosened. He held one arm away from his body in a stance that would allow immediate access to the handle of his weapon. His bronze-plated name tag said Deputy M. Hanson. He studied me appraisingly for a moment or two and then relaxed a little.

"What seems to be the problem?" I asked.

"Is this your vehicle?"

"Not mine. Rented, yes."

"Mind opening it up?"

"Not at all, but what seems to be the problem?"

"Let me ask the questions, please, Detective Beaumont. Unlock the door and then step away from the vehicle."

I did as I was told. As soon as I turned the key in the lock, Hanson pulled a penknife from his pocket and gingerly lifted the latch. When the door swung open, he leaned inside, carefully examining the floor mats of both the front and back seats. When he was finished, Hanson straightened up and stepped away from the car, studying me carefully.

"Did you disturb the vehicle in any way when you found it here in the lot this morning?" he asked.

"I got in it," I said. "On the driver's side. The keys had been left in the ignition. I took them out and put them in my pocket."

"Did you touch anything else?"

"I unlocked the glove box to check the rental agreement. I wanted to see how far the car had been driven. What exactly is going on here?" I asked, exasperated. "I call to report a car prowl. You turn up three hours later and act as though the case has suddenly turned into a major crime and I'm somehow at fault for stealing my own car."

"It has turned into a major crime, as you call it," Deputy Hanson said seriously. "It's my understanding that you believe your roommate, Joseph Rothman, took your vehicle, drove it?"

"Joey. That's correct. I left the keys in my desk drawer. He must have lifted them from there."

Hanson nodded. "That could be," he said. "We'll have to check all that out later. In the meantime, I'll have to impound this vehicle. I'll need you to ride along up to Prescott with me after a bit. We'll need your fingerprints."

"Impound my car! Take my prints! What the hell are you talking about? I tell you, I didn't steal my own damn car!"

Hanson looked at me first with a puzzled frown

and then with dawning awareness. "I'm sorry. I thought you'd been told."

"I haven't been told a goddamned thing except to get my butt up here and bring my car keys along."

"Your roommate is dead, Detective Beaumont."

That stopped me cold. "Dead?" I repeated.

"That's right. A rancher just up the road found the body hung up on a mesquite tree along the bank of the river about six-fifteen this morning. That's why I'm so late getting here. It was right on the boundary, so it took a while to figure out if the body was found in Maricopa or Yavapai County. The line runs right through Don Freeman's ranch. Don's an old geezer, ninety-one if he's a day. He got all confused and thought it was on the Maricopa side. Then, when Mrs. Crenshaw called to report one of her residents missing, we started putting two and two together."

The news staggered me. Joey Rothman dead? A parade of one-word questions, detective questions, zinged through my head like so many bouncing Ping-Pong balls in a lottery bottle: How? When? Who? Where?

"You said they pulled him out of the water. Drowned?"

Deputy Mike Hanson shook his head. "Nope."

"What then?" I demanded, feeling a clammy sinking in my gut, remembering the acrid odor of burnt gunpowder in the car when I opened the glove box of the Grand AM at four-thirty in the morning, the smell that had told me the Smith and

Wesson had been fired sometime within the previous few hours, to say nothing of the two missing rounds.

"You can tell me," I insisted. "I'm a homicide cop."

"Not here you're not," Hanson replied decisively.

He didn't add that here in this god-forsaken corner of Nowhere, Arizona, I was just another one of the suspects. Hanson didn't have to *say* it, because I already knew it was true.

Desperately my mind swung back and forth as I tried to decide on the best path to follow, given the incriminating circumstances. It seemed as though I'd be better off making full disclosure right away than I would be letting Deputy Hanson find out about the gun later—the recently fired gun with my fingerprints on it and hopefully the killer's as well. If I told Hanson first, it might look a little less as though I was withholding information.

"Deputy Hanson," I said quietly, "you should probably know that my departmental issue .38 is locked in the glove box."

The startled look on Deputy Hanson's face confirmed my worst suspicions. Joey Rothman hadn't drowned. Somebody had plugged him. And I knew with dead certainty that the murder weapon had to be my very own Smith and Wesson.

Just then I heard the sound of laughter and approaching voices. Finished with the Round Robins, early morning Group had broken up. Family members from my session and others were on their way to an outlying portable, this one a new addition across the parking lot. The group had to pass down the aisle directly in front of where Deputy Hanson and I were standing.

Several people gave us curious glances as they went by. Kelly walked past without acknowledging my existence. Karen nodded but didn't stop. Scott walked past but then turned and came back, frowning.

"Dad, is something wrong?"

"No," I said quickly. "I'm fine. It's nothing."

Scott smiled. "Good," he said. He started away again, but stopped once more. "I just wanted to tell you in there that it's all right. Kelly's a spoiled brat. She carries on like that all the time, and Dave and Mom let her get away with it. You know how it works."

"Yeah," I said. "I know."

"And I . . ." Scott paused.

"You what?"

"I just wanted to tell you that I love you," he said.

The lump returned to my throat. I grabbed Scott then, right there in the parking lot with a puzzled Deputy Hanson looking on, and held him tightly against me, feeling his strong young body next to mine, marveling at how tall my little boy had grown, how well built and capable.

"I needed that, Scotty," I said at last, when I could talk again. "You've no idea how badly I needed that."

CHAPTER
5

Despite the extraordinary circumstances, Louise Crenshaw sent word through her secretary that I was to return to Group until the sheriff's department investigators were ready to speak to me. Deputy Hanson reluctantly agreed to let me leave the parking lot only after cautioning me not to mention Joey Rothman's death to anyone at all until after a decision had been made on an official announcement.

Bearing that in mind, I returned to our portable where Burton Joe was leading the client group through a meandering discussion about denial and its impact on dysfunctional, chemically dependent families. The bottom line revolved around the catch-22 that denying you have the disease of alcoholism is in and of itself a symptom of the disease. Naturally, until you admit you have a problem, you can't fix the problem. According to Burton Joe, breaking through denial is a major step on the road to recovery.

I've heard it before, and I must confess I didn't pay very close attention during the remainder of the morning. My mind wandered. There was no denying I had a problem all right. Regardless of the fact that the weapon belonged to me, the presence of my fingerprints as the most recent prints on a possible murder weapon clearly posed a very touchy problem, one that had nothing to do with alcoholism or liver disease, although I'd say that in terms of potential for long-term damage it rivals either one.

I could feel myself being sucked inevitably into the vortex of circumstances surrounding Joey Rothman's death. If any homicide cop worth his salt started asking questions, it wouldn't take much effort to discover that J. P. Beaumont had both motive and opportunity. I took small comfort from the fact that all the circumstantial evidence pointing at me also pointed at Lieutenant Colonel Guy Owens. (In the course of the long night and longer morning, his official title and rank had surfaced in my memory.) Whatever fatherly motive I might have had, Owens had more. In spades. Kelly Beaumont wasn't pregnant. Michelle Owens was.

Blocking out Burton Joe's psycho-babble, I wondered about the official time of death. Lacking that critical piece of information, I couldn't assess exactly how much trouble I was in. If the coroner happened to declare that the murder occurred while Guy Owens and I were together in the cabin, then life would be good. Each of us could provide the other with an airtight alibi.

But if Joey Rothman died later than that, I

thought uneasily, if the autopsy indicated that the crime occurred sometime after Guy Owens left my cabin and before I went to see Lucy Washington and to report the problem with my car, that would be a white horse of a different color.

Around eleven o'clock, Nina Davis came to the door of the portable and crooked a summoning finger in my direction. Annoyed at the barrage of unexplained interruptions, Burton Joe nonetheless nodded that I could go. I followed Nina out the door, wondering why Louise had once more sent her secretary instead of coming herself. This was exactly the kind of one-woman show Louise did so well, playing the part of a *grande dame* puppet master, jerking the strings of anyone dumb enough to let her.

But even outside, Louise Crenshaw was nowhere in sight. Instead, waiting on the path was an attractive Mexican-American woman in her mid-thirties. Nina Davis introduced her as Yavapai County Sheriff's Detective Delcia Reyes-Gonzales.

I've survived a good portion of my career in the fuzzy world of affirmative action. Years of departmental consciousness-raising seminars have taught me better manners than to call women girls, especially not the ladies who make their way up through the law enforcement ranks and land on their feet in detective divisions.

The female detectives with the Seattle police are women who definitely carry their own weight. Although I can't say the trail-blazers have always been welcomed with open arms, they've done all right for themselves and for the department as well, because the ones who really make it in a man's world, quotas notwithstanding, have to be smart and capable both.

Detective Delcia Reyes-Gonzales seemed to qualify on both counts. She was only about five six, slim and olive-skinned, but I sensed tensile strength packed in that slender body. Lustrous ebony curls were pulled away from her face while silver earrings dangled from each delicate earlobe. She was far and away the prettiest and most exotic detective I've ever seen, but there was nothing frivolous about her dignified carriage. Her brown eyes sparkled with intelligence and purpose.

Delcia Reyes-Gonzales inclined her head and held out her hand, acknowledging Nina's introduction. She smiled slightly, revealing a row of straight white teeth.

"Sorry to disturb your session," she said. "Hopefully this won't take too long."

"No problem," I replied. "I was getting a little antsy in there. Can I do anything to help?"

"We'd like to go through your cabin, if you don't mind, since it belonged to you as well as the deceased. We'll need to search your vehicle as well since presumably he was in it shortly before he died.

"I have someone standing by in Prescott ready to obtain search warrants if necessary, but that will take several hours. In the meantime, I have a Consent-to-Search form here. If you'd be so good as to sign that, it would certainly speed things up."

"I don't mind at all," I said. "Hand it over."

The detective withdrew the consent form from a maroon leather briefcase and handed it to me. Using the case as a writing surface, I signed the paper on the spot.

"I suppose you've already called in a crime scene team," I commented, passing the signed paper back to her.

Detective Reyes-Gonzales shook her head. "We do our own crime scene work," she replied, "although the state crime lab in Phoenix does the actual analysis. This way, please, Detective Beaumont. We're to use Mrs. Crenshaw's office. Mr. Crenshaw will be making the official announcement as soon as people come to the dining hall for lunch."

In the course of the morning a new bank of lowering clouds had blown in from the west. Now it began sprinkling in earnest. Walking briskly through the spattering rain, Detective Reyes-Gonzales led the way up the path to the main building, through the deserted dining room, and down the tiled hallway to Louise Crenshaw's office. She opened the door without knocking and motioned me into a chair before pausing to speak briefly to someone who had followed us down the hall. Finished with that, Detective Reyes-Gonzales closed the door firmly behind her, then settled herself easily into Louise Crenshaw's executive chair.

"I take it things weren't particularly cordial between you and your roommate, Detective Beaumont," she said, opening our discussion with both a shrewd statement and an equally disarming smile. That's a killer combination for a detective—one few male detectives ever master. It did as expected and suckered me right into talking when I probably should have been listening.

" 'Not cordial' isn't the expression I'd use," I replied shortly. "Joey Rothman was a punk kid. I've never liked punk kids."

"Tell me a little about him," she said. "For instance, what do you mean by the term 'punk kid'?"

"You know the type—a spoiled brat. His family has way more money than good sense. He was a braggart, especially where women were concerned. Claimed he could screw anything in skirts. And then, there were all those rumors."

Detective Reyes-Gonzales seemed to become more alert. "What rumors?"

I had opened my mouth and inserted my foot. "About him being a hotshot drug dealer," I answered. "Legend has it that he was a big-time operator, that he was still dealing right here at Ironwood Ranch."

The detective arched one delicate eyebrow. "You're saying he was still dealing while a patient at the recovery center?"

"As I said, that was only a rumor. I'd take it with a grain of salt if I were you."

"Why?"

"I'm telling you, Joey Rothman was a braggart. He thrived on attention. Bad attention, good attention, it was all the same to him. Joey knew I was a cop. I wouldn't be surprised if he started that rumor himself just to see if I'd try to do anything about it."

"Did you?"

"I ignored him as much as possible. I'm not here dropping a grand and a half a week to play games of cops and robbers with some young twerp. Joey and I shared the same cabin, but that's as far as it went. I kept away from him except when absolutely necessary."

"What happened last night? I understand from one or two people I've talked to that there was some kind of problem in the dining room just before your family went back into town to their motel."

That was a lie. The detective hadn't talked to one or two people to get that piece of information. She had only talked to one—Louise Crenshaw herself. I remembered the disapproving glare Louise had leveled at me as she walked by Kelly and me just when our battle over Joey Rothman was reaching fever pitch.

"He was messing around with my daughter. Kelly's only seventeen. He was leading her on when he'd already—"

I broke off, but too late. Detective Reyes-Gonzales was on point. "When he'd already what?" she asked sharply.

Lamely I shrugged my shoulders. "I suppose by

now you know all about Michelle Owens."

"What do *you* know about Michelle Owens?" Detective Reyes-Gonzales returned.

"That she's pregnant and claims Joey Rothman is the father."

"And how do you know so much about it? Did Joey tell you?"

"Are you kidding? Of course not. I talked to Guy Owens, Michelle's father."

"After he got the results back from the doctor?"

Clearly, Detective Reyes-Gonzales had already done a considerable amount of homework among the players.

"Yes," I answered. "After he got the results."

"Where?"

"Where what?"

"Where did you talk to him?"

"At the cabin. Joey's and my cabin. Guy came there looking for Joey."

"When?"

"Last night."

"After lights-out?"

"Yes."

"What time did he leave?"

"I don't know. It must have been around midnight. Maybe a little later."

"And then what happened?"

"I kept waiting for Joey to come in, but I must have fallen asleep. When I woke up around four-thirty, that's when I discovered the car keys were missing."

"And?" she prompted.

"I went up to the parking lot, expecting the car to be gone, but it wasn't. It was parked right where it is now. The keys were in the ignition."

"You should have turned your gun in to the treatment center when you checked into Ironwood Ranch four weeks ago. It shouldn't have been left in the vehicle."

Detective Reyes-Gonzales was no longer smiling. Deputy Hanson had already told her about the Smith and Wesson in the glove box, and her understated reprimand was well deserved.

"I know. I've been telling myself the same thing over and over all morning long. I just didn't, that's all. No good reason for it either except that we've been through the wars together, that .38 and I. Maybe I'm paranoid. I don't feel comfortable if I can't get to it if I want to. If I need to. You know how it is."

From the level, detached look she gave me, I wasn't at all sure Detective Reyes-Gonzales did know how it was. Maybe female cops don't have the same kind of meaningful relationship with their weapons that male cops do. Maybe they don't have to.

There was a sharp rap on the door behind me. "Come in," she called.

The door opened to reveal Deputy Mike Hanson standing outside, waiting anxiously for the door to open. "Excuse me, Delcy, but could I have a word with you?"

Detective Reyes-Gonzales stood up. "Do you mind?" she asked.

"Not at all. Go right ahead."

She stepped outside and closed the door. For several moments I could hear them speaking urgently back and forth. When she came back into the room, Delcia Reyes-Gonzales was frowning.

"I'm afraid something's come up, Detective Beaumont," she said. "We're going to have to go check it out. Can we finish this interview later?"

It was my turn to smile. "I'm not going anywhere," I answered. "What about fingerprints? The deputy said you'd want a set of mine for comparison."

Detective Reyes-Gonzales nodded, but absently, as though she wasn't really listening. "That will have to wait. This is more important at the moment. It's almost lunchtime. I'll get back to you later this afternoon." She went out and closed the door then reopened it far enough to stick her head back inside.

"And if you don't mind, Detective Beaumont," she added, "stay away from your cabin until after we finish searching it, would you?"

"Of course."

She hurried away then, leaving me sitting alone in Louise Crenshaw's office. It was only a few hours since I had been in that room, but I felt as though the major part of a lifetime had passed. When I had come in that morning, it had been because I was pissed that Joey Rothman had taken my car. Now Joey Rothman was dead. Shot dead with my very own .38. Nobody had mentioned that outright. Delcia Reyes-Gonzales had hinted at it, in a roundabout way. Sooner or later she'd come back to it head-on. If she was any kind of detective at all, she'd have to.

An ominous feeling of apprehension washed over me. I couldn't help wondering what urgent piece of business had summoned Detective Reyes-Gonzales away from her interview with me. It had to be something of vital importance concerning Joey Rothman's death. Homicide detectives don't break up those sensitive initial interviews with material witnesses unless there's some over-whelmingly compelling reason.

I desperately wanted to know what the hell that reason was, but Detective Reyes-Gonzales wasn't going to tell me, and nobody else would, either, because on this alien Arizona turf, J. P. Beaumont wasn't a detective at all. He was an outsider—a visiting fireman without benefit of boots, jacket, or water hose.

More than being an outsider, he was also a logical, viable suspect. Even I had to admit that. Throughout our interview, Detective Reyes-Gonzales had treated me with the professional deference and respect police officers use when dealing with fellow cops, but once they verified that the murder weapon was indeed my Smith and Wesson . . .

The dinner bell rang, interrupting my reverie and summoning those who were still in Group to come to lunch. Automatically, I got up and walked to the dining room, not because I was particularly hungry but because I was too filled with a sense of foreboding to want to sit alone any longer in the depressing oak-lined cell that was Louise Crenshaw's office.

As people filed into the dining room, they were strangely silent, as though somehow word had spread through the general Ironwood Ranch population that something was dreadfully wrong. As yet, nobody seemed to know exactly what it was, but all were equally affected by it. There was no playful banter in the serving line, no joking or calling back and forth as people headed for tables. At the far end of the room, Calvin Crenshaw paced nervously back and forth in front of the huge fireplace. His hands were shoved deep in his pockets, and he stared fixedly at the floor as he walked.

Ed Sample sidled up to me in line. "What the hell's going on?" he demanded. "Everybody's acting as though their best friend died or something."

I glanced at him quickly, trying to assess if his comment was merely an innocent coincidence or if he had some inside knowledge of what had happened. Despite my questioning look, Sample steadfastly met my gaze, his countenance blandly open and indifferent, his smooth features the picture of a man with nothing to hide. Had I been the detective on the case, I would have paid attention to his comment and done some discreet digging into Ed Sample's personal life to see if there was a connection between him and that miserable dead excuse for a human being, Joey Rothman.

You're not the detective, I reminded myself silently. Go have some lunch and stay out of it.

"Beats me," I said aloud, and hurried over to Dolores Rojas' serving window. I collected a plate filled with her version of corned-beef hash along with a generous portion of steamed fresh vegetables. I glanced around the room and found that Karen and the kids were already settled at a table. Scott had saved a chair for me. I hurried over to it, wanting to be there as a buffer when Calvin Crenshaw made his inevitable announcement.

As I walked across the dining room carrying my plate, that's when the inconsistency struck me full force. Why was Calvin Crenshaw making the announcement? Why not Louise? For someone who was always front and center, for someone who had insisted that she be the one to notify the authorities of any irregularities, this sudden reticence seemed totally out of character. Understated elegance wasn't Louise Crenshaw's style.

Karen looked at me questioningly as I walked up. Kelly feigned an engrossing conversation with the person next to her so she wouldn't have to see me. I took the chair Scott offered, sat down, and glanced around the room, making a quick mental roll call.

Cal was still pacing in front of the fireplace. Louise was nowhere to be seen. Michelle and Guy Owens weren't seated at any of the tables, nor were they standing in line waiting to be served. That was just as well. Their absence confirmed my suspicion that they must have been the first to be notified of Joey Rothman's death when Nina Davis had pulled them out of the room before the beginning of our early morning session.

When the last straggler left the serving window, Cal cleared his throat with a tentative cough that carried throughout the room. The already subdued crowd hushed expectantly.

"I regret to inform you," Cal began slowly and deliberately. "I regret to inform you that something tragic has happened here today. Joey Rothman was found in the river early this morning."

Calvin stopped speaking. The people in the room looked uncertainly at one another. "What I'm trying to tell you," Calvin Crenshaw continued, "is that Joey Rothman is dead."

There was a moment of stark silence followed by a shocked, betrayed shriek. Sobbing, Kelly leaped from her chair and stumbled blindly from the room.

It was going to be one of those days. All day long.

C H A P T E R
6

Karen shoved back her chair and went after Kelly while Scott caught my eye. "Geez, Dad," he said. "What's going on here?"

I didn't have much of an answer.

Once lunch was over, the dining room cleared out as though someone had pulled a plug. People wanted to talk about Joey Rothman's sudden death, and they wanted to do it in relative privacy. Ignoring the rain and taking their family members with them, they quickly dispersed to individual cabins rather than hanging around the main dining room as they usually did to linger over cigarettes and coffee.

Because of the murder investigation, I was forbidden to return to my own cabin. Adding insult to injury, Burton Joe corralled Karen and the kids and vanished with them into his private office for some kind of confidential powwow. Within minutes I found myself alone in the dining room, stewing in my own juices. I had nowhere to go, nothing to do, and no one to do it with. Willing to settle for a much-needed nap as a dubious consolation prize, I settled down by the fireplace to wait out the remainder of the lunch break.

I had barely closed my eyes when the front door banged open. James Rothman, Joey's father, strode into the room with Jennifer, his seven-year-old, blonde-haired daughter, trailing forlornly along in his wake. He paused briefly at the entrance to the hallway leading to the administrative wing of the building and looked down at his daughter. Stopping and kneeling beside her, he spoke briefly, motioning for her to return to the dining room and wait for him there, then he hurried on down the hallway.

The child, alone and hesitant, stood looking longingly after him, hoping he'd relent and let her accompany him. He didn't. Down the hall and well out of sight, a door slammed shut, giving voice to James Rothman's final answer. Dejected, Jennifer turned her back to the closed door and surveyed the long dining room with its empty tables and chairs.

Uncertain of my reception with her, I waved tentatively across the deserted tables. As soon as she saw me, her desolate elfin features brightened. In a day of sudden upheaval, I was someone vaguely familiar, someone she recognized. After all, I had been her brother's roommate.

Dubiously, she waved back.

"Would you like to come sit here with me?" I called.

Jennifer Rothman had come to Ironwood Ranch the previous week as part of her brother's family week experience. In my book, she was the proverbial sweet-tempered petunia trapped in an onion patch full of schmucks. She was a beautiful child—fair-skinned with straight long blonde hair and deep blue eyes. When Joey had initially introduced us, I fully expected her to be a brat. After all, chronic phoniness seemed to run in the family.

Her half-brother was an out-and-out jackass. Jennifer's parents, unrepentant yuppies, showed up at every group session dressed in matching sets of Fila sweats. Daddy was a loud, obnoxious blowhard—Joey came by his boorishness honestly—and Marsha, his stepmother, moved in a cloud of resentment that belied the skin-deep show of marital harmony suggested by their matching outfits. I figured Jennifer would make it four for four.

But she fooled me. Jennifer Rothman turned out to be well-behaved and cheerful to a fault. Wide-eyed and innocent, she faced the world with an unfailingly sunny disposition—a latter-day Pollyanna. Her only apparent defect was what I regarded as an incredibly misplaced case of hero worship which she lavished on her no-good half-brother. During family week she had spent every free moment dogging Joey's footsteps like some adoring but ignored puppy, waiting patiently for him to pay her the slightest bit of attention or to toss her the smallest morsel of kindness.

That's how I had gotten to know her. She would come down to the cabin at mealtimes and hang around while Joey finished showering and dressing so she could have the dubious honor of escorting him back up to the dining room. He had carelessly accepted her unstinting devotion, shrugging it off as though it was no more than his just due, all the while making jokes about it behind her back. His callousness toward the child had made my blood boil.

Now, nodding wordlessly, Jennifer Rothman threaded her way through the scattered tables and chairs, stumbling toward me while her cornflower eyes brimmed with tears. I half expected her to throw herself into my arms and fall sobbing against my chest. Instead, she checked herself a few feet away.

She stopped short and with well-bred reticence climbed up onto the far end of the couch where I was sitting, discreetly distancing herself from me. Someone had drilled impeccable manners into Jennifer Rothman. Daintily she crossed her legs at the ankle and then smoothed the skirt of her plaid pinafore before she looked up at me and spoke.

"Joey's dead," she observed quietly, glancing at me surreptitiously under tear-dampened eyelashes, curious to see how I would receive the shocking news.

"I know," I replied.

"Somebody already told you?"

I nodded.

"Daddy had to come get me from school," she continued. "He's talking with a detective right now. He says for me to wait here until Mother comes to get me."

"Your daddy's right," I said. "It's much better for you to wait out here."

I was grateful James Rothman had shown at least that much sensitivity. Seven-year-old children should never be subjected to the gruesome details of homicide investigations, particularly an investigation into the death of someone they love.

A long, uncomfortable silence followed. Every once in a while she would sniffle or mop away at the determined tears that continued to course down her reddened cheeks.

"Dead means he won't ever come back, doesn't it?" she asked eventually.

I nodded. "That's right. Not ever."

"How come?"

How come people don't come back after they're dead? Where the hell do kids come up with questions like that, and how the hell do you answer them? I'm a cop, not a goddamned philosopher.

I searched my memory banks for some lingering scrap of Sunday school wisdom that might not answer her question outright but would at least offer a smidgen of comfort. I came up totally empty-handed.

"Daddy told me Joey's in heaven now," Jennifer continued when I said nothing. "Is that true?"

"Yes." I answered quickly, not daring to hesitate. "I'm sure he is."

I tried to sound as convincing as possible although I personally had grave doubts as to her brother's eternal destination. The Joey Rothman I knew seemed a most unlikely prospect for halo and wings.

There was another long silence while Jennifer waggled the toe of her scuffed baby tennis shoes. Reeboks, naturally.

"What's Mother going to do now?" she asked, breaking the silence with another totally unexpected question. I wasn't at all sure I understood what she was asking.

"What do you mean?"

More tears spilled out of Jennifer's eyes, but she maintained a surprising level of composure. "Mother always liked Joey best." She spoke the words slowly and guardedly, but with unwavering conviction. She paused and swallowed hard before she continued. "If Joey's dead, will she still love me?"

Jennifer Rothman had dragged me entirely out of my depth in the child psychology department. The Smothers Brothers may have elevated the old "Mom always liked you best" shtick to a money-making art form. The same routine coming from a mourning, grief-stricken seven-year-old child was anything but funny. Her look of utter abandonment sliced through my heart like a hot knife.

Before I could tell her I was sure she was mistaken, before I could offer the reassurance that I was sure her mother loved her just as much as she had loved Joey, the dining room door crashed open once more. Marsha Rothman, Mother herself, hurried inside.

"Mother, Mother," Jennifer wailed, letting loose

a cloudburst of noisy sobs. She clambered off the couch and raced toward her mother, catching Marsha Rothman in a desperate tackle as the woman started across the room.

"Joey's dead," Jennifer whimpered, burying her face in her mother's woolen skirt. "Joey's dead."

"I know."

Marsha Rothman's usually unemotional face was distorted by her own grief. Distractedly she placed both hands on Jennifer's heaving shoulders. "Where's Daddy?" she asked.

Jennifer sobbed all the harder and didn't answer.

Feeling like an eavesdropper, I followed Jennifer across the room and stood waiting for the two of them to notice me. Melting mascara had left muddy tracks on Marsha's pallid cheeks. Her skin had the leathery look of someone who has spent years in search of the perfect tan, but now there was no trace of color in her skin. She looked pale, gaunt almost, but not a lock of her perfectly sculpted haircut was out of place.

I was only a few feet away, but she didn't see me. I didn't necessarily like the woman, but at a time like that, personal preferences don't mean much. Marsha Rothman's stepson was dead, and I would do whatever I could to help.

"I'm sorry about Joey," I said quietly, wanting to let her know I was there without startling her.

Despite my cautious tone, Marsha Rothman jumped when I spoke but regained her composure. My words of condolence seemed to strengthen her somehow. She swallowed and stiffened.

"Thank you," she answered formally. "Thank you very much. Do you have any idea where I could find my husband?"

"He went down the hall," I told her. "Probably into Louise Crenshaw's office. The detectives have been using that for a base of operations."

She nodded and then looked down at the weeping Jennifer, who still clung to her mother's waist. "I've got to go, Jennifer," Marsha said, trying to disengage herself. "Can you stay here with Mr. Beaumont?"

Jennifer shook her head and held on even more desperately. "Don't leave me, Mother. Please don't leave me. Can't I come too? Please?"

Marsha's answer was firm. "No, Jen. I have to go be with Daddy. You have to wait here."

One clutching finger at a time, Marsha pried loose Jennifer's grasping hands. There was no anger in the gesture, but nothing very motherly either, no caring, warmth, or comfort, just a practiced indifference. I caught myself wondering if maybe Jennifer was right. For whatever reason, maybe Marsha really *had* liked Joey Rothman best.

Sobbing and bereft, Jennifer allowed herself to be handed over to me while Marsha paused only long enough to straighten her skirt and give her hair a superficial and unnecessary pat before walking away. As she left, Marsha Rothman didn't favor Jennifer with so much as a backward glance.

I picked up the weeping child and held her, letting her bury her head against my shoulder while I rocked back and forth. I held her for some time, listening to her cry, watching the pelting rain falling outside the windows, and wondering how the hell to ease the hurt she was feeling. Suddenly, I caught sight of Shorty Rojas. Slouched under a huge yellow slicker, he rode past the ranch house on an ancient plodding gray horse. Behind him he led a wet string of bridled but unsaddled horses. It was a heaven-sent but guaranteed diversion.

"Look at all the horses," I said, pointing out the window with one hand while boosting Jennifer off my shoulder with the other. "Would you like to go outside and see them?"

It worked like a charm. Little girls and horses are like that. Jennifer's sobbing stopped instantly. "Could we? Really? Maybe I could even ride one." Then, just as suddenly, her face fell again. She ducked her chin to hide the disappointment. "It's raining outside. These are my school clothes. Mother doesn't like for me to get them wet."

Screw Mother, I thought savagely. For a moment I was stymied, but then I remembered seeing Dolores Rojas leave the ranch's kitchen to walk back to her mobile home, a stately mountain of a woman moving slowly under the shelter of an immense black umbrella.

"Hold on," I said. "I have an idea."

Carrying the child into the kitchen, I found Dolores Rojas elbow-deep in sudsy dishwater. "Could we borrow your umbrella for a little while, Dolores? This is Joey Rothman's sister. She'd like to go outside with Shorty to see the horses."

A quick look of sympathy and understanding flashed across Dolores' broad, brown face. "Sure," she answered. "It's right over there by the door."

I retrieved her umbrella from the metal milk can that served as an umbrella stand. We were about to step outside into the rain when Dolores stopped us.

"Wait," she said, drying her hands on a towel. "I may have a few old carrots around here somewhere."

Of course there was nothing wrong with the handful of carrots she pressed into Jennifer's eager hands. Dolores Rojas was another soft touch. It takes one to know one.

We caught up with Shorty just as he closed a barbed wire gate behind the last of the unsaddled horses and was remounting the gray. When I told him who Jennifer was, Shorty clicked his tongue sympathetically and then asked if she would like to help him bring the rest of the horses up from the stables to the higher pasture. In response to her delighted affirmative, he swept her out of my arms and set her in front of him on the gray's high horned saddle, wrapping her snugly in the folds of the slicker.

"I'll bring her back to the ranch house when we finish," Shorty promised. "They're going to be awhile."

I was sure Marsha Rothman wouldn't approve

of the wet horsy odor that was going to permeate Jennifer's private-school pinafore, but that was just too damn bad. Helping Shorty move horses would be a whole lot better for Jennifer Rothman than sitting abandoned in the ranch house while grown-ups finished sorting out the ugly aftermath of her brother's death.

By the time I returned Dolores' umbrella to the milk can, it was time to go into afternoon Group. People were already filtering into the various meeting rooms, and I hurried to mine.

I'm not sure what was originally scheduled to happen in Group that afternoon, but it turned out to be a serious and subdued discussion of life and death. If nothing else, Joey Rothman's death had reminded all of us of our own mortality and underscored the importance of making the most of whatever time each of us had left.

Burton Joe's private meeting with Karen and the kids seemed to have had a salutary effect on both Karen and Kelly. I don't know what he told my daughter. Maybe he spilled the beans about Michelle Owens' condition. At any rate, I was back in their good graces for the time being. As we left the room for mid-afternoon break, Kelly caught up with me by the door and gave me a quick hug, one I returned gratefully.

It was still raining outside. Sunny goddamned Arizona.

We hurried to the dining room for coffee and iced tea. With a mixture of sadness and relief I noticed that Jennifer Rothman wasn't back on the couch beside the fireplace. With any kind of luck, her parents had taken her home.

Bringing my coffee with me, I went out on the front patio to watch the falling rain. While standing there, I glanced curiously down the trail toward my darkened cabin, trying to ascertain whether or not the Yavapai County Sheriff's department had completed its search. There was nothing to see one way or the other, no sign of life or investigative activity. The lights in the cabin were off, and no vehicles of any kind were visible in front of or behind it.

Before we could reconvene in our various groups, Calvin Crenshaw rang the dinner bell and summoned everyone back to the dining room. Once more in a time of crisis Louise Crenshaw was not in evidence, and once more Calvin was thrust into the limelight.

"We've just had a call from Yavapai County Flood Control," he said quickly, once the group was silent. "The river's expected to crest at one and a half feet over flood. We need volunteers to help sandbag the Rojases' mobile home. Otherwise it could be washed off its footings."

Which is how, in the last few hours of daylight on the day Joey Rothman died, I found myself, along with several other able-bodied volunteers from Ironwood Ranch's collection of misfits, slogging knee-deep through icy water and mud, filling sandbags with shovels full of wet sand, and heaving the bags in a stack along the base of Shorty and Dolores Rojas' double-wide mobile home.

It was cold, backbreaking, hard labor, but it was also exhilarating to be out in the open again, to be exerting physical effort, to be using muscles I'd forgotten I owned for a change instead of sitting around endlessly talking. When we finished the job, it was almost time for dinner. There was just enough time to grab a quick shower before rushing off to dinner and the in-town AA and Al-Anon meetings that make up Ironwood Ranch's unvaried Tuesday night and Thursday night agenda.

Hurrying back to the cabin, I paused on the porch long enough to strip off my wet shoes and make sure there was no crime scene tape that would still keep me from entering. Seeing none, I slipped inside, shedding dripping shirt and jacket as I went.

The cabin, the last one in the row, was farthest away from the main ranch house. It was also a long way from the hot water heater. Consequently, it usually took some time to coax a reluctant stream of hot water out of the shower head.

Bearing this in mind, I stepped into the bathroom long enough to turn on the faucet and begin warming the water before I went back out to empty my pockets at the dresser. I did all this without bothering to turn on a light. With my pockets empty, I stripped off my sodden pants and tossed them on the floor somewhere in the general direction of the outside door.

And that's when I heard the snake. Even over

the rush of water in the shower, the chilling sound of the rattlesnake's rattle was unmistakable.

With a sinking clutch in my gut I recognized it as a sound I had learned from watching hundreds of Saturday afternoon serials and westerns as a kid, first at the old Baghdad Theater and later at the Bay in Ballard. When I threw the pants toward the door, I must have unintentionally scored a direct hit.

I froze, squinting my eyes at the murky darkness. Fortunately, the pissed-off rattlesnake continued to sound its ominous warning. I was exceedingly grateful it did so. Armed with infrared sensors, the snake knew my every movement, all the while remaining totally invisible to me. If the rattling ever stopped, I'd have no way of knowing where he was.

Waves of goose bumps surged up and down my legs. My pulse pounded in my temples. I listened desperately over the noisy rushing of my own blood, trying to pinpoint the exact location of that bone-chilling rattle.

It had to be coming from somewhere near the door. If that was the case, I was lucky as hell that I hadn't stepped on the damn thing when I came inside. But now I was trapped. And in the dark. Not only was the snake beside the door, so was the light switch.

Holding my breath, I took one cautious step backward, dreading the feeling of snake's fangs sinking deep into the naked flesh of my leg or ankle. When nothing happened, I tried another step. The rattle stopped for only for a moment, then it began again in what seemed like a slightly different position.

I took another backward step, wondering how far it could possibly be—not inches, not feet, but miles—before I reached the relative safety of the bathroom.

Two more cautious steps and I felt the welcome cool of the tiled bathroom floor beneath my feet. Sick with relief, I sprang backward and slammed the door shut. Quickly I turned on the light and then looked down at what seemed suddenly to be an immense crack beneath the door. It may have been irrational, but all the same, I plugged it with a bath towel just in case the snake might be able to squash itself flat and somehow squeeze under the door to come after me.

While I stood there shaking with relief and resting my head on the door, I watched the towel for any sign of movement. Seeing none, I finally pulled myself together enough to turn off the water and take stock of the situation. The ringing of the last-call dinner bell greeted my ears. By now everyone would have gone up to the dining room except for a few flood-fighting stragglers like me who might possibly still be showering.

I tried to think. I may have been safe in the bathroom, but it was a hollow victory at best. I was still trapped. I still couldn't get out. Yelling wouldn't help. Once they left for dinner and the meetings, no other clients would be within earshot for hours. The trip into Wickenburg usually lasted until around ten, unless . . .

A sudden thought spilled over me like a bucket of icy water. Unless they noticed I was missing and sent someone to find me.

What if they sent Kelly or Scott? I thought with my heart sinking. What if one of my own unsuspecting kids walked directly into the snake? I wouldn't be able to see them coming in time, wouldn't be able to warn them.

I had to get out! Somehow I had to do it, but I'd be damned if I was going to open that bathroom door.

I looked at the shower. A combination tub and shower. Five feet above the bottom of the tub was a window, a discreet frosted jalousie window. Small, and tough to get to, but maybe I could make it work.

Adrenaline is wonderful. It surged through me, giving me a strength I didn't know I had. I'm reminded of the five-foot-two grandmother from Tulsa, Oklahoma, who single-handedly lifted a 327-cubic-inch GMC engine off her husband's legs when it fell on him in their garage. That dame didn't have anything on me.

Wrapping my hands in towels, I opened the window and managed to punch out the three tiers of glass. Then, amazed that I was able to do it, I pried the window frame loose from its moorings. I tried yelling for help through the open window, but as I had expected, it was useless. By then every last straggler had gone to the dining room.

The Rojas mobile home was much closer at hand than the ranch house, but yelling for Shorty wouldn't work either. The roaring of the bloated river blanked out every other sound.

Standing there with my escape hatch open, I realized suddenly that I had another serious problem—I was buck naked. All my clothes were in the other room along with the snake.

Public opinion and shards of broken glass were nothing compared to my dread of the snake, which I imagined was lying in wait, lurking there just outside the bathroom door.

Casting my fate to the winds, I gathered one more towel, tossed it out the window in front of me in hopes it would protect my bare feet from the broken glass. Then, standing on tiptoe on the edge of the tub, I clambered up the wall and wiggled my bare butt out the window.

Thank God I didn't get stuck.

CHAPTER
7

Shorty Rojas seemed a little surprised when I turned up on his doorstep wearing nothing but a towel and an off-the-shoulder smile. Unperturbed by my tale of the snake, he gave me a bathrobe and a pair of rubber thongs. The robe, a shocking pink chenille, evidently belonged to Dolores and came close to wrapping around me twice. The thongs, blue rubber dime store jobs, were definitely Shorty's. They were wide enough for my feet, but my heels hung off the back end by a good inch and a half.

I wanted him to exhibit some visible reaction when I told him about the snake. I wanted him to act like it was something out of the ordinary, for him to be more upset, but Shorty Rojas wasn't the excitable type.

"Happens every time we have a flood," he said with a shrug. "Them snakes hole up in the bank along the river. When high water gets to 'em, they go looking for someplace warm and dry. What'd you do, leave your door open? Hang on a minute. I'll go get my snake stick and a burlap bag."

He pulled a much-used Stetson down from a hook on the wall near the door and shoved it on his head.

"You mean this kind of thing happens often?" I asked.

Shorty didn't answer. When he returned to the door, instead of packing a gun, which was what I wanted and expected, he was carrying a gunny-sack and a stick the size of a cane with a leather noose hanging off the bottom end.

"What the hell are you going to do with that thing?" I demanded.

Shorty looked down at the stick. A leather thong ran up one side of the stick. He slipped it up and down, tightening and loosening the noose. "I'm gonna catch me a snake," he said impassively. "Take it back outside where it belongs and let it loose."

"You mean you're not going to kill it?"

"No, I'm not going to kill it." He sounded offended, not only by the question but by the implied stupidity behind it. "If every snake in this danged world disappeared off the face of the earth tomorrow, we'd all be overrun with varmints in two shakes of a lamb's tail."

With a derisive snort and a shake of his head, Shorty Rojas headed up the trail. Chastened, I followed meekly behind.

"Where is it?" he asked over his shoulder as we trudged along.

"I never turned on the lights so I didn't actually see it," I admitted, "but it's somewhere right near the door. At least that's what it sounded like when I left."

"If the snake's by the door, how'd you get out without getting bit?"

"I climbed out the bathroom window."

He stopped in the glow of a yard light and looked up at me, consternation written on his face. "Out the window, no shit? Musta been a tight fit."

"I broke out the glass."

"I see," he said, and continued on.

Feeling like a cowardly jackass, I stayed outside, hovering nervously on the rim of the porch while Shorty cracked open the door, switched on the light, and peered inside.

"See him?" I asked.

"Nope. Not yet. Probably slipped under a bed or into the closet, looking for someplace to hide, I reckon. You stay outside," Shorty added. "I've got boots on. You don't."

Carefully he slipped inside the cabin, easing the door shut behind him. I stood outside, gazing forlornly in at the window while he searched the cabin for the snake. For several anxious minutes I was afraid he wouldn't find the snake at all, that people hearing the story would assume I had made the whole thing up in a fit of alcohol-withdrawal-induced paranoia.

But then, much to my relief, I saw Shorty struggling with the stick inside the closet. A few minutes later he returned to the door and opened it. Behind Shorty, I saw the empty snake stick leaning against the wall beside the open closet door. In one triumphant hand Shorty held a writhing burlap bag.

I recoiled from the bag in alarm. "Don't worry," Shorty said reassuringly. "It can't hurt you now. Come on in and get some clothes on." Holding the bag well away from his body, he tied the neck of it in a solid knot, shaking it once to be sure it would hold.

Gingerly I stepped in over the threshold, warily watching the bag, but also looking around the room for any further sign of danger. "What if there's another one?" I asked. "Is that possible?"

"I suppose," Shorty replied. "Possible, but not likely, especially since this one here's a pet."

"A pet?" I couldn't believe my ears. "Are you kidding? I thought you said it came from the riverbank."

"Not this one. It's somebody's pet snake all right, one that got loose somehow. And not very long ago, either, from the looks of it."

"How the hell do you know that? What's he doing, wearing a dog tag?"

I had given up all hope of taking a shower. Instead, I went to the closet to get some clothes, pulling everything to one side and examining every corner of the closet before I took down my shirt and trousers. In the process I noticed that all of Joey Rothman's belongings had been removed, not only from the closet but from the rest of the cabin as well. It was as though someone had come through the place and erased every trace of his occupancy.

Shorty set the wriggling bag down near the door and walked into the bathroom, where he examined the broken window. "How come you didn't take the glass out?" he asked.

"Pardon me?"

"The glass, how come you broke it? Those panes just sit in the frame, you know. They lift right out."

"You could have fooled me," I told him with a nervous laugh. "I must not have been thinking too straight. That snake scared the living shit right out of me."

Shorty retrieved his stick from beside the closet and set it near the bag while the snake rattled ominously. Even muffled by the burlap bag, the sound was enough to make my skin crawl. But Shorty didn't seem remotely disturbed. If anything, he seemed to be struggling to suppress a grin.

"What the hell's so damned funny?" I demanded.

"Him too," Shorty answered, allowing himself a discreet smile.

"What do you mean?"

"Look over there," he said, pointing. "See that mess there under the corner of the bed?"

I looked where he pointed and was rewarded with the sight of a small, stomach-turning mass of white fur and tiny tails.

"What the hell is that?"

"Snake's dinner—dead white mice," Shorty answered. "He scared you, but you musta scared him pretty good too. He barfed his guts out. You ever see any white mice in the wild, by the way?"

"You're saying I scared *him*?"

The idea of the snake being frightened of me was so laughable that I felt an almost hysterical chuckle welling in my throat. But Shorty Rojas wasn't laughing.

"You bet. Coiling up and striking is hard work for snakes. Bothers 'em. Upsets their digestive tracts, especially if they've just been fed."

I wondered suddenly if Shorty was having a bit of old-fashioned cowboy fun with a tenderfoot city-slicker from Seattle, but there was no hint of amusement about him as he spoke. The smile no longer flickered around the corners of his mouth. The twinkle was gone from his eyes. He seemed dead serious.

"How do you happen to know so much about snakes?" I asked.

"My cousin's kid, Jaime. He went to the university and works in Tucson now at a place called the Arizona-Sonora Desert Museum. He claims snakes are more scared of people than we are of them. He says that after a captive snake gets fed, it needs to be left alone and quiet until it has a chance to digest the meal, twenty-four hours or so anyway."

Shorty was quiet. The snake rattled one more time as if to remind us that it was still present. Hurriedly, I pulled on a pair of socks and stuffed my feet into my other pair of shoes. I glanced in his direction and found Shorty staring at the lumpy burlap bag, regarding it with a puzzled expression on his face.

"Even without the mice, I would have known," he said.

"What do you mean?" I was back at the closet pulling out a sports jacket. I was cold, much colder than the temperature in the room warranted.

"It's the wrong kind of snake," he answered. "We have diamondbacks around here, and some Mohave rattlers. Even a few speckled, but this here's charcoal gray with no markings whatsoever. I'd say it's an Arizona black from up around the Mogollon Rim. I can't remember seeing one of them around here before, not ever."

"If it's somebody's goddamned pet snake, what the hell was it doing in my cabin?"

For the first time the full implication of the snake being a "pet snake" hit me. If somebody had planted it in my room, then that somebody had tried to kill me with it as sure as I was standing there. Assault with a deadly weapon. A living deadly weapon.

I turned on my heel and stalked out the door, not even thinking now about the snake in the burlap bag as I walked by it. Someone had just tried to murder me. I wanted to know who the hell that person was.

"Where are you going?" Shorty asked, following me out onto the small porch.

"To call the sheriff. If somebody's trying to knock me off, I want a detective down here on the double, taking prints and finding out what the hell is going on."

"There's already been so much trouble today, with the boy and the flood—" Shorty began, but I cut him off.

"The flood's one thing, but believe me, Joey Rothman's murder and this snake are connected. Whoever killed Joey just tried to get me as well. I'm calling the sheriff."

With that, I left Shorty there on the porch and bounded up the trail. At the door to the dining room I almost collided with people coming out. Not bothering to apologize, I stormed past them. Halfway down the administrative wing's hall I ran full tilt into Lucy Washington, who was coming from the opposite direction.

"What's got into you now?" she demanded, stopping in her tracks and barring my way with both hands on her hips. Her full lips ironed themselves into a cold, thin line. She was still packing a grudge from our previous encounter.

"To see Mrs. Crenshaw," I answered.

"Like hell you are. She's not here and neither is the mister. What do you want?"

"To call the sheriff's department."

She bared her teeth in a forced smile. "Oh, do tell. We're not going to go through all that again, are we, Mr. Beaumont?"

"We sure as hell are," I muttered.

Instead of backing away from me, Lucy Washington stepped forward until the top of her head almost touched my chin. There was no getting past her on either side. Lucy Washington was almost as wide as she was tall. Her ample breadth filled up the hallway.

"Now you listen to me, and you listen good. Mr. and Mrs. Crenshaw gave orders that they are not to be disturbed. Period. By you or anybody else. And if you pull the kind of stunt you did last night, if you go near a telephone without permission, I'm calling the cops myself. I'll have your ass thrown in jail. Understand?"

I tried to be reasonable. "Look," I said. "Somebody put a snake in my room, a rattlesnake. Shorty Rojas just now got it out."

Santa Lucia smiled. "Sure he did, and Jesus Christ himself is out in the kitchen helping Dolores Rojas wash all the dishes."

Out of nowhere, Kelly appeared at my elbow. She was evidently ready to let bygones be bygones.

"Daddy, where were you? We got you a plateful of food, but if you don't come right now, there won't be time enough to eat before we have to leave for Wickenburg."

"That's right," Lucy Washington said, flashing me another smile, square-toothed and insincere. "You just do that, Mr. Beaumont. You go have yourself some dinner with your family and get yourself all calmed down. You'll feel better once you have something to eat."

"What's the matter, Daddy?" Kelly asked. "This has been such a terrible day already, how could anything else go wrong?"

Santa Lucia had me right where she wanted me and she knew it. I wasn't about to say anything more about the snake in front of Kelly or Karen or Scott. It would have scared them to death.

"Nothing's the matter, honey," Lucy said. "You take your daddy along with you, feed him his supper, and take him to the meeting. If I happen to talk to either Mr. or Mrs. Crenshaw, I'll let them know you want to talk to them. They might call in."

Provoked but letting it pass, I turned and marched away with Kelly following close at my heels. Karen and Scott were still waiting at a table near the center of the almost deserted room. A plate full of cold roast beef and mashed potatoes sat at a clean place setting next to Scott. I wasn't hungry, and I didn't want to have to sit down and make some kind of phoney excuse or polite conversation. It was far easier to avoid the situation entirely.

Halfway across the room I stopped abruptly and turned around, catching Kelly by surprise. "I've got to go see somebody, Kelly. Thanks for getting my food, but I just can't eat right now. I'm not hungry."

Hurt, she looked up into my eyes. "You can't? Daddy, tell me. What's the matter?"

"Nothing," I said. "Everything's fine."

Unfortunately, I've always been a terrible liar. Kelly knew it, saw through what I said, but I hurried away before she had a chance to call me on it. Once outside the ranch house, I half walked half ran back down the muddy path to Shorty's mobile home. He was standing outside, hat pulled low on his forehead, smoking a cigarette, and peering through the inky darkness in the direction of the roiling flood.

"Still hasn't crested," he said, looking up as I stopped next to him. "But I think we're going to be fine. Those sandbags will do the trick."

"I didn't come to talk about the flood, Shorty. Where do the Crenshaws live?" I asked.

"In town. Why?"

"That damn nurse again, Lucy Washington. She won't let me near a phone to call the sheriff. What about you? Would you let me use yours?"

"Would if I could," Shorty replied, "but the phones are out of order. Have been for a while. Half an hour or more. I tried calling Jaime just as soon as I got back from your cabin. I wanted to ask him what to do with your friend."

"What do you mean what to do with it?"

Shorty tossed his cigarette. "Hell, man, if I turn it loose here, the damn thing will die. It's probably never lived in the wild. Besides, it doesn't belong here. This isn't its territory. I thought maybe Jaime could keep it in the museum, but I couldn't reach him. Incidentally, you want to see him? Not Jaime, the snake, I mean. I put him in one of Dolores' big gallon jars."

I didn't much want to see the snake, and yet I did, too. Shorty led me inside. On the floor just inside the door sat a commercial mustard jar with the snake coiled up in the bottom. A series of air holes had been punched into the jar's lid. The snake must have been at least three and a half to four feet long. Folded back upon itself to accommodate the shape of the jar, its exact size was difficult to discern. It was a deep charcoal gray, black almost, with no markings of any kind. The rattles, somewhat lighter in color, stood upright almost like an antenna in the center of the coil. The snake regarded me malevolently while its wicked-looking forked tongue flickered in and out.

An involuntary shudder shook me, bringing me back to the problem at hand. "I've got to talk to the Crenshaws," I said. "Would you take me to their place?"

Shorty glanced at his watch. "You're not going to the meeting? The vans will be leaving in a few minutes."

"Goddamnit, Shorty. Person or persons unknown tried to kill me this afternoon. It's about time someone at Ironwood Ranch took that news seriously. I sure as hell do."

I doubt Shorty Rojas had ever quite come to grips with the essential differences between wrangling horses for a dude ranch and doing the same thing for a rehab joint. He hailed from a simpler, less complicated time long before the red-taped vagaries of the Louise Crenshaws and Lucy Washingtons of the world reigned supreme. People were people to Shorty Rojas, regardless of whether they were dudes or drunks.

I'm sure he shouldn't have, but when I asked him for a ride, he looked at me appraisingly, then shrugged. "Don't suppose it'll hurt nothin' if I take you there. When you finish, I can still drop you off at the meeting later."

I followed Shorty outside to an elderly Ford pickup parked ten yards up the hill. "Get in," he said. "She ain't pretty, but she'll get us there."

The pickup fired up after only one try. It slipped and slid some in the muddy track. As we started up the hill, an unopened can of Coors rolled out from under the seat and banged against the side of my shoe. When I reached down to pick it up, it was icy cold.

"Sorry about that," Shorty said sheepishly as I handed it back to him and he returned it to its place under the seat. "I like to have a cool one of an evening."

"No problem," I returned.

We sailed out of the parking lot just as people were beginning to climb into vans for the ride to the meetings in town.

The Crenshaws' house was located near the outskirts of Wickenburg, on a high bluff overlooking the highway. When we pulled up in front, Shorty stopped the pickup and turned off the engine. "Wait here," he said, climbing out of the truck and starting up the walk. There was no porch light shining on the flagstone patio, but there were lights on inside the house. The porch light came on moments after Shorty rang the bell.

Calvin was the one who came to the door, stepping back in surprise when he saw who it was. They talked for a few moments before Shorty motioned for me to get out of the truck and come to the door.

"Mr. Beaumont, what are you doing here?" Calvin Crenshaw demanded when I stepped into the light.

"Who is it, Cal?" Louise Crenshaw called from out of sight somewhere inside the house.

"It's nothing, hon. I'll handle it," he said, moving as if to close the door behind him before Louise got a look at who it was.

"Please," he began hurriedly, "my wife has been through too much already today. She can't handle any more . . ." But he was too late. Louise Crenshaw appeared in the lighted doorway before he managed to pull the door shut behind him.

At least someone who resembled Louise Crenshaw stood there. She wore a long blue robe and held a glass in one hand. I thought at first it might be Louise's much older sister, or maybe even her mother, but then I realized that for the first time I was seeing the real Louise Crenshaw, one washed clean of all her war paint. Her sallow face looked like a death mask, a pale reflection of the woman I'd argued with early that morning.

As soon as she recognized me, however, the look of cold fury that further disfigured her face left her identity unmistakable. It was Louise Crenshaw, all right. The one and only.

"What are *you* doing here?" she inquired imperiously.

"Somebody tried to kill me today," I answered reasonably enough, I thought, considering the circumstances. "In my cabin. Naturally, Lucy Washington wouldn't let me report it without your permission, so I'm here to find out what you intend to do about it. In case you haven't noticed, the phones aren't working."

"You say someone tried to kill you?"

Louise Crenshaw's question was couched in a dismissively sarcastic mode, derogatory but still slyly coy, almost like her old bitchy self.

"Come now, Mr. Beaumont. Surely your imagination is playing tricks on you. If you were female, I'd say you were overwrought, but men don't get overwrought. Or do they?"

"I'm not overwrought, as you call it. Somebody planted a damn rattlesnake in my cabin this afternoon. It's a wonder I didn't step on it in the dark."

Louise laughed then, uproariously, almost hysterically. Calvin Crenshaw hurried to his wife's side, a worried frown on his face.

"Come on inside, Louise. You really must sit down."

She pulled away from his grasp. "I'm all right, Calvin, but I want this man out of here. Now."

"We'll talk about this tomorrow," Calvin said to me, turning as if to take Louise back into the house.

"No, we *won't*," I insisted before he could hustle her inside. "We'll talk about it now! Tonight. Don't you understand? I'm telling you, somebody tried to kill me."

Calvin Crenshaw stubbornly shook his head. "Rattlesnakes are part of the natural order of things around here, Mr. Beaumont. They do turn up occasionally, especially when it rains."

"That's what I'm trying to tell you. Shorty says the snake isn't from around here, that it must be somebody's pet."

Louise came to life and spun around, her eyes wide. "Who says?"

"Shorty Rojas. He came to my cabin and caught the snake with a stick. It was in my closet."

Louise's face went suddenly slack. "You're right, Cal," she said weakly. "I want to go lie down, please."

"Sure, hon. Right away." Cal turned back to us. "Wait right here."

As gently as if she were a damaged porcelain doll, Calvin Crenshaw led his wife into the house, closing the door behind them. He was gone for several minutes. The longer he stayed away, the longer I had to wait, the more aggravated I became. When he finally returned to the door, though, I noticed a subtle change in the man. He was grim-faced but determined.

"Louise and I have talked it over. Our clients have had enough disturbances for one day. You're to go back to the ranch, Mr. Beaumont. Tomorrow we'll decide what's to be done."

My mouth must have dropped open half a foot. "Tomorrow? Are you crazy? I'm talking attempted murder here. Homicide. I'm not going back to that cabin, and I'm sure as hell not staying there until there's been a full police investigation."

"Then you won't be going back at all." Calvin

Crenshaw spoke with a quiet assurance I had never seen in him before. "That being the case, Mr. Beaumont," Calvin continued, "I suggest you have Shorty here take you back to the ranch to pick up your belongings. If you hurry, you may be able to catch the Greyhound into Phoenix."

"Wait a minute. Pick up my belongings? Does that mean you're throwing me out?"

"If you're not prepared to do as you're told, Mr. Beaumont, you don't leave us any choice. We have a treatment center to run, and we must look to the welfare of all our clients."

"What the hell do you expect me to do? Forget that someone tried to kill me? Go back to my cabin and act like it never happened? You expect me to *sleep* there?"

Beside me on the porch, Shorty Rojas shifted uneasily, but Calvin Crenshaw gave him a warning head shake that stifled any objection Shorty might have had. I couldn't blame him. I had no doubt that if he had crossed this newly transformed Calvin Crenshaw, his job would be on the line.

"It's up to you, Mr. Beaumont," Calvin said, turning back to me, relaxing a little now that he felt he was once more in control. "If you go back to the ranch tonight, you're welcome to stay. If you leave Ironwood Ranch without permission, however, you won't be coming back."

Aggravation and mystification turned to rage. "That remains to be seen, Mr. Crenshaw," I replied, barely holding my temper in check. "I will be back, in the morning, along with someone from the Yavapai County Sheriff's Department. If anybody goes near my cabin between now and then, you can tell them for me that they're running the risk of becoming prime suspects in a felony investigation."

"Good night, Mr. Beaumont," said an unperturbed Calvin Crenshaw, closing the door in my face as deliberately as if I'd been a pushy door-to-door salesman.

I turned to Shorty. "What the hell got into him?"

But Shorty Rojas didn't answer. He pulled his cowboy hat down low on his forehead and turned away from me, walking quickly back toward his pickup.

"Sorry about that, Mr. Beaumont," he said. "Come on. I'll drop you in town, then I'd better get home and see what the river's doing. It'll be cresting pretty soon now."

I stopped long enough to look back at the house just in time to see the living room and kitchen lights go out. The message was clear. Calvin Crenshaw was shutting the place down and going to bed. J. P. Beaumont and his problems weren't important enough for the Crenshaws to lose any part of their good night's sleep.

Deep in the interior of the house another light went off, a hall light this time, while behind me the engine of Shorty's pickup roared to life.

I stood there for a moment longer, angry and puzzled both. Before my very eyes, Calvin Crenshaw, the lamb, had turned into a lion. A tough-minded lion at that. I had been there, seen it happen, and yet I had no idea what had caused it. What the hell had I missed?

It had something to do with Louise Crenshaw, Joey Rothman, and me. Of that much I was certain, but I'd be damned if I had the foggiest idea what the connection was.

Joey Rothman wasn't talking, so Louise Crenshaw would have to. Whether she wanted to or not.

CHAPTER
8

Wickenburg, Arizona, a one-horse town with a non-snowbird stable population of about 4,500, is divided more or less in half by the usually dry bed of the Hassayampa River. On this dark October night, with the river half a mile wide and flowing bank to bank, the division was much more serious than usual.

As Shorty drove us down toward the town's single stoplight where two secondary highways intersect, it was clear there was some kind of major problem on the roadway. It looked for all the world like a big-city traffic jam, on a somewhat smaller scale than the ones we have in Seattle.

"Bridge must be closed," Shorty muttered, stopping the truck and getting out.

"Sounds like home," I said.

"I'll go check it out. Wanna come?"

"No thanks. I've had more than enough of the Hassayampa River for one day," I told him.

The trip downtown from Crenshaw's house had been a conversational wasteland. Shorty Rojas hadn't wanted to talk, and neither had I. As we drove, however, I made up my mind that I'd get to Phoenix that night, one way or the other, and enlist the help of my attorney, Ralph Ames, in doing whatever needed doing. After all, he was the one who was ultimately responsible for my being at Ironwood Ranch in the first place. It was only fair that he help me fix the problem.

Shorty came back to the pickup and wheeled it around in a sharp U-turn. "Water's scouring out the bridge supports," he said. "Probably be closed most of the night. The deputy says they've still got one or two rooms up at the Joshua Tree Motel over on Tegner. It's nothing fancy, but it'll be better'n nothin'."

"Any place at all will be fine," I said. "Thanks for all your help, Shorty. Not only for the ride tonight, but also for what you did with Jennifer this afternoon. Having her go along when you moved horses was just what the doctor ordered."

"Poor little tyke," Shorty agreed. "Felt real sorry for her. Dropped her off with her mother when I saw Mrs. Rothman packing the boy's things out of the cabin and loading them into the car. As I walked away, Jennifer was getting her ass chewed because her uniform was wet. That's one mean mama," he added.

"Don't worry about it," I said. "From the delighted look on Jennifer's face when you put her down on the saddle in front of you, I'm sure she thinks the ride was worth it."

We drove to the Joshua Tree Motel, four blocks from downtown Wickenburg proper. Shorty let me out and drove away, reaching under the seat for the no longer cool Coors. Even though beer isn't my drink of choice, it was still thoughtful of him to wait until I was out of the truck before he opened it.

The Joshua Tree Motel turned out to be a barely habitable relic from another era. I found myself standing in front of a run-down office where a faded but hand-lettered cardboard vacancy sign still leaned against the glass in one corner of a bug-speckled window.

The place consisted of a series of crumbling stucco edifices, cabins I suppose, that must have dated from the earliest days of motels. Or before. The AAA rating, if one ever existed, had fallen by the wayside years ago. Tiny arched carports, far too narrow for many contemporary vehicles and ideally suited to Model Ts, were attached to every free-standing unit. Inside the office all available flat surfaces were covered with price-tagged, church-holiday-bazaar-type bric-a-brac and hand-icrafts.

At the counter, a pillow-faced, cigarette-smoking manager pushed a leaky pen and registration form in my direction while announcing that the Joshua Tree didn't take American Express—only Mastercard, Visa, or cash. I paid cash, twenty bucks, and considered myself lucky.

As I finished filling out the form, the office door opened again to admit a harried young father trailed by three obnoxious little kids. The father eagerly snatched up the Joshua Tree's only remaining room. It was, he told me with obvious relief as he began filling out his own registration form, the last available room in town. While the three children raced around the office, screeching with joy at being let out of the car and manhandling the handicrafts, I retreated to the welcome safety and solitude of my own threadbare room.

Clearly most of the furnishings, interior design, and plumbing were still the original equipment. The room reeked of years of cigarette smoke, mold, and benign-to-active neglect. Dingy wallpaper peeled away from the walls and ceiling. The fitfully meager spray of lukewarm water from the shower head hit me somewhere well below the shoulder blades, but even the short, tepid shower with a tiny sliver of nondescript soap was better than no shower at all.

Putting the same clothes back on, I tried the phone, an ancient black model with no dial, but was told by the manager that the phones in Wickenburg were all out of order. That wasn't exactly news.

Unable to reach Ames, I sat there being frustrated for several minutes before I realized that part of what was wrong with me was hunger. My afternoon of unaccustomed physical labor hadn't been followed by dinner. I had walked out on my plate of roast beef and mashed potatoes. That was a problem with an accessible solution, so I left my room and walked the four blocks back down to Wickenburg's main drag, where the entire three-block area between the stoplight and the bridge was full of parked cars and milling people.

If a town is small enough, I guess any excuse for a party will suffice. This sociable group, made up equally of stalled travelers and curious locals, laughed and talked and carried on like a spirited crowd eagerly anticipating a dazzling Fourth-of-July fireworks display. There's nothing like the possibility of a collapsing bridge to bring out the local thrill-seekers.

Center Street, Wickenburg's main thoroughfare, was lined with several restaurants, all of which were doing land-office business. Every visible table was fully occupied, and each restaurant doorway held a queue of people waiting to be seated. I chose a place at random, the Silver Spur, and managed to work my way across the threshold and into a crowded vestibule.

Before reaching the hostess, however, I found myself standing in line directly behind the young couple from the motel with their three screaming banshees. Life is too short. Stumbling over the man behind me, I managed to elbow my way back outside. A few feet farther up the street was another door, still part of the Silver Spur, but this entrance opened into the bar. Saloon, the sign said. It was noisy inside, noisy and crowded, but it was my kind of place. There were no kids within hearing distance. Not a one.

Counselors at Ironwood Ranch had issued all kinds of dire warnings and predictions about what would happen to clients foolhardy enough to attempt returning to the bar scene. Bars were, to quote Burton Joe, "bad medicine," and those who went back were "tempting fate." If drunks wanted to recover, if they wanted to lead lives of upstanding sobriety, they needed to change their ways, their habits, and their friends in order to find other things to do with their time besides drink.

But I was no longer a client at Ironwood Ranch. Calvin Crenshaw had thrown me out. Tempting fate or not, I wanted a place where I could eat in peace without some hyperactive kid spilling a glass of Coke down the back of my neck or dropping a ketchup-laden French fry on my sleeve. The hell with Burton Joe. I pushed open the swinging door and went inside.

At first the place seemed almost as full as the restaurant had been, but then two people got up and left. I set off through the crush, aiming at one of the two empty stools at the far end of the polished mahogany bar. I jostled my way through the crowd of happy imbibers and reached one of the two stools just as a middle-aged man in a natty three-piece suit claimed the other.

"This seat taken?" I asked.

"No. Help yourself."

When the bartender came by, I ordered a hamburger and a glass of tonic with a twist. I might have returned my backside to the familiar world of barstools, but, Burton Joe aside, that didn't mean I had fallen off the wagon.

I sat there fingering my drink, looking around the bar, and feeling a little out of place. It was as though I had been away from bars and drinking for a long time, although in actual fact it had only been just shy of a month. I glanced at the man next to me. Sitting there among Wickenburg's casually dressed tourists and cowboy-type locals, he looked ill at ease in his citified gray suit and dandified paisley tie. Meanwhile, I felt as though the indelible aura of Ironwood Ranch still clung to my body. I couldn't help wondering if it showed, like some kind of religious stigmata.

"Where are you from?" I asked, turning to the man seated next to me and thinking that a little friendly conversation might make both of us feel less uncomfortable.

"California," he answered, spinning a newly filled beer glass around and around between the palms of his hands while he stared deep into its depths. I recognized the gesture as a drinking man's version of examining tea leaves.

"Get stuck by the flood?"

He shook his head and smiled ruefully. "If you can believe it, right here in Wickenburg is where I wanted to be. It really does seem like the end of the earth. I drove over from the coast this afternoon, planning to surprise my wife and kids, but they're not in their rooms, so I guess the joke's on me. I left a note saying that I'd wait here until they got back."

There was a hint of marital disharmony in his answer, and I was happy he spared me the gory details. Friendly conversation I could handle. Shoulder crying, no way.

My hamburger came. I doctored it with liberal doses of mustard and ketchup and ordered another tonic with another twist. The noise level in the room went up a notch as still another group of revelers—locals or stranded tourists, I couldn't tell which—crowded into the already packed bar.

"Do you have floods like this often?" the guy in the suit asked, erroneously assuming I was on my home turf.

I started to tell him that I wasn't from Wickenburg any more than he was, but that would have necessitated explaining where I was from and what I was doing there.

"They're calling it a hundred-year flood," I answered, quoting my local fountain of knowledge, Shorty Rojas. "Personally, I've never seen one like it," I added with what I thought was artful candor.

The hamburger was all right, if you don't mind fried lettuce, and the French fries were soggy with grease, but food is food if you're hungry enough. I downed the main course and ordered a dish of vanilla ice cream for dessert. It was the first time in years I had ordered ice cream in public. Watching me curiously, the man next to me ordered another Bud.

"What do you do for a living?" I asked. By asking questions first, I thought I could at least direct the flow of conversation.

"I'm an accountant. You?"

But that's the problem with casual conversations. Every answer evolves into another question, tit for tat.

"I'm a cop," I answered.

"Oh," the guy grunted. Not, What kind? Not, Where? Just, Oh, and since he didn't ask for any more specifics, I didn't offer them. An old loose-jawed guy one seat over asked Gray Suit for a light, which he didn't have, but the two of them struck up another conversation, leaving me out of it. With the life- and property-threatening flood surging past outside, everyone in the room found it easy to talk to strangers. While Gray Suit was preoccupied, I asked the bartender for a pay phone. He directed me to one in the grungy yellow hallway between the dining room and the bar, but when I picked up the handset, the phone was dead.

"Phone's out of order," a dishwasher said unnecessarily as he trudged past me lugging a huge plastic tub laden with dirty dishes.

"I noticed," I said, and made my way back into the bar, where a third glass of tonic had reserved my place. I had just hunkered onto the stool and was in the process of raising the glass to my lips when someone spoke directly behind me.

"If this isn't cozy. What are you two doing, sitting around comparing notes?"

I recognized the icy voice. Instantly. It was Karen, my ex-wife Karen, on a rampage. Stunned, I turned to look at her, almost spilling the full drink down my front. What the hell was she doing here?

Carefully I set my drink back down on the bar. When in doubt, attack, so I took the initiative. "I thought you were going to the meeting."

There was such blazing fury in her eyes that I almost would have preferred tangling with the rattlesnake in Dolores Rojas' glass jar.

"Meeting? You're damned right I've been to a meeting, but I'm here to tell you you've suckered me for the last time, Jonas Piedmont Beaumont."

"Karen," I said reasonably, "it's not what you think."

"It isn't? I'll tell you what I think. The kids and I took a full week out of our lives. We came all the way over here and squandered our time willingly, on the assumption that we were doing you a favor, helping you get well. That's what all the counselors told us on the phone when they were begging us to come. Just now we've spent a good hour and a half attending a goddamned Al-Anon meeting, while you're already back in the bars and drinking again."

"Karen, I . . ."

But before I could say anything more, the man in the gray suit, who seemed almost as surprised as I was, managed to find his voice.

"Honey," he said, standing up, "I think I can explain everything."

She glared at him, her face awash in tearful anger. "You'd better get started then, David, unless you prefer his company to mine."

With that, Karen Moffit Beaumont Livingston turned on her heel and swept regally out of the

Silver Spur Saloon, with gray-suited David, her second husband, trailing miserably behind. Somehow sensing incipient danger, people in the crowd parted, stepping aside to let them pass.

The bartender came by and collected David Livingston's abandoned glass. "Who was that?" he asked, pausing for a moment to polish the top of the bar in front of me.

"My ex," I replied grimly. "And her second husband."

I couldn't exactly call David Livingston Karen's *new* husband. After all, he had been around for some time now, ten years in fact, although I personally had never before laid eyes on the man. From the way he handled his glass, from the way he stowed away the Bud, I wondered if Karen had screwed up and reeled in a second drinker. It happens; at least that's what the counselors say.

"Did you know who he was?" the bartender asked, staring at me curiously.

"I do now," I said.

The bartender grinned and shook his head. "You look like you could use something stronger." He set a glass of amber-colored liquid on the counter in front of me. "On the house," he added.

I sat there looking at it for several moments, debating whether or not I should pick it up, when somebody tapped insistently on my shoulder. I turned around expecting to find Dave Livingston standing there ready to punch my lights out. Instead, Shorty Rojas peered up at me.

He motioned his head toward the door. "Come on," he said. "I got somebody who wants to talk to you."

Call it fate, call it superstition, but I had the uncanny feeling that somebody was looking over my shoulder, watching out for me, making sure I didn't take that first drink. That Somebody had nothing to do with Shorty Rojas.

I waved my thanks to the bartender with an apologetic shake of my head. "Some other time," I said, and followed Shorty out into the street. His truck was nowhere in sight.

"Who is it?" I asked, figuring that Calvin Crenshaw had changed his mind and was ready to call the sheriff's department.

"Joey Rothman's mother," Shorty said. "She wants to talk to you."

"Marsha? What does she want with me?"

"Not his stepmother," Shorty answered. "His real mother."

"Where did she come from?" I asked.

I knew vaguely that Joey Rothman's mother existed, but she had been conspicuously absent during Joey's family week.

"She drove down from Sedona this afternoon. She just got in a little while ago."

"Where's Sedona?"

"North of here, a hundred miles give or take. She tried coming down the Black Canyon Highway, but she had to backtrack and come around the other way because of the river."

Karen had told me about the kinds of pressure

Ironwood Ranch personnel had exerted on her in order to get her and my kids to drive over from Cucamonga. If Joey's mother lived only a hundred miles away, how had she managed to resist the hard sell and stay away from Joey Rothman's family week?

"Where is she now?" I asked.

"I left her back at your motel and told her I'd come find you."

"Why?"

"Didn't figure she'd be able to pick you out in this crowd."

"But what does she want with me?"

Shorty shrugged. "Beats me. I just follow orders. Lucy told me to bring her to you, and that's what I'm doing."

A decrepit-looking, dark-colored Fiat 128 was parked in front of my unit at the Joshua Tree Motel. Shorty's looming pickup stood guard behind it.

"That's her," he said. "I'll leave you two alone to talk. I've got to get back home."

He hurried into the Ford and it turned over with its customary roar. Tentatively, I approached the Fiat and knocked on the driver's window. There was a lone woman sitting inside the car. She opened the window a crack.

"Are you Joey's roommate?" she asked.

"Yes," I answered. "My name's Beaumont. J. P. Beaumont."

"And you're the cop, right?"

"Yes."

"Will you help me?" I assumed she meant would I help her get out of the car. I reached for the door handle but the door was locked. She made no move to unlatch it.

"We can talk in my room if you want to, Mrs. Rothman."

"My name is Attwood," she corrected. "Rhonda Attwood. I took back my maiden name when I divorced Joey's father. But before I get out of the car, I want your answer, yes or no. Will you help me find the man who killed my son?"

"That's a police matter, ma'am," I said politely. "This isn't my jurisdiction. It's not my case."

"That's not what I heard."

She was peering up at me through the open crack of window with a look that was almost conspiratorial while the glow of the halogen streetlight behind her made a lavender halo of her lush blonde hair.

"Maybe you'd better tell me what you heard," I said guardedly. "This is all news to me."

"Joey said he thought you were a plant, a narc working undercover. I'm sure that's why he tried to kill you."

Women drive me crazy. They're forever trying to tell you things while leaving out vital details, those critical specifics that make what they're saying understandable.

"Why *who* tried to kill me? Lady, you're talking in circles."

"Joey, of course. My son. Who did you think? Ringo belonged to him, you know."

"I don't know anything of the kind," I responded irritably. "Besides, who the hell is Ringo?"

"The snake. Joey's rattlesnake. I ought to know. I lived in the same house with that damned thing long enough that I'd recognize Ringo anywhere, even in somebody else's glass jar a hundred miles from home."

Understanding dawned. Joey's snake.

"You're right," I said. "You'd better come inside. We need to talk."

"But will you help me?" she insisted. "I'm not getting out of the car unless I have your word of honor."

At that point, I would have agreed to almost anything. "Yes," I told her. "You have my word."

I reached down to take hold of the door handle, but Rhonda Attwood didn't wait long enough for me to prove myself a gentleman. She had already unlocked the door, opened it herself, and was getting out.

She straightened up and looked around uncertainly. She was a medium-sized woman, five-five or so, with a dynamite figure.

"Which is your room?" she asked.

"Right here. The one with the burned-out porch light."

She started toward the door. If she felt any concern about entering a strange man's motel room alone at night, it certainly didn't show. She paused on the unlit doorstep and waited for me.

I closed the car door behind her, first checking

to be sure both doors were properly locked. They weren't, and so I locked them. After all, I'm from the big city.

She laughed at my precautions. "Thanks, but I'm sure the car would have been fine," Rhonda Attwood said, as I opened the door to let her in. "Nobody's going to bother stealing a broken-down old wreck like that."

Considering Ringo's unannounced presence in my room at Ironwood Ranch earlier in the day, potential car thieves were the least of my worries.

"Better safe than sorry," I murmured.

I glanced around the room nervously, trying not to appear too obvious about it, but checking for snakes just the same. Right about then I felt a certain kinship with the little old ladies in this world who are forever checking in their closets and under beds, searching for prowlers.

Maybe I was being paranoid, but I wanted nothing more at that moment than to be out of Arizona and back home in Seattle, where the rattlesnake population is exceedingly low.

And where Karen Moffit Beaumont Livingston can't make unscheduled surprise appearances.

CHAPTER
9

In terms of quality, the Joshua Tree Motel is a long way from, say, the Westin Bayshore, and I was embarrassed to show anyone, especially an unknown lady, into that dingy hovel of a room, but Rhonda Attwood appeared to be totally unaffected by the bleak surroundings. Without waiting to be invited, she settled herself at the spindly-legged kitchen table with its chipped and mottled gray Formica top.

Seeing her out of the car and in the light, I was startled by her uncanny resemblance to Marsha Rothman. At forty-one or so, Rhonda was a good ten years older than her husband's second wife, but they were both uncommonly attractive women—small-boned, narrow-shouldered, blue-eyed blondes with similarly delicate facial features and classic profiles. Both wore their hair in below-the-ear bobs, but Marsha's flawless honey blonde was courtesy of Lady Clairol herself. No hair dared wiggle out of place in Marsha Rothman's chiseled, precision cut. Rhonda's seemed more nonchalant, breezy, and genuine. The ash blonde was highlighted by marauding streaks of premature silver from Mother Nature's own paintbrush.

"What's the matter?" she asked, settling back against the ragged plastic-covered chair and regarding me curiously. "You look like you've seen a ghost."

"It's just that you're so much alike," I mumbled in confusion.

Her lips curled into a tight smile with just a hint of rancor. "You mean Marsha and me? You're not the first to mention it, and I don't suppose you'll be the last. JoJo Rothman never drew a faithful breath in his life, but he's certainly true to type."

"JoJo?" I asked.

"He goes by James now. He got rid of JoJo when he got rid of me. He *always* picks blue-eyed blondes, but I've got some bad news for Marsha Rothman. She's going to lose her gravy train. JoJo ditched me around the time I hit thirty. She'll reach that soon enough herself. He'll give her the slip then, too. Women age, you see. JoJo doesn't."

She paused for a moment, unabashedly meeting my gaze and giving me an opportunity to study her more closely. Everything about Rhonda Attwood seemed contradictory. Her skin glowed with a healthy, wholesome vitality that showed little assistance from makeup of any kind. A softly feminine pink angora cardigan was worn over a garish Powdermilk Biscuit T-shirt and faded, belted jeans. Her feet were shod in much-used waffle-stomping hiking boots with thick leather thong laces.

A complex woman, I thought, internalizing the full paradoxical effect. Rhonda Attwood was pretty, not beautiful, but capable of making a stunning appearance. At the moment she simply chose not to.

"I don't believe you came here to tell me about your former husband's marital difficulties with his present wife," I said, tentatively, trying to bring her back to the subject at hand.

She nodded, allowing herself to be herded. "You're absolutely right, Mr. Beaumont. I came because I need your help. I came to talk to you about Joey. About my son, and, as I said outside, to ask for your help."

Until she spoke Joey Rothman's name aloud, there had been little outward evidence of the grieving mother about her. Her distress was muted and kept firmly under control. People who succeed in not showing emotions under these circumstances come from the two opposite ends of the grieving spectrum. Either they genuinely don't care about what happened or they're afraid to show it for fear it will tear them apart.

"I'm sorry about what happened," I said, trying to smoke out which definition applied.

She looked at me appraisingly. "I suppose you think I ought to cry or something, don't you," she said.

"We're all different," I assured her. "No two people react in exactly the same way."

She nodded thoughtfully. "I'm sure most mothers do cry, but I can't anymore. You see, I used up all my tears years ago. Maybe Joey finally died last night, at least his body did, but he's been gone a long, long time. The only thing left for me to do is bury him. After that, I plan to get even.''

Her voice was low and husky and deadly serious.

"Get even?" I asked, playing dumb. "What do you mean?"

"I think you know what I mean. Like in the Old Testament. An eye for an eye, and a tooth for a tooth. I'm going to find whoever did this to him, and I'm going to take them out.''

Her words seemed totally at odds with a lady of her demeanor, but there was a chilling certainty about them, a dogged, unemotional resolve, that put me on edge. Determined women who decide to even scores scare hell out of me.

"That's a job for professional police officers," I cautioned.

Unblinking, she stared at me. For a scary moment or two I wondered if maybe that was why she had come looking for me. Maybe she was operating under the misapprehension that I was somehow personally responsible for her son's death. She had laid a narrow purse on the table in front of her. With tension tightening across my shoulders, I gauged how thick the bag was and wondered if it was big enough to hold a handgun. Unfortunately, the answer was yes.

"I had nothing to do with Joey's death," I said.

She arched one finely shaped eyebrow. "Oh? Convince me.''

"Convince you of what? That I'm not a narc? That I'm a drunk, dammit, just like everybody else at Ironwood Ranch? We're all drunks or addicts, one way or the other. Believe me, I wasn't there on some kind of undercover assignment. I was there under protest, on doctor's orders."

"That's not what Joey thought," she countered.

"I don't give a damn what Joey thought. He was wrong."

"He said you didn't seem that sick to him, that you made his suppliers nervous."

"I made them nervous? That's a laugh. Why the hell would he tell you something like that?"

"He was afraid you'd do something that would blow the whole operation. He thought he might have to leave the state for a while until things blew over."

"But he wasn't afraid you'd turn him in," I suggested.

"Evidently not," she replied, but the piercing blue-eyed gaze never left my face.

"When did Joey tell you all this?"

"Last night," she said.

"What time?"

She paused before she answered, her blue-eyed gaze cool and assessing. When the answer came, it seemed as though she had reached a decision about me.

"Eleven o'clock maybe. It was fairly late, but I didn't notice the time exactly. He called to ask me for money and a place to stay after he got out."

"He asked you for money? How much?"

"Ten thousand dollars. He said he wanted to go somewhere and start over."

I whistled. "That's a lot. Did you agree to give it to him?"

"Are you kidding? I may have been his mother, but that doesn't make me stupid. I knew what my son was."

"And what was that?"

She smiled bitterly. "A liar and a cheat. A chip off the old block."

"You mean like his father?"

She nodded again. "JoJo uses people too. I'm sure Joey had absolutely no intention of starting over someplace else. Not really. That was a lie to see if I would bite. He would have used the money to bankroll himself into some other deal, and if he got caught again, I'm sure his father could have fixed it again."

"You mean the plea-bargained MIP?"

"That's right. His father's a big-time developer with lots of friends in high places."

"What exactly did they catch him doing?"

"When he got sent to Ironwood Ranch? I suppose he was dealing drugs, but I'm not sure. JoJo passes information along to me only on a need-to-know basis, and he doesn't think I need to know much."

"It doesn't sound like you approve of the plea arrangement."

"I don't," she returned coldly, "but no one bothered to ask my opinion. If my son really was a drug dealer, he should have been in jail, not at

Ironwood Ranch. I know they call it a hospital, a treatment center, but it looks more like a resort to me."

I couldn't help feeling a certain grudging admiration for this tough-minded woman. In my experience, most mothers of punks opt for whatever plea bargains are available when their little boys get caught doing what they shouldn't. That made Rhonda Attwood a very unusual specimen. Mentally ticking off what I had learned so far, I went back to something she had said earlier, while we were still outside, her unflinching assumption that Joey had tried to kill me by turning his pet rattlesnake loose in our cabin. That too wasn't exactly standard mother-of-scumbag behavior.

"So you think Joey tried to kill me?"

"Maybe I'm wrong. Maybe it was nothing more than a practical joke and he was only trying to scare you."

"It worked," I said grimly. "It scared hell out of me."

She laughed ruefully. "I know how you feel. Joey turned Ringo loose in my house once as well. It was a full week before I found him hiding behind the detergent in the laundry room. Joey claimed it was all a joke, that he wanted to see what I'd do."

"Nice kid," I interjected. "I'd have moved out of the house, or moved him out."

"I couldn't, at least not then. I tried to get him into counseling, though, but his father wouldn't hear of it. He said there was nothing wrong with him."

She closed her eyes and seemed to wander far away from the Joshua Tree Motel. I watched her for a moment, marveling once more at what a tough, remarkable woman she was. Eventually I dragged her back to the present.

"Supposing it wasn't a joke. Why would I have been the target?"

"I'm sure it was just like what he said on the phone. The suppliers thought you were a narc and they told him to get rid of you."

"Instead, someone got to him first."

Rhonda nodded pensively while a shadow of grief flitted briefly across her face, then her blue eyes hardened once more in the harsh light from the overhead fixture.

"You have to understand, Mr. Beaumont, Joey Rothman was my son, but I lost him years ago. I had to emotionally disassociate myself or be a party to my own destruction. No. I didn't promise him the money, and I told him he wasn't welcome to come live with me, either. I couldn't afford to be drawn into his machinations."

Hers was an odd perspective. She seemed to differentiate between her loss of Joey and his death. They were two separate and distinct occurrences. For some reason, his death hurt her less than whatever had happened years earlier, although the anguish in her voice was real enough.

"How did you lose him?" I asked, following her lead.

She shrugged hopelessly. "That question has plagued me for years. The divorce, I guess, although sometimes it seems like the trouble started well before that. At the time of the divorce, I couldn't take him, not in good conscience. I didn't have the money. I never would have been able to provide for him financially the way JoJo could—private schools, the swimming pool, his friends."

"Money isn't everything," I said.

"If you don't have any, it seems like it. If I had fought for it hard enough, the court probably would have ordered JoJo to pay child support, but collecting it would have been something else. It was easier to give in. By my letting his father have custody, Joey was able to have some continuity in his life, to stay in the same school system, have the same friends. It hurt like hell, but at the time I thought I was doing what was best for all concerned."

She paused and bit her lower lip. Talking about her divorce and losing custody still bothered her. She smiled sadly. "I wish you could have seen Joey when he was little, when he was smart and kind, both. He was only five when he rescued a Gila monster that came washing by on a piece of driftwood during a flash flood. I was standing on the bank and watched him do it. He managed to catch the branch as it floated by and drag it to high ground."

"A Gila monster?" I asked. "Aren't they just as dangerous as snakes?"

She laughed then. The memory of that experience seemed to ease her pain. "That one wasn't. It was so pale I thought it was dead, but Joey said it would be all right. And sure enough, after the sun warmed it and it dried out, it got up and wandered away.

"And that was the beginning of Joey's interest in snakes and lizards. He pored over books, begged us to take him to zoos and museums. He wanted to be a herpetologist when he grew up. A herpetologist or a writer. He caught Ringo that same year, up near our summer cabin in Pinetop. The snake was just a baby then. Joey dragged it home in a quart jar. I didn't find out until years later that it's illegal to keep snakes in captivity, but by the time I figured it out, it was too late. I didn't live there anymore. It was no longer any of my concern. Marsha said he could keep it."

"I see," I said.

"Do you?" she demanded, her voice rising until it verged on shrill. "I'm not so sure I do. Marsha got everything—JoJo, Joey, the house, although they have a different house now—with another child they needed a bigger one—and the cabin in Pinetop."

To say nothing of the snake, I thought. I said, "Where did she come from?"

"Marsha? She was my babysitter once." There was no concealing the bitterness in her answer. "I had begged JoJo to let me go back to the university and get my degree. Marsha lived two houses up from us in Paradise Valley. She was still in high school when they started screwing around behind my back. It took me three years to figure out what was going on. I'm a slow learner."

"Nice guy," I said. "Like father, like son."

"I've wondered sometimes if Joey didn't know about it before I did. I asked him once. Of course he denied it, but that's about when he started going haywire. By the time I got the divorce, even if I had gotten custody, I'm not sure it would have made any difference. I think by then the damage with Joey was already done. Besides, by then I had too many problems of my own." Close to tears, she stopped, swallowing hard.

"Giving up isn't a crime," I said.

She smiled gratefully. "Thank you for saying that, Mr. Beaumont. Maybe it isn't, although I've blamed myself for years. I tried to get him back later, after I got through school and was back on my feet financially and emotionally, but whenever he came to stay with me, he lied and stole and cheated. At first I chalked it up to genetics. Later on I told myself it was because of the drugs. It would kill me if I had to think that it was my fault."

I tossed her the nearest, handiest platitude. "I'm sure it wasn't."

"Maybe not. I hope not," she added.

Rhonda Attwood sat quietly for a moment before continuing. "So that's how it happened. I locked Joey out of my heart so he couldn't hurt me any more, the same way I locked out his father. And now, I don't have anything else to lose. Nothing."

"And with nothing left to lose, you're forming a one-woman posse, is that it?"

"Why not?"

"Because it's illegal for one thing and dangerous for another."

"I don't have any faith in the criminal justice system, Mr. Beaumont. They let my son off, and they'll let his killers off the same way. That's why I came to you for help."

"You haven't been listening, dammit. I can't help you. You need to go to the detective on the case. The one from Prescott. Talk to her."

"A lady detective?"

"Her name's Delcia Reyes-Gonzales. She's with the Yavapai County Sheriff's Department up in Prescott. She seems to know her stuff. I ought to talk to her myself and let her know where I am."

Abruptly, Rhonda Attwood stood up. "Let's go, then," she said.

"Go where?"

"I'll take you there, to Prescott. We'll talk to the detective together, if that's what you want."

"Now?"

"Yes. Why not? They say the phones here could be out of order all the rest of the night. I want to get moving on this."

That wasn't exactly what I'd had in mind, but it did give me a way to get out of Wickenburg. "Tell me one thing," I said. "What exactly do you intend to do once you catch up with these characters, the drug suppliers or whoever the people are you think are responsible for Joey's death?

What are you going to do then? You said earlier that you planned to 'take them out.' You didn't really mean that, did you?"

"Didn't I?" she returned.

It wasn't a reassuring answer. In fact, it was a downright crazy answer. Nice middle-aged ladies don't go up against big-time drug dealers, at least sane middle-aged ladies don't. Fortunately, I'm not a psychologist, and it wasn't my job to talk her out of it.

Still, crazy or not, Rhonda Attwood had wheels and she was offering me a one-way immediate departure ticket out of Wickenburg, Arizona. Maybe in Prescott I could rent another car and still get to Phoenix before morning to see old Mr. Fixit, Ralph Ames.

"So let's go," I said. "What are we waiting for?"

I knew at the time that I was misleading her some, offering an implied alliance that I had no intention of honoring, but I let her draw her own conclusions. If anyone asked me later, I'd tell them that I had just gone along for the ride. Literally.

It turned out not to be such a wonderful bargain.

Happy to escape my one-night sentence at the flea-bitten Joshua Tree Motel, I left the room key on the table, locked the door behind us, and followed Rhonda Attwood outside to her Fiat for what turned out to be one of the most hair-raising rides in a lifetime of hair-raising rides.

To begin with, my six-foot-three body was never intended to fit inside a 128 Spider. At first

I thought I'd have to spend the entire trip sitting with my head cocked to one side. Fortunately, once the car was moving, the convertible's canvas top ballooned up enough that I was able to put my head into the bubble created by air movement. That way I could sit up straight, but it also cut my line of vision down to a few feet in front of the car and an acute angled view of what was directly outside the rider's window.

Highway 89 climbs abruptly up from the desert floor, winding around the flank of a mountain locals call Yarnell Hill. That's what they call it, but believe me, it's a full-fledged mountain.

Rhonda Attwood drove with the heater turned on high and the driver's window wide open. Wind whipping through her hair, she pushed the aging Fiat like a veteran sports-car-rally driver, coaxing more speed and life out of that old beater than she should have been able to.

My left shoulder was jammed against hers. There was only one spot in the V-shaped foot well big enough to hold my feet, and they promptly went to sleep. I felt like a horse with blinders on, for all I could see was the vast darkness falling away from the side of the car and the fast-dwindling lights of Wickenburg and Congress Junction twinkling fitfully in the valley far below.

Every time Rhonda swung around a bend in the road, the Fiat clung like a bug to the white line on the far outside edge. Vainly groping for a steadying handhold, I wondered what would happen if the wheels slipped off the blacktop. How far would the car plunge down the pitch-black side of the mountain before it came to rest on solid rock? Or maybe in the branches of some scruffy desert tree.

Twice, with no warning to me, we came around hairpin curves only to have Rhonda set the car on its nose because traffic was flagged down to only one lane. Looking out the driver's window as we crept past, I caught glimpses of muddy slides where stove-sized boulders—three-man-rocks they call them in the landscape business—had broken loose from the steep embankment and washed down onto the roadway to block the inside lane.

I don't like backseat drivers, and I most particularly don't like being one, especially when I'm hitching a free ride in somebody else's vehicle. At one point I mentioned offhandedly that the Yavapai County Sheriff's Department was most likely a twenty-four-hour operation and that they'd still be there once we arrived in Prescott, no matter how long we took making the drive. Rhonda didn't acknowledge the comment one way or the other, and she didn't ease her foot off the gas pedal, either.

So I shut up and hung on for dear life, remembering all the while what my mother always used to say: Beggars can't be choosers.

CHAPTER
10

Unlike those in Wickenburg, the phones in Prescott were working. At midnight I awakened Ralph Ames out of a sound sleep. It served him right.

"What time is it?" he grumbled. "And why are you calling me at whatever ungodly hour it is!"

"I need your help, Ralph. Come get me."

"Come get you! You're not due to be out for another two weeks. Besides, what's the matter with the rental car? I distinctly remember asking my secretary to make arrangements for one."

"They've impounded the rental, Ralph. I'm in Prescott, not Wickenburg. Nobody rents cars in Prescott. Not only that, Calvin Crenshaw threw me out."

"Of Ironwood Ranch? You're kidding." There was a pause. "Maybe I should have enrolled you in the Dale Carnegie course first. They're the ones who teach you how to win friends and influence people."

"This is no time for jokes, Ralph. I really need you to come get me."

"Who said I was joking? Where are you, Whiskey Row?"

"I'm at the sheriff's department, waiting to talk to a female homicide detective named Delcia Reyes-Gonzales. They've called her at home, and she's on her way, should be here any minute. Did you get the name?"

"Detective Reyes-Gonzales," Ralph Ames repeated. Then, with a sudden change of inflection that told I had his undivided attention, he added, "Did you say with homicide?"

"I certainly did."

The sound of muffled movement told me Ralph was throwing off his covers and scrambling out of bed. "It'll take me two hours or so to get there. This sounds serious, Beau. Are you all right?"

"I am now. My roommate's dead, though. From what I can gather, I seem to be fairly high on the list of possible suspects."

"Great," Ralph said. "Make that a little less than two hours. I'm on my way."

I put down the phone and turned back to the center of the lobby where Rhonda Attwood stood waiting. Just then Detective Reyes-Gonzales appeared at the opposite end of the room. She stepped forward swiftly and was gravely shaking hands with Rhonda when I joined them in the middle of the room.

"I'm so sorry about your son, Mrs. Attwood. I understand that the deputies weren't able to reach you until late this afternoon," Detective Reyes-Gonzales was saying.

Rhonda nodded. "I was out working all day. They were waiting for me at the house when I came home." Rhonda turned to me, drawing me into their conversation. "I guess you already know Mr. Beaumont here."

"Yes," Detective Reyes-Gonzales said, nodding curtly in my direction. She didn't appear to be overjoyed at the prospect of seeing me again. "We met earlier today, although I guess it's yesterday now. Would you mind stepping into my office, Mrs. Attwood?"

I'm sure the invitation was directed to Rhonda alone, but when I started to drop back, Rhonda took my arm and led me along with her. Detective Reyes-Gonzales shrugged as though it didn't much matter to her one way or the other. She conducted us through a secured door and into a compact two-desk office where she motioned Rhonda into the lone visitor chair and left me standing, making no effort to bring me the extra chair from the other desk.

Her message was clear—just because I had entered the office with Rhonda Attwood didn't necessarily mean I was welcome. Visiting detectives who might try to horn in on Detective Reyes-Gonzales' case and/or territory could damn well stand. I got the chair myself and pushed it over next to Rhonda's while the detective watched, sitting perched on the desk with her arms crossed and her head cocked to one side. As soon as I was seated, she asserted her authority by coming after me with no holds barred.

"I understand you were the subject of a number of interdepartmental communications last night, Detective Beaumont." She said it carelessly enough, but I knew she was sniping at me, baiting me.

"Is that so?" I replied innocently, wondering if maybe Calvin Crenshaw had come to his senses after all and had decided to report the snake incident himself. "I'm certainly relieved to hear that."

It wasn't the answer she expected. Detective Reyes-Gonzales raised one impeccably arched eyebrow. "You are?"

"Absolutely. If I had known Cal was going to report it, I wouldn't be here bothering you."

She smiled, a belittling, patronizing smile. "Report what, the snake in your room, you mean?"

Her attitude was starting to irritate me. "Yes, the snake in my room! You're damn right! Somebody was trying to kill me."

"I think you're overreacting, Detective Beaumont. Rattlesnake venom isn't instantly fatal, you know. I haven't yet been in direct contact with Mr. Crenshaw, but I was told to inform you, if you did by any chance happen to show up here, that the snake is safely on its way back to wherever it came from."

"Gone back to where it came from?" I echoed. "What does that mean? How could it? Snakes don't drive, do they?"

She threw me a quizzical look. "Drive? What are you talking about? That snake wasn't driving anywhere. The last I heard, Shorty Rojas was supposed to take it outside and let it go. In this state it's illegal to keep snakes in captivity, unless you happen to be operating a legitimate museum. By now that snake is probably safely back in its cozy little nest or den or whatever it is snakes live in."

Up until then, Rhonda Attwood had kept completely quiet. Before I could launch a verbal counterattack, she cut in.

"That snake hasn't lived in the wild for the past fourteen years, Detective Reyes-Gonzales," Rhonda commented quietly. "Ringo was my son's snake, you see. He's lived most of his life in a terrarium in Joey's bedroom."

Frowning, the detective focused her attention fully on Rhonda. "But Mr. Crenshaw told the sheriff—"

"I don't care what Mr. Crenshaw said or why. That snake was a pet snake—my son's pet snake—and if they've turned it loose in the desert by Wickenburg, Ringo will most likely die. Black rattlesnakes from the Mogollon Rim can't live in the low desert, you know. It's not their natural habitat. Not only that, Ringo hasn't lived in the wild since he was tiny. He's old for a snake, and he doesn't know how to hunt. Without someone to feed him regularly, he'll probably starve to death."

Detective Reyes-Gonzales seemed genuinely taken aback. She looked first at Rhonda and then back at me for confirmation. "My understanding was that the snake had been displaced by the flood waters."

Rhonda shook her head. "No. That's not the case here at all. I'm sure Ringo was deliberately planted in Mr. Beaumont's room, probably by Joey himself, unless I miss my guess."

Detective Reyes-Gonzales' eyes narrowed, but she was obviously intrigued by what she was hearing. So was I. Even if they know it's true, perpetrators' mothers don't generally voice those kinds of accusations to law enforcement personnel. Detective Reyes-Gonzales evidently found it as disquieting as I did.

Leaving her perch on the desk, she went around to the back of it and sat down in her chair, leaning back with her fingers crossed and regarding Rhonda Attwood intently.

"Why would your son do a thing like that, Mrs. Attwood? And how?"

Her questions were asked with disarming directness. Rhonda responded in kind.

"How is easy. My guess is that Ringo was there for several days. Snakes can be in a room without people being aware they're there."

For a moment an echo of atavistic fear lurched through me. Rhonda was right. Ringo could have been there for some time without my knowing it, just as he had been loose in Rhonda's house years before.

"As for the why," Rhonda was saying when I came back to the discussion, "Joey believed Mr. Beaumont was a narcotics agent planted at Ironwood Ranch for entrapment purposes."

I caught the sudden shadow of doubt that flitted briefly across the detective's face. She looked at me questioningly. "Were you there on assignment, Detective Beaumont?" she asked.

"No way. Joey Rothman may have *thought* that," I countered, "but that doesn't mean it's true."

Detective Reyes-Gonzales nodded, gravely acquiescent. "I see," she said.

There was something odd in her manner toward me, but I couldn't put my finger on it. She regarded me for a long moment, studying me, assessing my reactions, wondering. Was I fish or fowl, ally or enemy, suspect or potential witness? Her attitude was equal parts professional courtesy and professional jealousy. I wasn't offended. If anything, I respected her for it. After all, it was far too early in the investigation for a careful detective to remove any names from the list of possibles—including that of a visiting fellow detective.

Detective Reyes-Gonzales turned from me to Rhonda Attwood. "How did you come to be aware of your son's suspicions about Mr. Beaumont here?"

"He called me last night and told me."

"You mean the night he died?"

Rhonda nodded. "That's right. It's tomorrow already, isn't it."

"What was the purpose of his call?"

"He wanted to hit me up for some money."

"Why?"

"I'm not sure. I used to lend him money all the time, but then I stopped because he never paid any of it back."

"So his calling you was unusual?"

"Yes."

"How much did he want?"

"Ten thousand dollars. He said he was planning to leave the state, but that was probably a lie."

"Did you give your son the money he asked for?" Detective Reyes-Gonzales asked.

Rhonda shook her head. "I don't have that kind of money, at least not at one time. Even if I had it, I wouldn't have given it to him. I learned the hard way. My son was a liar and a cheat. I quit lending him money years ago. I thought it would help him grow up and learn to stand on his own two feet."

"Mrs. Attwood, do you believe your son was involved in drug trafficking?" Detective Reyes-Gonzales asked the pivotal question gently.

"Yes," Rhonda replied.

"According to what I've seen so far, he got sent up on a Minor In Possession, an MIP. I can't find anything official that links him to drugs."

"Keep looking," Rhonda said grimly. "It's there."

"How do you know?"

"Because he told me. He told me JoJo had gotten him off."

"JoJo?" Detective Reyes-Gonzales asked.

"James Rothman, his father, my ex."

"And you believe that's possible?"

"Where JoJo is concerned, anything is possible."

Detective Reyes-Gonzales nodded. "All right. I'll do some more checking into that end of it. By the way, in his discussion with you, did your son ever mention someone by the name of Michelle Owens?"

"No," Rhonda returned decisively. "Not that I remember."

Detective Reyes-Gonzales continued. "Michelle's young, only fifteen, a girl your son met while they were both in treatment at Ironwood Ranch. She told us Joey was in the process of 'working some deals' and then they were planning on running away together."

Rhonda Attwood laughed. "Run away?" she asked.

"As in elope," Detective Reyes-Gonzales replied seriously. "When I talked to her this morning, the girl showed me a ring. She claims they were engaged." Reyes-Gonzales paused for just a moment before adding, "Michelle Owens is pregnant, Mrs. Attwood."

For the first time in the entire interview, Rhonda Attwood looked stunned.

"Pregnant?" she said. "Joey got a girl pregnant?"

"Eventually you may want to confirm it with a paternity test, but for the time being, we're taking the girl's word that your son is the father."

Rhonda sat perfectly still, her face ashen. I'm sure that, like me, Detective Reyes-Gonzales had assumed that someone else had given Rhonda the news. "I'm sorry. You mean you didn't know?"

"No," Rhonda answered weakly, almost in a whisper. "I had no idea."

"It's just that your husband—"

"I don't have a husband," Rhonda cut in.

"Excuse me, your former husband seemed to know all about it, and I thought you would too."

"My former husband and I aren't exactly on speaking terms," Rhonda said testily. "Thank you for telling me." Abruptly, she stood up and turned to me. "Can we go now, please? I'm not feeling well."

To my surprise, Detective Reyes-Gonzales didn't object. "Of course, Mrs. Attwood. I'll be happy to finish going over all this with you some other time."

"Thank you," Rhonda murmured and fled from the room. Without moving, Detective Reyes-Gonzales watched the door swing slowly shut behind the departing woman.

"So that's it?" I asked.

"For right now," she replied. "If I have any more questions, I can ask them tomorrow."

Being this close to the action and at the same time being totally shut out of it was driving me crazy. I decided to try a direct approach. What did I have to lose?

"How about your answering one for me, then?" I asked.

"Such as?"

"Yesterday when you were interviewing me in

Louise Crenshaw's office, something happened. Somebody came to get you, and you got up and left me, just like that."

A curtain of wariness fell across the detective's face. "What about it?"

"What was it? Why did you leave?"

"A lead," she answered coolly. "I'm not at liberty to say what kind."

"Just tell me one thing. Was it something to do with Joey Rothman's murder?"

"You're not listening, Detective Beaumont," she said, standing up. "I can't say anything more without jeopardizing my investigation. Won't," she added.

"But you do have a suspect?" I insisted.

I had turned the questioning tables on her suddenly enough that I caught her off guard. An affirmative answer flashed in the lucid brown eyes before she could properly mask them. Yes, she did have a suspect.

"Who is he?" I asked, pressing my luck. By then, Detective Reyes-Gonzales was back in control. She ignored my final question as though it had never been asked.

"I understand you're no longer staying at Ironwood Ranch." It was a statement not a question, and I didn't answer.

"Do you have any idea where you will be staying? For the time being, I would prefer your not leaving the state of Arizona."

I had seen that request as a distinct possibility. "I'll probably stay with my attorney, Ralph Ames.

In Phoenix. His office is in Phoenix but he lives in Paradise Valley." I gave her Ralph's telephone numbers and addresses.

"What about my car?" I added.

"Oh, that." She shrugged. "A minor detail. Have the rental agency call us. Better yet, have them call me personally. The car is still impounded, but you won't have to pay any charges from the time we took it into custody. At least that's my understanding of how it's supposed to work."

The detective got up and escorted me to the door. We found Rhonda Attwood pacing up and down the hallway. Pacing and seething.

She stopped as soon as she saw us, her face still contorted with anger. The change was remarkable. This new woman barely resembled the one with whom I'd spent the past few hours.

"I take it you spoke with my former husband at some length?" Her words were clipped and staccato, while the question itself reeked with sarcasm.

"Why, yes, as a matter of fact, we did. We were able to reach him early on during the day, long before the deputies were able to locate you."

"And while you were chatting with him, he didn't happen to mention when the services for Joey are scheduled, did he?"

Detective Reyes-Gonzales frowned. "That depends on the autopsy, but I believe he said something about Monday. Somewhere in Paradise

Valley, I believe, but I can't remember where or what time. When you talk to him—"

"I won't be speaking to JoJo Rothman," Rhonda said icily. "I haven't spoken to him since before the divorce, and I see no need to change that now." With that, she turned and stalked away down the hallway. I started after her, but Detective Reyes-Gonzales stopped me.

"What's going on with her? Are you two involved in some way?"

"You mean romantically? No."

"But you came here with her. She brought you along into my office like you were an advisor or a close personal friend."

"I never met her before tonight. She offered me a ride out of Wickenburg, that's all. The road is closed going the other way, remember?"

"And that's all?"

"Of course that's all," I answered, exasperation creeping into my voice.

Detective Delcia Reyes-Gonzales smiled, but there was no humor in it. "Let me remind you, Detective Beaumont, that you are now in Arizona, not Washington. Yavapai County, not the City of Seattle."

"In other words, butt out and mind my own business."

"I couldn't have said it better myself."

The course of the interview had taken so many sudden twists and turns that I had almost lost sight of my initial reason for wanting to talk to her. I had come to report an attempt on my own life, but that original intention kept getting buried under other issues. Resentment boiled to the surface.

"And let me remind you, Detective Reyes-Gonzales, that no matter what you were told by the sheriff or Crenshaw or anybody else, somebody, most likely Joey, tried to kill me with that snake yesterday afternoon. I'm not going to let up until I know for sure."

The detective flashed me a winning smile. "If I were you . . ." she began.

"You're not me," I reminded her, and strode away.

Rhonda Attwood was waiting in the lobby with a night clerk hovering in attendance when I came out of the office area. She seemed to have gotten herself under control.

"There's a message for you," she said.

I turned to the clerk. "For me? For J. P. Beaumont?"

"Yes. Mr. Ames said to tell you that he's chartered a helicopter and that he expects to be in Prescott within the hour. He said for you to wait right here. We've sent a cab out to the airport to meet him."

"Who's Ames?" Rhonda asked, showing some interest.

"Ralph Ames. My attorney. He's coming up from Phoenix."

"By chartered helicopter?" she asked.

"He thought I was in some kind of trouble," I answered lamely. "So did I."

"I'll wait with you until he gets here," Rhonda said.

I thanked the clerk for the message then led Rhonda over to some chairs by a blind-covered window.

"Tell me about her," Rhonda said.

"The detective? What's to tell?"

"Not her, the girlfriend. Joey's girlfriend . . . the pregnant one."

"Her name's Michelle, Michelle Owens."

"Where's she from?"

"Ironwood Ranch."

"You mean she lives there?"

"No, she was a client, same as everybody else. They met there. Like the detective said, she's only fifteen, a mousey little girl. The last time I saw her she looked like she was scared to death."

"I don't care what she looks like. Where does she live?"

"With her family, her father anyway. He's in the service, a lieutenant colonel in the army, I believe."

"From here in Arizona?"

"I think so, but I can't remember where exactly. Fort something. It seems like the name starts with a W."

Rhonda thought about that for a moment. "Fort Huachuca, maybe?"

"That's it. I told you it starts with a W."

"It starts with an H," she corrected. "It's Spanish."

"You could have fooled me," I said.

Suddenly, a light came on in my head. Detective Reyes-Gonzales had mentioned a suspect. She hadn't said so in so many words, but her manner had hinted that I wasn't it. I was off the hook and somebody else was on, and I wondered if that somebody was Lieutenant Colonel Guy Owens.

"I'm going to talk to her," Rhonda said determinedly.

Absorbed in my own thoughts, I hadn't been listening. "Talk to who?" I asked.

"Michelle, and her father, too."

The mention of Guy Owens made me feel as though Rhonda had somehow been peering into my brain. Talking with Guy and Michelle Owens was the last thing Rhonda should do, especially if the lieutenant colonel really was Detective Reyes-Gonzales' prime suspect.

"Don't," I said. "Leave them alone. Don't go messing around with things you don't know about."

"What I don't know about!" Rhonda repeated venomously. "After all, he *was* my son."

"What I mean is . . ."

Rhonda didn't wait for me to finish. She got up from the chair and bolted toward the door, where she ran headlong into Ralph Ames. He stopped abruptly, grabbed her elbow to keep her from falling, apologized, and then looked around the room frowning until he caught sight of me.

"There you are," he said. "How are things?"

"Fine."

"I don't see any handcuffs. Does that mean you're free to go?"

"As near as I can tell."

"Are you telling me this whole thing was a false alarm?"

"There's nothing false about it, Ralph. My roommate's still dead. This is his mother."

Standing quietly beside him, Rhonda Attwood hadn't moved during the course of Ralph's and my exchange. He looked down at her and seemed to see her for the first time.

"Excuse me," he said politely, releasing her arm and then holding out his hand. "Allow me to introduce myself. I'm Ralph Ames, Mr. Beaumont's attorney. His roommate was your son? I'm so sorry."

She took his proffered hand and shook it. "Thank you," she said. "My name is Rhonda Attwood."

While a look of total consternation passed over his face, Ralph Ames did a complete double take. He stepped back a step, a full step.

"The water-colorist!" Ralph evidently knew the lady. If not personally, at least by reputation.

Rhonda inclined her head gracefully. "Yes," she said.

"But your son's name . . ."

"Attwood was my maiden name," she explained.

"Of course," Ralph said, nodding. "If there's anything I can do to be of service . . ."

"I'll let you know," Rhonda said, completing

his sentence. "And since you're here to pick up Mr. Beaumont, I'll be heading back to Sedona."

She started away then stopped and turned to me. "I heard you tell the detective inside that you will be staying with Mr. Ames here. Is that where I could get in touch with you if I needed to?"

Ralph groped in his pocket and extracted a card. He handed it to her. "Both my office and home numbers are on there," he said. "Feel free to call any time. If we're not in, be sure to leave a message."

Rhonda nodded her thanks and walked away.

"Who the hell is that?" I asked.

"You should know. You were with her."

"But you acted like you knew her."

"You mean you don't?"

"No, dammit. All I know is her son was my roommate and he got himself killed. When they shut down the bridge in Wickenburg tonight, she gave me a ride here to Prescott. Let me tell you, she may be a nice lady, but as a driver she's scary as hell."

Ralph Ames looked at me and shook his head sadly. "She's developing quite a reputation throughout the state as one of the most up-and-coming young water-colorists. As far as I'm concerned, she's still terribly underpaid, but she's also very, very talented. She does such marvelous work and yet here you are complaining about her driving?"

"Somehow water-coloring didn't come up in the course of conversation. Survival takes precedence over aesthetics. Now shut up and take me home, Ralph. I'm dead on my feet."

CHAPTER
11

When I woke up it was two o'clock in the afternoon. I lay there for a while on the huge bed in Ralph Ames' guest room, looking out the window and across a pristine backyard swimming pool at the huge mass of ocher sandstone that forms the hump of Phoenix's famed Camelback Mountain.

There was a discreet tap on the door. "Come in."

Ames entered wearing a three-piece suit but playing butler. He handed me a snazzy cordless phone. "Telephone for the birthday boy," he announced.

Birthday? Was today my birthday? Somehow the arrival of my birthday had gotten lost in the frenetic shuffle of the past few days.

"Hello?"

"Dad? Is that you? Are you all right?"

It was Scott. His voice sounded tight and worried. "Of course I'm all right, Scotty. Where are you?"

"Home," he said. "In California. We all drove

home to Cucamonga last night. I don't know what you said to Mom. She was furious. I've never seen her that mad. I don't think Dave had ever seen her like that, either."

"She thought I was out drinking."

He hesitated. "Were you?"

"No. It was all a big misunderstanding. Your mother saw me in a bar and jumped to the wrong conclusion."

"That's what Dave tried to tell her," Scott said ruefully, "all the way home, but she wouldn't listen. Anyway, I just called to wish you a happy birthday."

"How did you know I was here?"

"I didn't. I called Mr. Ames to see if he could tell me where you'd gone, and he said you were right there in his house, that you were still asleep." He paused. "Is it true that you found a rattlesnake in your cabin and that's why you left?"

"Yes, it is."

"You didn't drop out of the program because of us, did you? Decide not to finish because of anything else that happened, I mean, like with Kelly or anything?"

"Somebody tried to kill me, Scott, and the people at Ironwood Ranch weren't the least bit interested in finding out who that person was. Calvin Crenshaw threw me out rather than call the sheriff and report it."

"Oh," Scott said. He sounded relieved.

"And I'm planning to go back," I added with

considerably more conviction than I felt. "As soon as all this business gets straightened out, I'm going to make them take me back into the fold. You just wait and see."

"Good. I'll tell Kelly. She was afraid you wouldn't go back. Oh, and one other thing."

"What's that?"

"Yesterday, when we were in that private conference with Burton Joe, he told us all about that other girl, Michelle, about her being pregnant and everything. It seemed like he really was on your side. He told Kelly she was being unreasonable. Anyway, Kelly wants you to know that she's not mad at you anymore."

"Good. Tell her I'm not mad at her, either."

There was something else I wanted to say, a question I wanted to ask, but I hesitated. In the past few days, Scotty had more than demonstrated his loyalty. I didn't want to push him away again, but I needed information. Despite the strictures against tattling, he was the only person I could turn to.

"Did Kelly say anything about what went on?"

"What do you mean, Dad?"

"Between her and Joey."

"Like did they go to bed together or something?"

His answer was far more blunt than my question. "No, that's not what I meant," I backpedaled. "I was wondering if he might have said something to her that would be helpful in the investigation. Is Kelly there? Can you put her on the phone?"

"Sorry, she's not here. I'm back at school."

"When you talk to her, tell her to give me a call, would you?"

"Sure thing, but I don't know when I'll talk to her again. You could call her at the house."

I thought about the way Karen had looked at me in the Silver Spur Saloon. I didn't want to have to fight my way through a verbal war zone without having a guarantee of actually speaking to Kelly on the phone.

"No, I don't think so," I told Scott. "Give her this number. I'll wait for her to call me."

"Kelly's not bad for a girl," Scott said as a brotherly afterthought. "She just has terrible taste in men."

They were words to chill the cockles of a father's heart. "I noticed," I said bleakly.

"Come on, Dad," Scott said. "It's your birthday. Cheer up. She'll probably grow out of it."

As I hung up the phone, I was feeling better. After all, Scott had given me a very real gift for my forty-fourth birthday—himself. I felt closer to him, in fact, closer to both my kids, than I had in years.

I was still holding the phone in my hand when Ralph Ames returned to my room carrying a tray laden with a coffeepot, cups and saucers, and two glasses of freshly squeezed orange juice.

"What exactly did you do to Louise Crenshaw?" he asked pointedly, pouring me a cup of

coffee in a handsome cup and saucer with geo-
metric borders designed to look like some brand
of Indian pottery.

"I never did anything to her."

Ralph Ames shook his head. "You're on the
lady's list, Beau, and I'm not talking Christmas
cards here."

"What do you mean?"

"I called Ironwood Ranch this morning to see
what we'd have to do to get you readmitted.
You'll have to go back, you know. If you don't
complete the program, the insurance won't pay,
which isn't all that big a deal, but it could cause
trouble with the Seattle P.D. since you're down
here on sick leave. When I talked to her, though,
Louise Crenshaw said not only 'No' but 'Hell no.'
She doesn't want you back up there, period. As
far as she's concerned, it's all your fault."

"What's all my fault?"

"Everything. The whole mess."

"How can that be? I didn't do anything. I was
supposed to be a second victim, remember? Somebody planted a rattlesnake in my room."

"Mediawise, all hell is breaking loose, and as
far as the Crenshaws are concerned, you're a convenient scapegoat. If only you'd turned in your
handgun . . . If only you'd taken care to secure
your car keys . . . If only you'd reported Joey Rothman's curfew violations . . ."

"Don't tell me she's blaming all of it on me?"

"And that's barely scratching the surface,"
Ames replied dryly. "I'm telling you, the lady's

mightily provoked. You have to understand, I'm sure the Crenshaws are looking at all this adverse publicity in the long term—how it's going to affect their viability in the treatment center community."

"What adverse publicity?"

"According to Louise, the Joey Rothman story is headline news all over the state because of the prominence of his family. Both sides," Ames added.

"Terrific," I said.

Ames nodded. "Not only that, now someone has leaked the snake story to the press as well. They're saying it's one successful homicide and one not so successful."

"What's wrong with that?" I demanded. "It's the truth, isn't it? That's better than newspapers usually do."

"Louise Crenshaw is categorically denying the snake story, saying the snake was obviously an unfortunate refugee from the flood and that he inadvertently strayed into an occupied cabin."

Ralph Ames allowed himself another slight smile. "Actually, in terms of adverse publicity, I don't think it matters that much if the snake was a stray or if it was deliberately planted. Either way, Ironwood Ranch doesn't sound like the super-safe, squeaky-clean kind of place you'd want to send your addicted husband or wife or child, whatever the case may be."

"Who leaked the story?" I asked.

"Nobody knows."

"They didn't mention me by name, I hope."

"Or the snake either, thank God," Ralph added. "If they'd done the story with names included, the wire services would be jumping on it, and Captain Powell would be reading it in Maxwell Cole's column in the *Seattle Post-Intelligencer* tomorrow morning at breakfast."

"And you expect me to count my blessings?"

"Something like that. It could be worse."

We sat there silently for a few moments, both of us sipping our coffee and lost in our own private thoughts. The more I considered the situation with Louise Crenshaw, the more puzzled and offended I became.

"Ralph," I said finally. "Louise Crenshaw is crazy. She's got to be. None of this is the least bit logical."

"Who says women have to be logical?"

"Don't make jokes, Ralph, I'm serious. She's given every indication of hating my guts since the first day I checked into that damn place. She as good as said right then and there that I'd never make it, and she's been riding me hard ever since."

"Sometimes there's no accounting for personal animosities," Ames suggested.

"I can buy that, but in the last two days, her reactions as far as I'm concerned have been totally out of proportion to what's been going on. Joey Rothman was my roommate. Luck of the draw. I sure as hell didn't ask for him. He's dead, and frankly I don't care that much one way or the other. But Louise Crenshaw is carrying on like Joey was the Second Coming himself. How come?"

"I don't know," Ralph said, standing up and moving toward the door, taking his half-filled coffee cup with him. "Get up and shower, Beau. We've got things to do."

"What am I supposed to wear?"

"I almost forgot to mention it, Louise had someone pack up your stuff. She sent it down with somebody named Shorty. He dropped it off about an hour ago. The dirty clothes are out in the laundry. The suitcase is in the closet. Shorty said for me to tell you that the sandbags held."

"Wait a minute. You mean the Crenshaws sent my luggage? Before or after somebody from the sheriff's department went over the room?"

"I wouldn't know about that," Ralph answered. "Shorty didn't say. Neither did Louise. Get a move on, Beau. I have to go by my office for a little while. After that, we have dinner reservations between five-thirty and six. It's a good thing Scott called. Otherwise I might not have remembered your birthday."

Fuming with frustration, I crawled out of bed and headed into the shower. Over my objections, Louise and Calvin Crenshaw had ordered someone to pack my things and send them to Phoenix. There was no point in calling Ironwood Ranch to raise hell or to check to see if anyone from the sheriff's department had gone over my room searching for evidence. They hadn't. Louise hadn't let it happen.

Ringo was gone, let loose to starve in the desert somewhere, and my room had been stripped clean of all personal belongings. Any trace of evidence my attempted killer might have left behind would have disappeared as well. If, after our talk in Prescott, Detective Reyes-Gonzales went looking for something, there wouldn't be anything left to find.

The problem with credibility is that once gone, it's hard as hell to regain. I didn't much relish the idea of some bright female homicide detective in Prescott, Arizona, thinking about J. P. Beaumont as a complete fruitcake.

I stood in Ralph Ames' steaming shower and vowed that one way or another Calvin and Louise Crenshaw were going to have to eat their words. Somehow I'd force them to admit that I had indeed been the victim of an attempted homicide. Once they agreed to that sticky stipulation, once they admitted that, they might take me back as a client. They might have thrown me out once, but I'd graduate from their pukey little program or know the reason why.

I was still lost in thought as I stepped out of the shower and toweled myself dry. Something was out of kilter with Calvin and Louise Crenshaw, but I couldn't quite put my finger on what it was. It was enough of a thought to file away for later consideration. After all, that's what we homicide detectives look for—things that are slightly out of place.

Just then a light tapping on the door cut short the thinking process. Ralph was champing at the bit and ready to go. I hurried into my most respectable shirt and sport jacket. Ralph had brought along one of his own ties, which he tossed in my direction. "You'll need it," he said. "For dinner."

Ralph, my friend as well as my attorney, drives an automotive anachronism, a huge whale on wheels—a white Lincoln Town Car. Unlike Rhonda Attwood's Spider, the Lincoln had plenty of headroom and legroom both, even for the likes of me. The smooth gray leather interior was plush and classy enough to suit even the most fastidious of clients, but as one who is making heavy monetary contributions to Ralph Ames' personal lifestyle, I appreciate the fact that he buys American. (After all, the Porsche 928 was *given* to me.) I don't want to pay the freight on the kind of conspicuous consumption that thrives on Mercedes or Jaguars.

We drove first to Ralph's office, a brass-and-glass high rise at Indian School and Central, an area that seems to be close to but not exactly in downtown Phoenix. I'm not sure there *is* a downtown Phoenix, but the city had plenty of mid-afternoon stop-and-go traffic without a freeway or bridge anywhere in sight.

I'm accustomed to the steep, tree-studded glacial ridges of Seattle and the Pacific Northwest. Driving through Phoenix, I was struck by the unremitting sameness of it all. The city seemed brown and flat, an endless panorama of urban blight. Here and there, on the periphery, stark rocky ramparts, blue and gray in the distance, rose up abruptly from the desert floor into a hazy, smoggy sky. I had been in Arizona for more than a month, but the desert still had an alien look about it, alien and forbidding and full of snakes.

When we reached his office, Ralph disappeared into his inner sanctum, leaving me to linger in the finely appointed reception area, where I used the phone to negotiate a temporary peace treaty with Alamo Rent A Car.

It wasn't easy. They were not happy to hear that their vehicle was in the hands of the Yavapai County Sheriff's Department as part of the evidence in a murder investigation, and they weren't eager to rent me a substitute vehicle, either. The first three people I spoke to insisted that I was responsible for daily charges regardless of whether or not the vehicle had been impounded by a law enforcement agency, and none would agree to place a clarifying phone call to Detective Reyes-Gonzales. Finally, on the fourth try, I connected with a supervisor who did make the call. With some additional prodding, she reluctantly allowed as how I could have a Subaru station wagon if I came back to Sky Harbor International Airport that evening to pick it up. I told her I'd be there.

When Ralph emerged from his office an hour later, he was wearing a self-satisfied smile that put me on guard as soon as I saw it.

"What are you grinning about?" I asked.

"Oh, nothing," he said offhandedly, which worried me that much more. "We have an early dinner reservation. We're meeting someone."

"Who?"

"It's a surprise."

The surprise got unwrapped as soon as we pulled into the parking lot of Vincent's on Camelback. The car idling roughly in front of us under the valet parking canopy was a familiar one, a dark green Fiat Spider.

"Rhonda Attwood's here too?" I asked.

Ralph Ames grinned smugly. "That's right. She called and left a message this morning. When I got back to her this afternoon with the information she needed, she said she wanted to speak to you as well. I suggested that she meet us here."

"Information? She asked you for information? What kind?"

"You know I can't answer those kinds of questions, Beau. She asked me to make some simple inquiries for her, that's all."

Ralph's suddenly choosing to duck behind a curtain of professional confidentiality surprised me. Since when had Rhonda Attwood become a client of his?

"You know what she's up to, don't you?" I asked.

"Up to? She's trying to bury her son, and not getting a whole lot of cooperation from her former husband," Ames replied confidently, as though he hadn't a doubt in the world that he knew the whole truth of the matter. I had been too worn out on our trip down from Prescott to Phoenix to give him many of the disturbing details from my hours alone with Rhonda Attwood, but I could see now that I should have warned him.

"Don't get mixed up with her," I said.

The parking attendant parked the Fiat and came back for the Lincoln. Ames got out and handed him the keys.

"What's that supposed to mean?" he asked me over the car's roof as the attendant got inside to drive it away.

"She's dangerous, for one thing," I said.

Ames shook his head in obvious disbelief.

"Look, what if I told you she's another Anne Corley waiting to go off? What would you think of that?"

"I'd say you have an overly active imagination," Ralph Ames said, and started for the entrance.

"Ralph, wait. She told me so herself last night."

"She's arranging a funeral, Beau. Come on."

The small anteroom, furnished with a few chairs and a polished burled maple desk, was decked with bouquets of freshly cut flowers. We were met at the door by a lovely blonde hostess carrying a leather-bound reservation book. She cooed happily over Ralph the moment she saw him.

"Ah, Mr. Ames. So good to see you again. One of your guests has already arrived and been seated. If you will please follow me, I'll take you directly to your table. Vincent is busy with the grill right now, but he'll try to stop by your table in a few minutes, before we get too busy."

Ralph nodded. "Fine," he said.

She led us into the restaurant, which turned out to be an odd mixture of Southwestern-American and something else, Continental probably, although I wouldn't know Continental for sure if it got up and hit me smack in the face. The whole place was light and airy, with white walls and tall open-beamed ceilings. There appeared to be a series of several small, intimate dining rooms, each highlighting some piece of original artwork. A number of other tables were already occupied with parties of early diners, some of whom had drinks in hand although no sign of a bar was in evidence.

Rhonda Attwood was seated in the first room, talking animatedly to a tuxedo-clad man I assumed was our waiter. He shook hands with Ralph, introduced himself to me as Francis, and then turned back to Ames.

"The lady and I have been discussing wines. She says she's never tried Le Neilleur Du Chai."

Ralph beamed at Rhonda. "Good choice. That will be perfect, Francis. Is it '83?"

"Of course," Francis replied.

He started away from the table. Assuming he was our waiter, I wanted to catch him before he left. "I'll have coffee," I said.

Francis nodded. "I'll send your waiter with some right away."

"I thought he was the waiter," I said to Ralph.

"Oh, no. Francis is the sommelier and sometime maitre d'," Ralph answered with a smile. "He and Vincent have been together through several incarnations of local fine dining establishments. As chef, Vincent plays the starring role, but always with Francis backing him up."

Ralph focused on Rhonda. "How are you doing?"

"Fine," she answered. Her sleek hair, brushed back from her face, glowed in the muted, indirect lighting. She was wearing a softly belted knit dress that showed off her figure. There was nothing about Rhonda Attwood that looked the part of a grieving mother. And nothing about the evening had the feel of planning a funeral.

A spiffy waiter in a crisply pleated white shirt and black bow tie appeared moments later. Without having to ask who was who, he set a full cup of coffee in front of me. Before the waiter walked away, Francis was there as well. With suitable pomp and circumstance, he administered the Cabernet Sauvignon, first ceremoniously sampling it with a spoon before offering a sip to Ames and finally pouring the two glasses. Maybe that's why I never cared much for wine—it always involved too much ritual and not enough drinking.

I sat there unnecessarily stirring my black coffee and waiting for them to get on with it. Despite the fact that this was supposedly a dinner in honor of my birthday, the conversation between Ralph and Rhonda made me feel very much like the proverbial fifth wheel.

Eventually, Francis withdrew only to be replaced by Vincent himself, a brawny Swiss ex-patriot who believed in the old-fashioned, hands-on, innkeeper's approach to running a restaurant. He arrived at the table wearing his chef's hat and an eye-watering perfume of mesquite smoke.

Rubbing his hands together in anticipation and fixing Rhonda Attwood with a blazing smile, he said to Ralph, "So this is the lady you were telling me about?"

Ames looked pleased. "She certainly is, Vincent. Allow me to introduce Rhonda Attwood."

What followed was a long discussion of art and artists, of shows and galleries and commissioned paintings—things about which the three of them seemed to know a great deal, while I knew less than nothing. Rhonda Attwood flushed with obvious pleasure that Ralph Ames had such an extensive working knowledge of her artistic progress. The enthusiastic sales pitch Ralph was giving Vincent made me wonder if his attorney relationship with Rhonda Attwood involved a commission.

Art and artists have never been my strong suit. My only artistic achievement, drawing stick figures, went out of vogue between second and third grades. From then on art classes left me cold. The ability to draw a lifelike landscape or seascape or face or even an orange strikes me as something akin to witchcraft.

Talking about all those things is even more remote. Instead of paying much attention, I concentrated on watching the people coming into the restaurant. Vincent's was obviously a place to see and be seen, where Phoenix fashion plates of both sexes sized one another up and kept score. This was almost, but not quite, as boring as the art talk. I was only too happy when some crisis in the kitchen summoned Vincent away from our table.

"So what's good here?" I asked, picking up my menu and trying to turn the conversation back to a subject I could handle.

"You didn't tell me today was your birthday," Rhonda remarked reprovingly.

"It slipped my mind," I replied.

My answer sounded unnecessarily curt, even to me. Ames' raised eyebrow sent me into retreat. "After forty there's not much reason to keep track," I added lightly. "So what's good here?"

"Everything's good," Ralph offered smoothly. "It all depends on what you like."

I looked at my menu, but looking didn't help. It was in French, most of it. The only word that looked vaguely familiar was "tamale," and that was only on the appetizer list.

"I didn't think tamales were French," I objected.

Ralph smiled. "They're not, but these are made from duck and they're wonderful."

With his selection already made, Ralph lowered his menu and caught Rhonda's eye. "So, did you reach her?" he asked.

"Yes, thank you so much," Rhonda murmured. She took a delicate sip of her wine.

I had the distinct feeling I was once more being left out of the conversation. "Reach who?" I questioned.

Ralph didn't answer but Rhonda did. "Michelle," she said. "Michelle Owens. When I called him this morning, Ralph here very kindly agreed to try to help me locate her. He's very efficient. By this afternoon it was a *fait accompli*."

In view of Rhonda's and my conversation from the night before, the idea of her having anything to do with either Michelle or Guy Owens made me very uncomfortable. "Ralph helped you do that?"

Rhonda nodded. "Owens is stationed at Fort Huachuca. He lives in a town called Sierra Vista just outside the military base. It's down in the southeastern part of the state."

I turned from Rhonda to Ralph. Dismay must have registered all over my face. Ralph shrugged as though my concern was totally uncalled for.

"When Rhonda told me that Michelle and Joey had been . . . well, involved, and that perhaps the girl would be interested in attending the funeral, it seemed only reasonable. Under the circumstances, I think Rhonda's being very civilized to take Michelle's feelings into consideration. The funeral's Monday afternoon, by the way," he added for my benefit. "At St. John's Episcopal, right here on Lincoln Drive."

I glanced at Rhonda Attwood. She was gazing back at me innocently, as if daring me to refute any of what Ames had said.

"Excuse me," I said, "but did Rhonda happen to mention to you that Michelle's father, Lieutenant Colonel Guy Owens, is quite possibly a suspect in the investigation into the death of her son?"

Naturally, the waiter chose that exact moment to return to our table. "Are you ready to order?"

"Not yet," Ames told him, waving him away. Only when the waiter was out of earshot did Ames answer my question.

"Actually, Rhonda did mention it. I checked with Delcia before I gave out the number."

"Delcia?" I asked, uncertainly, feeling more and more like an outsider with every passing moment.

"You know, Delcia. Detective Reyes-Gonzales in Prescott. I talked to her early this afternoon. She said that she didn't have a problem with Rhonda inviting Michelle to the funeral."

"What the hell do you think you're doing, messing around in a homicide investigation like that?"

"We're not messing around in any investigation, Beau," Ames countered. "Inviting Michelle Owens to attend Joey Rothman's funeral has nothing whatsoever to do with his murder. Is she going to come, by the way?" he asked, turning to Rhonda.

"If she can," Rhonda replied. "At least that's what she told me on the phone. She seemed touched that I had bothered to call. According to her, she hasn't heard a word from JoJo and Marsha. I don't expect she will, either."

My brief warning to Ames on the way into the restaurant hadn't included Rhonda Attwood's exact words about intending to "take out" the people responsible for her son's death, so he wasn't playing with an entirely full deck, but I was still astounded at the conversation shifting back and forth across the table between them.

I had the sickening feeling that Ralph Ames was being royally suckered, neatly led into the trap, and there I sat, watching but helpless to derail the process. Sentence by sentence Rhonda Attwood deftly plied him for information, asking innocent-sounding questions that drew him further and further into what I saw as her own private vigilante agenda.

It galled me to watch Ralph Ames, my trusty, sophisticated, man-of-the-world attorney who should have known better, be led like a lamb to the slaughter, smiling and laughing all the while. After all, it wasn't the first time. For either one of us.

"What about Michelle's father?" I asked ingenuously. I folded my arms across my chest and waited to see how Rhonda would respond to that one.

"He wasn't invited," she responded carefully.

"I'll just bet he wasn't."

There was a sudden flash of anger in Rhonda Attwood's eyes, one that wasn't masked by the flattering candlelight. "What's that supposed to mean?" she demanded.

Our waiter reappeared as if on cue. It seemed

like a deliberate plot. "Are you ready now?" he asked.

Together, Ralph and Rhonda settled for something that roughly translated into mesquite grilled rack of lamb seasoned with thyme and garlic and served with jalapeño jelly and a still-burning sprig of rosemary. I ordered the Cornish game hen. Ralph insisted that we each try one of the appetizers—the tamales, cucumber soup, and red and yellow bell pepper soup.

The food was fine, but I would have enjoyed the dinner a whole lot more if I could have eaten without the sense that the artistic bullshit that passed for conversation around our table was nothing but a convenient camouflage for Rhonda Attwood's keg of emotional dynamite.

The fuse was already lit. The best I could hope for was to keep it from blowing sky-high and taking an unsuspecting Ralph Ames right along with it.

CHAPTER
12

While Rhonda and Ralph continued to talk about art and things artistic, I contented myself with people watching. The dining room grew crowded and noisy with fashion-plate people, including several who were evidently deeply entrenched in city politics. The women, dressed to the nines, were there to see and be seen. The men were there because the women were.

Our table afforded me an almost unobstructed view of the small grill area where no fewer than six men dove back and forth in a complicated ballet that was almost comic to watch although I have no quarrel with the quality of the food that ultimately ended up on our platter-sized plates.

Dessert, an unpronounceable *crème brûlée*, consisted of three flavors of custard served in sweet miniature taco shells and topped with a rich raspberry sauce. Ames must have cued someone about my birthday, because my chocolate-glazed plate arrived with a lit candle stuck right in the middle of one of my custards. Thank God they didn't light all the candles I deserved.

I kept waiting for Rhonda to steer the conversation back to her son's murder, but that didn't happen, nor was there any further reference to plans for Joey's funeral. Two and a half hours after we had been seated, we were waiting outside for the valet to retrieve our cars. He brought the Fiat first. As Rhonda was getting in, she turned back to Ralph.

"Thank you for getting me the room," she said, almost as an afterthought. "It's so convenient, but . . ."

If she was going to voice an objection, Ralph waved it away. "Don't worry about it. It's my pleasure."

"What room?" I asked, once Rhonda had roared out of the parking lot past a waist-high sign that through some inexplicable coincidence said "Beaumont Properties."

"At La Posada," Ralph said. "The manager and I are good friends. We trade favors back and forth all the time. It's just up the street from the church. I told her to stay there until after the funeral."

The drive to Sky Harbor in Ames' Lincoln was thorny. When I tried to recap some of what Rhonda had told me the night before, Ralph listened politely enough. When I finished, he brushed aside my concerns, telling me I was completely off base, out of my head. When I hinted that he might be losing his objectivity in regard to Rhonda Attwood, he came as close as Ralph Ames ever comes to losing his cool.

"Look," he said finally, sounding somewhat annoyed. "I appreciate your concern, Beau, but give me a little more credit than that. Right now Rhonda Attwood is a woman beset by numerous legal difficulties. She also happens to be a gifted artist whose work I've admired for some time. Certainly I jumped at the chance to be of service, but just because I've decided to help her, don't assume there's a whole underlying agenda for either one of us, because there isn't."

"So you're not interested in her personally?"

"Professionally, not personally."

"And you're not worried that she might try to draw you into the fray?"

"I don't believe there's going to be any 'fray,' as you put it, but I'll take your warning under advisement."

That was the best I could do.

At the Alamo office near the airport, Ames started to park and come inside with me, but I told him not to bother, that wouldn't be necessary. Promising to see him at home, I trudged into the office prepared to face down the folks at the rental desk. They treated me with an air of less than cordial distrust, regarding me as an auto-renting leper who, however inadvertently, had managed to involve one of their precious Grand AMs in a homicide investigation.

A supervisor, not the same one I had talked to earlier on the phone, was summoned from a back room. She subjected me to a lengthy and public lecture on my general automotive character and deportment. The lecture concluded with a recita-

tion of rental agreement no-nos, the strongest of
which was a forcefully worded prohibition against
taking my Subaru anywhere into the wilds of Old
Mexico. I received my keys only after promising,
cross my heart, that I had no such evil intention.

Relieved to escape the office, I retreated to the
welcome solitude of the Subaru, even though,
compared to the luxury of Ames' Lincoln with its
car phone and liquid-crystal dashboard instru-
mentation or to my own Porsche, the modest four-
wheel-drive station wagon represented a big step
downward. It seemed gangly and awkward, but
it still beat walking.

As I left the airport area, my first inclination
was to drive directly back to Ralph's place, but by
the second stoplight, I rethought that plan. I had
slept away most of the day, and it was far too
early for bed. I certainly didn't want to resume my
non-conversation with Ralph Ames regarding
Rhonda Attwood's questionable intentions.

My second inclination was to turn in at the very
next HAPPY HOUR sign on the right-hand side of
the street and buy myself a drink, a double, but
the place turned out to be a topless joint in an
exceedingly marginal neighborhood. Repelled, I
kept on driving. Besides, did I really want to stop
there with the dust of Ironwood Ranch still stick-
ing to the heels of my shoes? That thought
brought me abruptly back to the business with
Calvin and Louise Crenshaw.

According to Ames, Louise herself was spread-
ing the story that the snake in my cabin had some-

how wandered in from the wild. She was, was she? Maybe it was time to see about that.

I glanced at my watch and saw that it was only nine o'clock, still plenty of time to drive the seventy miles or so to Wickenburg and beard the lions in their cozy ranch-style den. With any kind of luck, I'd manage to see both of them at once. I turned left at the next intersection and headed west on McDowell, a major east-west arterial, figuring correctly that eventually I'd run into Interstate 17 headed north.

By ten-fifteen, I was parked in front of the Crenshaws' one-level rambler, where both the porch light and several interior lights were on. The flickering glow of a television set told me someone was home. I rang the bell.

Calvin, clad in a bathrobe and floppy slippers and wearing a sleepy yellow tabby cat draped across one shoulder, came to the door. He opened it and frowned when he saw who I was. "What are you doing here?"

"I came to talk. Can I come in?"

He hesitated for a moment before stepping away from the door and holding it open. "I suppose." It was hardly an engraved invitation. "What do you want?"

"To talk," I repeated. "With both you and Louise."

"She isn't here," he said.

"When will she be back?"

He shook his head. "Who knows? We don't keep very close tabs on one another."

He shut the front door and padded back into the living room, moving carefully so as not to disturb the cat. I followed a few paces behind him. Calvin settled comfortably into a high-backed chair that made me homesick for my own leather recliner back home in Seattle.

"Have a seat," he said, motioning me onto the couch.

The cat raised its head, blinked once or twice, then stood and stretched before climbing languorously down from its shoulder perch. In Calvin's ample lap, it circled several times and then settled contentedly into a compact gold-and-orange-striped ball. The cat's noisy purring could be heard all the way across the room.

Calvin scratched the cat's chin affectionately. "His name is Hobbes," he said to me. "You know, like in the comics?"

I didn't know someone named Hobbes from a hole in the ground. "I don't read the comics," I explained. "I don't read newspapers at all."

Calvin Crenshaw looked at me with one raised eyebrow and then he nodded. "I see," he said. "So what is it you came here to talk about?"

"The snake. Ringo. Joey Rothman's pet rattlesnake. Why is Louise insisting that the snake I found in my cabin was a wild snake that wandered in out of the rain? Rhonda Attwood saw it and positively identified it when Lucy Washington pawned her off on Shorty to come find me. Rhonda told me right then that it was Joey's snake, that he'd had it for almost fourteen years."

Calvin sighed. "It's gone. I told Louise that was a mistake, but by then she'd already ordered Shorty to get rid of it. It's useless to try to cover up that kind of thing, you know, but Louise was all upset at the time and not thinking very straight. She was in no condition to listen to advice from anybody, me included."

"You mean you already knew about the snake?"

"Shorty told me about Mrs. Attwood's identification. I knew right away that it was only a matter of time, but I try to let Louise handle things her own way. I thought a day or two might give her a chance to pull herself together. This has really been hard on her, you know."

"Hard on Louise!" I exclaimed. "How about me? Covering up an attempted homicide is a crime—obstruction of justice. I should think that detective from Prescott would have pointed that out to you by now."

"I've talked to her," Calvin said, "and straightened things out. It was unfortunate that the snake disappeared in all the confusion. The detective told me she'll be down tomorrow morning to take Shorty's statement."

It was some small consolation, but not much.

"I take it, then, that now you do finally believe that somebody tried to kill me?"

Calvin Crenshaw nodded reluctantly. "I suppose so."

"You wouldn't happen to have any idea who, would you?"

He laughed. "You're asking me?"

"That's right. You and your wife seem to have gone to a good deal of trouble to conceal what really happened. I'm wondering why."

"You're barking up the wrong tree, Mr. Beaumont. Murder, attempted or otherwise, isn't my bailiwick."

"Unless you were covering up for your wife."

That single blunt statement was a calculated attack, a ploy I had been planning on the drive up from Phoenix. I waited quietly, watching Calvin Crenshaw's reaction.

He blinked in what seemed like genuine astonishment. "Covering up for Louise? You've got to be kidding. Certainly you don't think *she's* the one who tried to kill you, do you?"

"Her behavior as far as I'm concerned has been totally irrational since the very first day I set foot on Ironwood Ranch."

"Oh, that," Calvin said, sounding immensely relieved, as if it had all suddenly become clear to him. "Of course. I can see how you could misread it."

"Misread what?"

"Her behavior toward you. Louise doesn't handle rejection very well. You hurt her feelings."

It was my turn to blink. "I hurt *her* feelings?"

"Joey Rothman was nothing but a temporary aberration," Calvin continued, "a ship passing in the night. You're far more Louise's type, far more to her liking generally. If you had given her the least bit of encouragement, I'm sure she would have tossed Joey aside completely, but you made it clear that you weren't interested. You didn't take the bait when she offered it. Yes, you hurt her feelings."

"Wait just a damn minute here. Take what bait? What the hell are you talking about?"

"The results of long-term drinking aren't always entirely reversible," Calvin said circumspectly, seeming to change the subject entirely.

"What's that supposed to mean?"

"I've been left with a rather permanent impairment in the sexual activity department."

"Oh," I said, although I still couldn't make out exactly where he was leading.

Calvin continued. "Louise doesn't seem to mind, at least not most of the time, but every once in a while, she does. When that happens, she tends to target one of the clients. For strictly recreational purposes, you see."

"You're telling me that periodically your wife gets her rocks off with one of your clients at Ironwood Ranch? That you know about it and let her?"

He shrugged. "It doesn't bother me particularly. None of it's ever serious. After all, you people are only here for six weeks at a time, and then you go away, back home where you belong, and Louise is fine for a few more months."

I was dumbfounded. Calvin Crenshaw, talking smoothly and without hesitation, discussed his wife's ongoing recreational infidelities among her patients the way he might describe her suffering from the ill effects of a common cold.

"And as I said," he added, "most of the time it's been with men like you—fortyish, good-looking macho types, fairly stable except for the drinking. Louise seems to prefer drinkers to other kinds of addicts, so I'll admit I was a bit startled when she took up with Joey, but then maybe he was the one who made the first move. It's been my observation that older women are always flattered when younger men find them attractive. Just like older men with younger women."

"So this has been a long-term thing and you've done nothing about it?"

"What would you have had me do, Beau? Throw the men involved out of the program? Not on your life, not at nine thou a crack. Get rid of her, then? No way. I need Louise here. She runs the place. Without her running the show, Ironwood Ranch would fall apart in two minutes flat. No matter what you think about her personal foible, Louise is a helluva good administrator. She may have her idiosyncrasies, but she doesn't miss a trick."

Calvin Crenshaw seemed unfazed by his own unfortunate choice of words. Maybe they didn't register with him. They did with me.

"I was under the impression that professional medical ethics preclude taking patients to bed," I observed sarcastically.

"My wife is a healthy, red-blooded, middle-aged, sexually liberated woman who has had the misfortune of marrying an involuntary monk.

She's making the best of a bad bargain."

"It doesn't sound like such a bad bargain to me. She gets you, complete with a suitable balance sheet and a going-concern business, along with blanket permission to screw around as much as she likes."

"Are you implying that she only married me for my money?"

"It seems possible," I returned.

"And maybe it's true," Calvin agreed. "In fact, the thought occurred to me a time or two in the early years, but she's been a tremendous help in this business, a tireless worker and a real asset. In your eyes our marital arrangement may seem a bit unconventional, but it's been eminently satisfactory to both of us. I don't have any complaints, and I'd be surprised if Louise did either. The status quo suits us both perfectly."

"It didn't suit Joey Rothman," I pointed out. "He's dead, and your satisfactory marital arrangement, as you call it, may very well have had something to do with his death."

Before, Calvin Crenshaw had been talking easily, confidently, something he was evidently capable of doing privately if not publicly. Now he bristled. "Is that some kind of accusation?" he demanded.

"It's a theory," I said.

"No. Absolutely not. Joey's death had nothing to do with Louise or me. I'm sure of that."

"Maybe not you," I countered. "But what about Louise? Look at the way she's been acting."

Calvin remained adamant. "It's a preposterous idea. Totally preposterous. All this may have left Louise a bit unbalanced in the short run, for a day or two at most, but she'll bounce back. You'll see. She's like that unsinkable Molly Brown."

"Where is she?" I asked.

"Taking the weekend off. In Vegas. R and R. She needs it."

"Aren't you worried about her bringing home a sexually transmitted disease?"

"I think it's time you left, Mr. Beaumont. You seem to have worn out your welcome. I'm sure you can find your way out."

I got up and stood there for a moment, trying to figure out what made Calvin Crenshaw tick, why someone who wouldn't give me the time of day earlier was now spilling his guts to me. Was he complaining about his wife's infidelities or bragging about them? I couldn't figure it out.

In his own way, Calvin Crenshaw was probably every bit as much of a crackpot as his wife was. Years of police work have convinced me that there's no point in arguing with nuts. It's a waste of time, breath, and energy.

His gaze met and held mine. "I must caution you, Mr. Beaumont, that if you mention any of what we've discussed here tonight to anyone else, I'll categorically deny it."

"And if you deny it, then it doesn't exist, is that the idea?"

Calvin Crenshaw smiled. "Generally speaking.

Something like that. My word against yours and all that."

"So that's how it is?"

Calvin nodded, smiling again. "I'm glad we understand one another, but I do have one question for you."

"What's that?"

"Louise tells me everything, you see. Everything. Sometimes she even lets me watch. The last time she was with Joey, he tried to borrow some money from her."

"How much?"

"Twenty-five thousand dollars. Naturally, she refused to give it to him, but considering what all happened, I've been doing some serious thinking about it since. At the time Joey asked for the money, he threatened to tell me about their affair."

"In other words, he tried to blackmail her."

"I suppose that's what you call it, but as soon as Louise told him it wouldn't work, that I already knew what was going on, he backed right off. Didn't seem to have the stomach for it somehow."

"So what's your question?"

"I know his parents are loaded, at least his father is. Why do you suppose he needed that much money?" Calvin asked.

Of all the questions Calvin Crenshaw could have been asking, should have been asking, that one seemed like one of the least likely, particularly since it pointed the loaded gun of motive directly back at his own head and at Louise's as well.

"I have no idea," I replied.

"Oh well," Calvin said resignedly, sounding genuinely disappointed.

I stood looking down at him, feeling a sense of total disgust. This voyeuristic little shit and his promiscuous wife, masters of the art of double-speak, played out their ugly little games behind a mask of helping-profession respectability. I realized then that this was just like my experience with Ringo. I had been in the same room with a snake, a human one this time, without sensing the danger, without realizing I was in jeopardy. I couldn't help wondering if Calvin Crenshaw wasn't just as dangerous as Ringo, and maybe even a little less predictable.

I turned to go. Carefully putting the cat down on the floor, Calvin got up and followed me after all. He stopped in the doorway.

"By the way, Louise and I have reconsidered. No matter what she said to that attorney of yours, you're welcome to come back and finish out your program."

I couldn't believe he was serious, but he was, continuing on with bland indifference.

"You'll need to check first and make sure we have room. We generally run a ninety-five percent occupancy rate, but we'll work you in."

"Thanks for the offer, Calvin," I said firmly. "I'll think it over."

With that, I stepped onto the sidewalk and hurried toward the Subaru, inhaling the clean, sharp air of the cool desert night. Above me, myriad yellow stars winked bright against the velvety black sky.

One of those distant, twinkling diamonds had to be mine, I thought thankfully—my own personal lucky star. After all, Louise Crenshaw had wanted me, and I hadn't even noticed. Unwittingly, without even noticing the trap, I had blundered away slick as a whistle.

I felt eternally and abjectly grateful.

CHAPTER
13

Ames had left the handset of his wireless phone just inside my door, and its cheerful chirping woke me early Saturday morning.

"Daddy," Kelly said when I answered. "Is that you? Are you awake?"

"I am now," I mumbled. "Barely. What time is it?"

"Just after seven, California time. Sorry to disturb you, but I've got a date to play tennis at eight. It's a little late, but happy birthday. Hope you had fun."

"Thanks. Ralph Ames took me out to dinner." My early morning engines hadn't quite caught fire. Since Kelly and I have never operated on quite the same wavelength, what followed was a long, awkward pause.

"Scott said you wanted to talk to me."

"That's right. I do."

"What about?" Her question was abrupt. She was worried about whatever was coming and wanted to get it over with.

"Joey Rothman," I answered quietly.

There was another long pause, but when she spoke she sounded exasperated. "Daddy, I already told you, nothing happened. I mean, we didn't go to bed or anything, if that's what you're worried about. Don't you trust me?"

Her whimpered question seemed to be verging on tears. That was the last thing I wanted. "Please, Kelly. Don't get upset. What you tell us may very well help us figure out what happened to him, that's all."

"You mean you're working on the case?"

"Something like that."

"Oh," she said, but she didn't volunteer any further information.

There was dead, empty silence on the other end of the phone. So that was how it would be. If I was playing cop and looking for answers, Kelly wasn't about to make it easy. It's the kind of diversionary strategy she learned at her mother's knee. My best countermeasure was to tackle the problem head-on.

"Did Joey tell you about Michelle Owens?" I asked. "Did you know they were going together?"

I heard the sharp intake of breath. "No." There was a small pause. "He lied to me about that, but it didn't matter."

"What do you mean, it didn't matter?"

"Daddy, are you listening to me? We weren't going together. It wasn't like that. We talked mostly, just talked. I thought he was really rad. You know, exciting."

"Like forbidden fruit."

"Maybe. Anyway, we were just getting to know each other."

As far as I can tell, the word "rad" roughly translates into something my generation would have called "cool." As for the words "getting to know each other"—those must have changed entirely since I was Kelly's age. The probing kiss I had seen Joey plant on Kelly's lips had been well beyond the glad-to-make-your-acquaintance stage of human sexual relations. I'm not so far out of touch that I'd mistake a kiss like that for a platonic one. My daughter and I were suffering from a classic case of failure to communicate.

"So what did the two of you talk about, Kelly?"

"You."

Her one-word answer surprised me. "Me?" I echoed.

"Joey was more interested in you than he was in me. He wanted to know exactly where you were a police officer and what kind of work you did. You know, robbery, homicide, that kind of thing. When I told him you had a lot of money, he said you were probably on the take. We almost had a fight about that, but I told him. You know . . . about Anne Corley."

She was finally opening up a little, telling me more than the bare minimum, but I knew the next question could turn her off again, just like a faucet, but she had brought up something that sounded like a common thread.

"Did he ask you for money, Kel?"

"No. Why would he do that?"

"I just thought he might have, that's all."

"Well, he didn't. He must have known I didn't have any."

I didn't know whether to be relieved or sad that my "common thread" had so quickly become a dead end.

"And then what happened?"

"We talked mostly and . . ."

"And what?"

"And stuff."

"What kind of stuff?"

"You know. I mean, you saw us."

"I saw you necking."

"Daddy, you don't understand. All the boys around here are such *children*, and Joey seemed so . . ."

"Experienced?" God help me, I couldn't keep from filling in the blank, although I wanted to bite my tongue as soon as the word passed my lips.

"Yes," Kelly whispered.

Joey Rothman was dead, but I think Kelly was still more than half infatuated with him. I wanted to shake her, tell her to wake up and smell the coffee. With any kind of luck, maybe she would grow up enough to see that being experienced is only half the battle. You also have to know what to *do* with those experiences.

"Joey was wrong about you, wasn't he, Daddy?"

"Wrong about what?"

"When he said you were working undercover for the DEA. I told him that was crazy, that you do homicide not drugs and that you were there for treatment just like everybody else." She stopped and took a breath.

"Yes, Kelly," I answered wearily. "I was there for treatment. Period."

"And you weren't working undercover."

"No."

"That's what Mr. Joe said, too. You know, the counselor back at the ranch? In his office that day he said you were a substance abuser just like the rest of them and that he was sure you didn't have anything to do with what had happened to Joey."

Suddenly, Scott's remark about good old Burton Joe being on my side clicked into focus.

"I've gotta go now, Daddy. My ride's waiting outside. Did that help?"

"As a matter of fact, it did," I told her. "A lot. Thanks."

"Okay."

"And, Kelly? One more thing."

"What's that?" A guarded wariness came into her voice, as though she dreaded what other intrusive questions I might ask.

"I love you, Kelly."

Her relief was apparent, even over the phone. "I love you, too, Daddy. Bye."

For a long time, I lay there on the bed, thinking about Joey Rothman and his fruitless quest for money. He hadn't asked Kelly, but he had tried accumulating cash in at least two other places. From the sound of it, his relationship with Kelly had been nothing more than a cover for intelligence-seeking about me, but with Rhonda and Louise, he sounded as though he was gathering getaway money. Rhonda was probably right. In all likelihood he would have moved elsewhere and then reinvested his capital right back in the same business—whatever that was.

I may have dozed again for a little while. The next time I opened my eyes, I had left Joey Rothman far behind and found myself wondering what to do with this unexpectedly unstructured day. At Ironwood Ranch, every moment had been measured and accounted for. Now, here I was in a strange limbo where I wasn't exactly on vacation, wasn't exactly in treatment, and couldn't very well go home, not when Detective Reyes-Gonzales had given me strict orders to hang around. Maybe Ralph Ames would have some brilliant idea. Besides, I wanted to have a heart-to-heart chat with him and let him know about the dark underbelly of Ironwood Ranch.

I headed for the shower. Later, when I came back out to get dressed, I was chagrined to discover that I was down to my last clean set of underwear. The only socks I had left were the mismatched pair consisting of one blue and one black. It was time to do laundry. It was past time to do laundry.

Once I was dressed, I gathered up the small pile that contained my newest dirty clothes and went in search of a washer/dryer and coffee, not necessarily in that order.

In the kitchen, on Ralph Ames' snow-white Corian countertop, I found an insulated carafe filled with hot coffee, a glass of freshly squeezed orange juice, and a note. The note, written in Ames' precise script, told me that unfortunately he had a prior commitment that would keep him busy most of the day, but that he'd be back late in the afternoon. Together we'd do something about dinner.

So I was on my own, for the whole day. Knowing that, I had no reason to rush into doing the laundry. I opened a sliding pocket door off the kitchen far enough to see that the room behind it was indeed the laundry. It smelled rotten in there. The penetrating stench seemed dreadfully out of place, especially in Ralph Ames' otherwise immaculate house. Quickly I dropped my bundle on the floor and shut the door again to keep the foul odor locked inside, then I turned to the serious business of coffee.

Awkwardly, holding the carafe with my arm, the glass of orange juice in one hand, and an empty cup in the other, I pushed open a sliding glass door with my shoulder and ventured out onto the patio to soak up some of Arizona's much-touted autumn sunshine. It was high time.

I settled down at a glass-topped patio table beside the pool and leaned back in the chair, with my eyes closed at times, feeling the warmth of the bright, brassy sun on the side of my face. Behind me I heard the usual city sounds—muted tires scrubbing on pavement, the sporadic rumble of occasional trucks, and once the blaring squall of a passing ambulance. The city was there all right, at my back and out of sight behind the glaring white stucco of Ralph Ames' rambling house, while before me loomed the rugged majesty of Camelback Mountain.

Ames had mentioned it to me once or twice, talked about how he considered himself privileged to live with that giant mound of red rock and its occasional internal grumblings as one of his closest neighbors. Sitting there quietly, sipping the sweet pulpy orange juice, I gradually came to understand what he had meant. A soothing, almost palpable silence drifted down the jagged sandstone cliffs like a veil of dense fog, wrapping itself around me and, for a brief while, blocking out all the disquieting circumstances of the past few days.

I may have actually slept for a moment or two, but finally, I roused myself and poured a cup of steaming coffee. Alternating the hot coffee with cool sips of orange juice, I sat for more than an hour, allowing myself to think about each of the players in turn, considering them individually and collectively:

Joey Rothman, a dead creep with no socially redeeming value, had evidently believed I was really some kind of undercover supercop sent to nail his ass. He had believed it enough, despite Kelly's protestations to the contrary, that he had sicced his pet rattlesnake on me. He hadn't tried to put the touch on Kelly in his search for investment capital, but I wondered how many others besides Louise Crenshaw and Rhonda had been approached in his quest for quick cash.

Rhonda Attwood, Joey's mother, seemed convinced that he was responsible for the attempt on my life, but despite the fact that nothing in her son's grubby life made his death seem worthy of revenge, and despite good advice to the contrary, Rhonda persisted in the illogical notion she could or should single-handedly take on whoever was responsible for her son's death. There was a good chance that her bungling around in the case would backfire and drive the killer or killers to ground.

Michelle, the dead man's pregnant "fiancée," had been jilted twice—once by Joey's behavior with Kelly and once by a bullet fired from my .38. I had asked Kelly if she had known about Michelle, and now I wondered if Michelle had known about Kelly. If so, what had been her reaction? On the surface, Michelle Owens had seemed insubstantial, almost a will-o'-the-wisp, and yet pulling the trigger on a handgun doesn't require much physical strength. Anger does wonders for itchy trigger fingers.

That brought me back to the lieutenant colonel, father of the pregnant non-bride. He was a definite possibility, having both motive and opportunity, but there was part of me that hoped it wasn't him. The two of us were too much alike, had too much in common.

Finally, I came around to the Crenshaws, those wonderful horrific folks, scum parading under the guise of small-town middle-class respectability.

Louise had snared the unsuspecting Joey for an insignificant sexual dalliance, with her impotent husband watching from the sidelines and urging her on. No wonder those two had been totally impervious to Joey's clumsy blackmail attempt. Of the three, I had a tough time choosing who was the most reprehensible.

And here was I, poor old J. P. Beaumont who never did anything to anybody, involved in this mess all the way up to my eyeteeth, stuck in the middle of this rogue's gallery briar-patch. The more I tried to get away, the deeper   sank, trapped in muck, hoping against hope that Detective Reyes-Gonzales would find a way to bring this impossible muddle to some kind of satisfactory conclusion. With any kind of luck, the lady would be good at her job.

Maybe I was no longer a prime suspect, but until Detective Reyes-Gonzales straightened things out, she wasn't likely to let me get on an airplane and go back home. The prospect of hanging around Arizona indefinitely with nothing to do but wait wasn't one I relished.

With that thought in mind, I put down my emptied coffee cup and went to start the washing machine. The smell in the laundry room hadn't gotten any better. Shorty Rojas or whoever had gathered up my personal effects from the cabin at Ironwood Ranch had evidently dumped my wet sandbagging clothes into the laundry bag and tied the damn thing shut. Anyone who's ever had the misfortune of forgetting a wet bath towel in a clothes hamper for a day or two knows what I'm talking about. There was another smell, too, hovering in the background, but the odor of the moldy clothes was so overpowering that at first I couldn't quite identify the other one.

My mother always insisted on sorting clothes into three stacks—whites, light-colored, and dark-colored. After first locating a large plastic bottle of bleach and pouring some into the filling washing machine, I began the sorting process. The ones on top, still dank and wet and shot through with sand, came out first and fell into a sodden heap. I left them there, figuring I'd wash those separately.

Next came a fistful of socks and underwear. I sorted out the socks. Loose sand had sifted down from the wet things at the top of the bag. When I shook a T-shirt to get rid of the sand, something small and white came free from the material and flew across the room like a guided missile, landing with a tiny soft thud several feet away on Ralph Ames' surgically clean kitchen floor. Not wanting to leave a mess, I went to retrieve whatever it was, and it turned out to be a mouse. A dead white mouse. A reeking dead white mouse.

For a sickening moment I was back in the cabin at Ironwood Ranch looking down at a regurgitated pile of fur and tail. I'm not scared of dead mice, but if a mouse could be concealed in my dirty clothes bag, I wondered what else could.

Dreading what I might find, I left the mouse where it was and went back to the laundry room.

Gingerly I shook out the entire bag, emptying the contents onto the floor and then kicking through the resulting heap to see if there were any other unwelcome surprises. There weren't. The only things left in my dirty clothes bag were moldy, dirty clothes.

By now the machine was full of hot soapy water, agitating wildly because no clothing had been added. I gathered up the white clothes, stuck them in the machine, and closed the lid before going back to the kitchen to deal with the mouse.

I located a plastic sandwich bag and put the mouse inside, lifting it by its tail when I picked it up. The plastic didn't succeed in containing all the odor, so I took bag and mouse outside and placed the malodorous package on the patio table.

For some time I stood looking down at it, trying to sort out what it meant. It was a clue of some kind, a message, but where had it come from and what was it trying to tell me? How had it gotten in my laundry bag? Who would have put it there, when, and why? Inarguably, the mouse had something to do with Joey Rothman, his rattlesnake Ringo, and hence the murder itself. But what? And what did all of that have to do with me?

Feeling more than a little silly, I went back into the house, picked up the kitchen telephone, and dialed information to get the number of the Yavapai County Sheriff's Department in Prescott. What the hell was I doing? Calling a goddamn homicide detective to report finding a dead mouse, for Chrissake? But gut instinct told me that the mouse was somehow related to Detective Reyes-Gonzales' case, and I couldn't afford to piss her off by withholding information no matter how trivial that information might seem at first glance.

The dispatcher told me the detective wasn't in. As a matter of fact, she was on the road, possibly somewhere between Wickenburg and Phoenix at that very moment. I left my name and phone number on the off chance that sooner or later Detective Reyes-Gonzales would check in with him.

"If it's an emergency of some kind, I can try patching you through," he offered helpfully.

An emergency? About a dead white mouse? Not likely. Not even I had that much nerve.

"Don't worry about it," I said quickly, giving him my name and number. "And don't go to any extra trouble. But if you do hear from her, tell her I called. There's no big rush."

I hung up the phone, drained the final cup of coffee from the carafe, and paced around in the kitchen, thinking and trying to decide what to do. Sitting still and doing nothing would drive me crazy. Homicide cops are action junkies, but in this instance, taking any kind of action at all could get me in a whole shit-pot of trouble.

I kept thinking about the dead mouse, cooking now in its plastic bag on the sunny patio table, and Ringo, the rattlesnake, starving to death somewhere on the banks of the swollen Hassa- yampa River. A dead mouse and an equally dead snake. Suddenly those two thoughts collided in my head, and a light bulb came on. Surely Marsha or JoJo Rothman would know when and how Ringo left their house. Why hadn't I thought to ask them about it earlier?

Quickly I searched through Ames' white laminated kitchen cabinets until I located a drawer full of telephone books. The number for James and Marsha Rothman listed a Carefree address. I dialed. Jennifer Rothman answered on the second ring.

"Hello, Jennifer, this is Detective Beaumont, from Ironwood Ranch. Remember me?"

"I know you. You're the one who helped me get to ride the horse."

"That's right. Are either one of your parents home?"

"No, they both had to leave for a while. The babysitter is here, but she's watching television. Cartoons. Want to talk to her?"

I tried to conceal my disappointment. A cartoon-watching babysitter wasn't going to be much help. I started to ask Jennifer when her parents would be home and to tell her that I'd call back later, when I thought better of it. Maybe Jennifer herself could provide some of the information I needed.

"Jennifer," I said casually, "do you remember Joey's snake?"

"Ringo? Sure, I remember him. Sometimes Joey let me feed him. I did it while he was gone."

Of course. I couldn't believe my luck. "You mean you took care of Ringo while Joey was away at Ironwood Ranch?"

"My brother showed me how to do it," she answered proudly. "And he paid me, too. Twenty bucks. I was always real careful, though. Rattlesnakes are poisonous, you know. I always thought Ringo was kind of creepy. I like kittens."

"When's the last time you saw Ringo?" I asked.

"The night Joey came to say good-bye."

"He what?"

"When he came to say good-bye and to get his books. It was in the middle of the night and he woke me up. He had Ringo in a bag. He said he was leaving, that I wouldn't ever see him again. Did he know he was going to die, Mr. Beaumont? Do people know they're going to die before it happens?"

Her distress radiated through the phone lines. My questions had reopened a painful wound.

"Sometimes they do," I answered.

There was a pause. Someone was speaking in the background, on the other end of the line. I heard Jennifer say, "No, it's for me. It's a friend of mine," followed by another pause.

"Jennifer?" I asked. "Are you there?"

"Yes," she answered, her voice small, tremulous.

"Tell me again what happened."

"I was asleep. Joey came into my room and woke me up. He had Ringo with him in a pillow-case that was tied shut. He told me that he came back for Ringo and his books. He said he was going away, so far away that I'd never see him again."

"What did you do?"

"I didn't want him to leave, and I started to cry. He said to keep quiet or I'd wake Mother and Daddy. So I kept quiet."

"And he left?"

"Yes. He got his books and left."

"What books?"

"You know. Like a diary. I always kept them for him." She laughed. "He always said the best hiding place is in plain sight, and that's where I kept them for him. On my bookshelf."

"And then what happened?"

"Like I said, he took the books and the snake and left. The next morning, I tried to tell Daddy about it, but he said it was all a bad dream or I made it up. That Joey would be back as soon as he got out of the hospital and that I shouldn't worry about it."

"Did you tell him about Ringo?"

"No," she answered. "I didn't have a chance. He was in a hurry."

Again someone was speaking in the background on the other end of the line. "The baby-sitter wants to use the phone," Jennifer said. "I have to go."

"Thank you," I told her. "You've been a big help."

"Is Ringo dead too?" she asked suddenly. "Is he dead just like Joey?"

"I don't know," I replied honestly. "He may be all right, but then again, I'm not sure."

"I didn't like Ringo," Jennifer said softly, "but

I don't want him to be dead. If he came back home, I'd take care of him, all by myself. No one would have to help me."

Jennifer Rothman was a little girl whose unappreciated goodness knew no bounds. My heart ached for her.

"Do you want me to have Mother or Daddy call you when they get back?" she asked, her voice brightening once more. "They'll be home pretty soon."

"No," I answered. "That won't be necessary, Jennifer. You've really been a big help."

CHAPTER
14

I put down the phone and stood looking at it for a long moment. Out in the laundry room, the washing machine rocked crazily into an uneven spin cycle, but I barely heard it. It was the morning after my forty-fourth birthday, and I was damn lucky to be alive.

Joey Rothman had indeed tried to kill me. His mother's worst suspicions were now confirmed by the innocent revelations of his adoring half-sister. But why? Had he been acting on his own authority or on somebody else's orders? Was it because he had truly believed I was there working undercover, or was it due to some other reason entirely? It was impossible to tell.

In twenty years of police work, I had no doubt racked up more than my share of enemies, people who wouldn't have blinked twice at the idea of Detective J. P. Beaumont being rubbed out of existence. Ostensibly, most of those people *should* have been in Washington State, preferably behind bars, but the justice system doesn't necessarily work that way. Creeps get out of jail all the time.

Sooner or later, they're back on the street, most likely still harboring grudges against the people who locked them up in the first place. Was it some pissed-off penal system graduate who had hired Joey Rothman to do his dirty work? If so, how had he known where to find me? Although I suppose that's a naive question. My checking into Ironwood Ranch had to be one of the worst-kept secrets of all time.

The wobbling washing machine rocked to a stop. Grabbing the clean clothes out of the tub, I took a whiff of them before placing them in the dryer. The dose of bleach had done its magic—the moldy odor was gone. Restarting the washer, I poured in another cupful of bleach before adding the lightly colored clothing. So what if some of the colored things faded? I much prefer faded to smelly.

When I came out of the laundry room, I could hear a voice speaking somewhere in the house. At first I thought Ames had returned, bringing someone with him. Then I recognized Detective Reyes-Gonzales' disembodied voice saying, "I guess you must have gone out, so I'll try back later."

Evidently I hadn't heard the ringing telephone over the laundry room's noisy equipment and running water. I dove for the phone and snatched it up. "I'm here," I said quickly. "Don't hang up." I caught her just in time.

"Detective Beaumont? Is that you?"

"Yes. The washer and dryer were both going full blast. I didn't hear the phone ring."

"I got a message from the dispatcher that you wanted to talk to me."

"That's right. Something's come up. We need to talk. When can I see you?"

"Not right now," she said. "I'm just now parking at the Department of Public Safety crime lab. The guy I need to see will be here for only a few more minutes. What about later, after I finish up with him?"

"Sure. Tell me where you'll be," I said. "I'll meet you."

"You have wheels?"

"At the moment," I replied.

I could almost hear her smiling. "Does that mean you convinced Alamo to rent you another car?"

She was having a little fun at my expense, but I didn't blame her, and I was operating under no delusions. Alamo would never have given me the keys to a second vehicle if Detective Reyes-Gonzales hadn't gone to bat for me over the telephone.

"As a matter of fact they did," I said dryly. "Thanks for the help on that score."

"No problem. I was happy to do it. Do you know your way around Phoenix?"

"A little," I replied. "Enough to get back and forth from the airport."

She laughed. "The DPS headquarters is at 19th Avenue and Encanto. Know where that is?"

"No, but I'm sure I can find it. Alamo gave me a map."

"Good. How about meeting me at La Piñata? It's a Mexican restaurant at 19th and Osborn. I'll be there by eleven-thirty or so, if that's all right."

Why wouldn't it be all right? I thought. I sure as hell wasn't doing anything else, although I was wearing a little thin on an almost steady diet of Mexican food. "That'll be fine," I said.

I found the restaurant without any trouble. A Yavapai County Sheriff's Department car was already parked outside. Going into the darkened, cavelike vestibule, I was temporarily blinded by the gloom. I gave my name to the hostess, who led me into the dining room. Detective Reyes-Gonzales, with two colorful menus on the table in front of her, was seated in the far corner of the room.

When I approached the table, she stood up and held out her hand in greeting. "Good to see you again, Detective Beaumont."

"Call me Beau, would you?"

She smiled. "Sure. And I'm Delcia."

The careless toss of ebony curls as she sat back down hinted that under the lightweight camel-colored suit she wore, with its carefully tailored ivory silk blouse, lived a fiery woman. A fiery and temptingly feminine woman.

Something uncomfortable stirred inside me. I remembered what Calvin Crenshaw had told me about the aftermath of his own years of drinking—the long-term damage. Maybe it was just a case of dry-out paranoia, but I wondered if I too had risked any permanent ill effects in that department. However, this was hardly the time or place to deal with that thorny issue.

"What's the matter?" she asked quizzically.

Caught without a plausible lie on my lips, I gave her a lopsided grin. "Nothing," I said more or less truthfully. "I was just thinking that you're probably the best-looking homicide dick I've ever seen."

Detective Delcia Reyes-Gonzales gave no evidence of being either amused or complimented.

"Why did you want to see me?" she asked, easily cutting through any attempt at sociable small talk. Before I could answer, our waitress, dressed in a bright yellow, flared Mexican peasant's dress, came by to deliver Delcia's coffee.

She reached up to take the proffered cup and saucer. When she did, I noticed a slight but telltale bulge under her left arm. The small swelling told me she was wearing a not-so-feminine loaded shoulder holster next to the elegant silk blouse. Seeing that, I found myself suddenly very lonesome for the comforting presence of my own AWOL .38.

In answer to the server's question, I ordered a cup of coffee as well. "Any chance of getting my Smith and Wesson back?" I asked once the waitress left our table.

"Not any time soon," Delcia replied with a smile. "You know how those things go."

Unfortunately, I did know—only too well. It was highly unlikely that I'd ever again see my old faithful handgun. Although I had more than qualified to carry a new semiautomatic when Seattle P.D. switched over, I had hung onto the .38 like a child clings to a worn but familiar teddy bear. If by some miracle it was actually returned to me, it would only be after a suitably long and paper-work-laden wait.

"Know where I could get a replacement?"

She studied me levelly before answering. "Lots of places, but only with the usual three-day wait-ing period. Why do you want one?"

"I feel naked without it, for one thing. And for another, I now know for sure that Joey Rothman was the one who tried to kill me, but just because he's gone doesn't mean somebody else won't try to finish the job."

My words had an electrifying effect on Delcia Reyes-Gonzales. Her eyes flashed fire and her whole body was electrically alert.

"Joey?" she asked, controlling her reaction enough that she put her coffee cup down without spilling any. "You say you know that for sure? How?"

The waitress returned and took our orders. As soon as she left us, I launched into the story of my enlightening conversation with Jennifer Rothman. By the time I finished, Delcia was nodding her head thoughtfully.

"The problem is, there's no way to tell if Joey Rothman was acting alone or in conjunction with someone else."

"Or why," I added gloomily.

"It's too bad snakes can't talk," she said with a

half-amused smile. "If they could, maybe Ringo could clue us in."

"Ringo?" I demanded in surprise. "What about Ringo? You mean he's still alive?"

"Didn't anybody tell you? It's one of the main reasons I'm in Phoenix today—to drop Ringo off at the Phoenix Zoo for safekeeping. I did that first thing, before I drove over to the crime lab. I didn't much like driving around alone with him in the car. In fact, that was my last stop before the Department of Public Safety."

"How did you find him? I thought he was a goner for sure."

"He was never lost. Shorty Rojas had him the whole time. Louise may have given orders to the contrary, but Shorty's too softhearted for his own good. He was afraid the poor old snake wouldn't be able to make it on his own. He hid him in the barn and planned to take Ringo down to a museum in Tucson on his next day off."

"Oh," I said. "The one where his cousin works—the desert museum, or whatever it's called."

Delcia nodded. "The Arizona-Sonora Desert Museum," she corrected. "Well, according to the keeper at the zoo here in Phoenix, Shorty was probably right to be worried—about the snake, I mean. Ringo's old—somewhere in his mid to late teens—which is pretty old for a snake. The keeper said Ringo would have died if he'd been left on his own in the wild, especially since he would have been so far outside his natural habitat."

"He may be old for a snake," I muttered glumly, "but age didn't make him any less scary when he had me cornered in the cabin. And it didn't slow him down enough so your guys found him when they searched my cabin, either."

"I asked about that this morning. At the zoo. The guy told me he probably found a hole somewhere and hid out in that until he thought it was safe to come out."

"Not a comforting thought," I said.

"No," Delcia agreed. "I suppose not. Anyway, Shorty kept Ringo out of harm's way until I picked him up, and now he's being held in protective custody at the Phoenix Zoo. The Yavapai County Sheriff's Department isn't exactly equipped to take care of live snakes in our evidence room. That's why we farmed him out to the zoo. Come to think of it, I believe it's the first time we've ever had a live deadly weapon in a felonious assault case."

Delcia looked at me across her raised coffee cup while her dark eyes sparkled with humor.

"Somehow I don't find it nearly as entertaining as you do," I pointed out. "And if you ask me, that damn snake seems to be getting a helluva lot more attention than yours truly, who just happened to be the intended victim."

"Sorry," she said evenly. "I didn't mean for it to sound that way. Believe me, Beau, nobody's treating this as a joke."

Mollified, I backed off. "I guess I'm a little edgy," I admitted, disgusted with myself for trying to pick a fight with someone who was offering to be an ally at a time when allies were in short supply.

"Perfectly understandable." Delcia nodded. "Don't worry about it."

I went on to tell her about the books Jennifer had said she kept for Joey, the ones he had retrieved from her along with the snake the night he came to tell her good-bye.

"From the way she talked, there must have been several volumes," I said. "In fact, I'm sure he was working in one like it while we were together at the ranch."

"He was?" Delcia asked, thumbing back through her notebook, scanning several pages. "What was it like?"

"Cloth-covered. Looked like a regular book almost, but the pages are blank inside so people can write on them."

Delcia frowned. "That's funny. I don't remember seeing anything like that either in his room or at the crime scene. It could be important." She paused long enough to write another brief note in her small spiral notebook.

Our food had come. I had ordered something they often call *taquitos* at Mexican dives in Seattle. In Phoenix they seem to be known as *flautas*. They were equally good if not better than the ones I'm used to having back home. For a while we ate in silence.

"Any idea when he put the snake in your room?" she asked.

I shook my head. For a moment Delcia sat chewing pensively before she spoke again. "I remember what Mrs. Attwood said the other night, that the snake could have been in your room for as much as a day or two, without your being aware of it. Do you think that's possible?"

"Beats me. It seems as though I would have heard something, noticed or sensed something, but then again, maybe not. It had been stormy for several days with lots of wind, rain, and thunder. The cabin has a tin roof and it's noisy as hell, so I could have missed it."

"Did Jennifer tell you what day she spoke with him?"

"No, and I didn't think to ask. The babysitter was bugging her to hurry and get off the phone."

Delcia made another note. I was sitting there watching her write when an odd thought occurred to me, one I hadn't considered before. Maybe I had jumped to the wrong conclusion. What if Joey's leaving the snake in the room had been nothing more than an ugly practical joke? According to Rhonda, he hadn't been above that sort of thing.

"What's going on?" Delcia asked.

That's why I never play poker. My face always provides a dead giveaway of whatever's going on behind it.

"Just a thought, that's all."

"What kind of thought?" she insisted.

"Is it possible he did it as a joke after all, to see what I would do? Remember what Rhonda told us about him turning Ringo loose in the house and her finding it a week or so later?"

"I remember all right," Delcia said with certainty, shaking her head, "but this is no practical joke, Beau. The two incidents happening in such close proximity have to be related. I can feel it in my bones. All we have to do is figure out the connection."

"We?" I said.

"I," she corrected.

But her comment had made me feel better, less paranoid somehow. And it was apparent that her earlier skepticism about me and my story had been replaced by belief. During our interview in Prescott, Delcia Reyes-Gonzales had clearly doubted my veracity. Now she was on my side.

Something had changed her doubt to trust, and I wanted to ask what, but instinct cautioned me to be wary. If I tried horning in where I wasn't welcome, I risked pushing her away. As the official investigator on the case, she needed to know about my conversation with Calvin Crenshaw, but if I told her, would she climb my frame for interfering? After all, she had just shot down my "we" and turned it into a singular "I." On reflection, though, it seemed worth the gamble.

"I talked to Calvin Crenshaw last night," I ventured cautiously.

"You what!" Delcia exclaimed. Her initial reaction wasn't good, but I forged on anyway. The damage was already done. What more did I have to lose?

"I drove up to Wickenburg last night and talked to him at home. It was a personal matter, Delcia," I said reassuringly. "Louise had told my attorney that I was a permanent *persona non grata* at Ironwood Ranch. I wanted to get that situation straightened out."

Delcia's face relaxed. Her sudden flash of anger dissipated. After all, my being thrown out of Ironwood Ranch wasn't her problem. "Did you come to some agreement?" she asked.

"Not exactly, because, based on what I found out, I don't ever expect to darken their doorstep again."

Alert and listening, she waited attentively. "And what exactly did you find out?"

"Louise Crenshaw was screwing Joey Rothman, among others. Calvin knew all about it. It was their own kinky little joke on the world."

Delcia Reyes-Gonzales seemed to rise in her seat by a good three inches.

"Who told you this?"

"Calvin," I said. "Good old Calvin Crenshaw himself. But he also warned me that if I tried to pass any of it along, he'd deny it. My word against his. No way to prove it."

Delcia sat forward in her seat with her dark unsettling eyes drilling into mine. "Tell me precisely what he said, verbatim, as much as you can remember."

And so I did, stumbling as witnesses sometimes do in an attempt to remember everything. Delcia seemed to hang on every word, not taking notes, but assimilating every detail. When I finished, she was nodding.

"In that case," she said quietly, "Joey Rothman's diary could be dynamite."

Before I could say anything more, she signaled for the waitress to bring the bill.

I had hoped my recitation would result in her returning the favor and letting me in on some of what she had going, but that was not to be. She reached for her purse and headed for the cashier with me trailing along behind.

"Wait a minute. Where are you going? What's going on?"

"I'm beginning to see a pattern here," she said, stopping in front of the cashier's desk. "One I don't like. I'm going to check it out."

The cashier ran Delcia's credit card through the machine while I waited impatiently in the crowded vestibule, which had filled up with lunchtime diners waiting for tables.

"But can't you tell me what it is?" I pleaded when we were alone outside, standing in front of her car.

"No," she said simply.

"Why not?"

"You seem to be forgetting something, Beau," Delcia Reyes-Gonzales returned sweetly, favoring me with a dazzling smile.

"What's that?"

"This is Arizona, not Washington, remember? Keep in touch."

With that, she got in her car and drove away,

leaving me fuming in the parking lot.

An old drinking buddy of mine once told me that when it comes to women, men don't know shit.

He sure as hell got that right.

CHAPTER
15

The way Delcia Reyes-Gonzales wheeled out of the asphalt parking lot leaving strips of rubber in her wake told me that she was a woman with a definite purpose in mind, a lady with a fire lit under her slender butt. I must have said something that jibed with information she already knew or suspected, something important enough to merit her immediate attention. It pissed me off that she hadn't bothered to tell me what that something was.

Frustrated, I got in my rented Subaru and drove home to Ralph Ames' house, intent on finishing the laundry. At the very least, sorting and folding clean clothes was a job with some resolution to it, with a tangible beginning and end, both of which were firmly under my power and control. That was a whole lot different from the people and circumstances surrounding Jocy Rothman.

There were two messages on Ames' answering machine, both from Rhonda Attwood, both anxiously trying to reach Ralph, and both saying she'd call back later. Hearing her voice made me crabby as hell. It reinforced my suspicions that she was up to no good and made me wonder what kind of subterfuge she was going to use to sucker Ames into helping her. I was sorely tempted to erase the messages entirely, but I didn't. My mother taught me to be a better houseguest than that.

MYOB, Beaumont, I told myself firmly. MYOB.

I had completed the only crossword puzzle in the house and was just folding the last load of wash, the once-muddy sandbagging clothes, when the doorbell rang. I saw the green Fiat through the sidelight windows. What the hell is Rhonda Attwood doing here? I thought as I opened the door.

She smiled up at me. "Is Ralph back from the golf tournament yet?"

"No," I answered with some vexation. Again I was odd-man-out. Ralph hadn't told *me* about being in a golf tournament, but he *had* told Rhonda.

"He said he thought he'd be done by three-thirty or four," Rhonda continued easily. "Mind if I come in and wait?"

"No," I said. "Come on in."

Someone else might have noticed my annoyance, but Rhonda didn't. She followed me into the spacious living room, where I motioned her toward the long white leather couch. Once again, Rhonda didn't take the hint. Instead of sitting down, she prowled around the room, examining the various pieces of artwork on the walls and tables, frowning at some and nodding in appreciation at others.

Finally she turned and looked at me. "Ralph certainly has the eye of a connoisseur, doesn't he," she said.

"I wouldn't know about that," I answered brusquely. I thought she had a hell of a lot of nerve to meander uninvited around Ralph's living room, treating it like a goddamned museum.

"Would you like a drink?" I asked, attempting halfheartedly to assume the role of stand-in host.

She glanced at her watch before she answered. "A Crown Royal if you've got it. Neat."

I made my way to Ralph's well-stocked wet bar. The Crown Royal was there. So was a bottle of MacNaughton's. I poured the Crown Royal and left the MacNaughton's alone. There was a tiny refrigerator-cum-ice-machine under the bar. I threw some ice cubes in a glass and poured a can of Sprite into it for me.

When I gave her the Crown Royal, she looked me straight in the eye.

"Most men find me attractive," she said, "but I get the feeling you don't like me much."

She had me dead to rights. "You worry me," I said.

"Why?"

"Women who do vendettas scare hell out of me, that's all. You know, the female of the species is deadlier than the male and all that jazz. You asked me to help you track down the people responsible for your son's death, remember? And now you're trying to get Ralph Ames to do the same thing."

"So that's it," she said, taking a sip of her drink.

"Of course that's it," I replied impatiently. "Ralph Ames happens to be a super-nice guy, and he's a good friend of mine. I don't want to see him bamboozled into your wild-haired scheme. He's a lawyer, goddamnit, and a good one. If he messes around in an ongoing homicide investigation, you could end up getting him disbarred."

Rhonda Attwood regarded me levelly over the rim of her glass. "It's not what you think," she said. "When I asked you to help me, I didn't know about the baby."

"Baby?" I asked.

"Joey's baby, my grandchild. You're right, when I first talked to you, I didn't care what happened. The only thing I could think of was evening the score. I'd lost him years ago, but I'd always had a secret hope of getting him back. I can't do that now, but I have something else, a grandchild, something of my son that will go on from here. That's why I want to see Ralph, to ask him to help me set up a trust fund for the baby, and the mother too, of course."

"When you change your mind, you do a complete one-eighty, don't you?"

Rhonda smiled and nodded. "So I've been told."

I sat there for a moment and let her words sink in. She was talking as confidently about that baby as though her grandchild were already a living, breathing entity. All I could think about was Michelle Owens' hollow-eyed misery and Guy

Owens' despairing pronouncement: "Fifteen and pregnant."

I hated to burst her bubble, but somebody had to do it.

"You'll never see that baby, Rhonda. Michelle is only fifteen. She's still wearing braces. Her father will never let her carry that baby to term. Even if he did, he wouldn't let her keep it."

Instantly two angry splotches of color appeared on Rhonda's cheeks. "It's a baby, Mr. Beaumont, not a stray puppy. Of course she'll keep it. I'll help her. Michelle can come live with me if she wants to. If she has to. Thanks to Ralph, I've just sold five paintings to Vincent at five thousand dollars apiece. That's what I want to use to start the trust fund."

"You're not listening, Rhonda. Twenty-five thousand is only a drop in the bucket of what it would take. We're talking about an adolescent here, a druggie with no education, no prospects, and no husband. What kind of life would that be for her or the baby, either one?"

Rhonda's glass, spewing Crown Royal all the way, sailed past my ear and shattered against the wall behind my head. At the same time, she launched herself from the couch, springing toward me like an outraged, unleashed tiger. I scrambled out of the way, slopping my own drink in my lap, jumping up and catching her wrists just in time to keep her sharpened fingernails from raking my face.

She screamed unintelligible words at me and

fought to get loose with surprising strength, but I kept her wrists firmly imprisoned. I don't know how long we struggled like that, but finally I felt the fight ebb out of her. She sagged against my chest, sobbing, as the dam she had built across her emotions broke free.

I let her cry, knowing she was weeping for two babies, not one, for her lost son and for the grandchild she was afraid of losing, for herself and for Michelle Owens as well. I patted her shoulder, murmuring what comforting words of consolation I could think of. They sounded empty and inept. Useless.

At last she gave a shuddering sigh and moved to disengage herself. When I let her go, she crouched near where the glass had smashed and began picking up the jagged pieces.

"Here," I said gruffly, "I'll do that."

She bit her lip. "I'm used to cleaning up my own messes," she said.

Together we cleaned up the splatters of Crown Royal that clung to the wall and the sticky Sprite that dappled the tile floor. Luckily, most of the mess had missed the mint-green oriental rug.

"I really would help her," Rhonda said as she scrubbed the wall. "If she kept the baby, I mean."

"It's not that simple," I returned.

I felt her turn and look at me, sensed the resurgence of anger. "What would you know about it?"

I bridled at the female arrogance that automatically assumes all men are unfeeling, insensitive clods. I wanted to lash out at her and put her in her place, but memories of my own mother's struggles raising an illegitimate son in Seattle in the forties and fifties tempered the fight in me as well.

"More than you know," I answered wearily. "Way more than you know."

For several minutes we worked on in silence. "But couldn't Ralph work out some kind of custody agreement? I could raise the baby myself. Michelle wouldn't have to be responsible."

"The chances for that are pretty slim."

She looked at me for a long time, but finally she nodded in defeat. "I guess you're right." Rhonda glanced at her watch. It was after five, close to five-thirty. "Damn," she said.

"What's wrong now?"

"No matter what I do with the money, I still have to get those paintings over to Vincent. He's already paid for them, and I promised to deliver them this afternoon. The problem is, they won't fit in my car. They're too big. I was hoping I could get Ralph to take me in his, since he's the one who put the whole deal together."

"Where are they?"

"At the Renthrow Gallery, on Main Street in Scottsdale. They close at six."

"I could take you," I offered, "if you think they'll fit in the Subaru."

"Would you mind?"

"Not at all. I'll just leave a note for Ralph so he'll know where to find us."

She looked down at the amber stain on her

blouse left by spilled Crown Royal. "I should stop by the hotel and change. It'll only take a minute."

"Sure," I said. "Lead the way."

In the gathering twilight I followed the Fiat out of Ames' driveway and back to MacDonald Drive, where we turned right and made our way to Lincoln Drive to the Red Lion's La Posada. We turned in by the main entrance and went past the huge pool with its immense waterfall. Rhonda led me through a maze of crowded parking lots to the hotel's farthest wing. She parked the Fiat in the only available spot then came up to me in the Subaru.

"Wait here," she said. "It'll only take me a minute to change."

When it comes to changing clothes, women's minutes and men's minutes are often quite different. She was back in less than one, still wearing the same clothes. "Let's go," she said, climbing into the car and slamming the door behind her.

"I thought you were going to change."

"Never mind that. Can't we go now, please?"

Something was seriously wrong, but she wasn't ready to tell me what it was, so I swung the Subaru in a tight circle and wheeled back toward the nearest exit on Lincoln.

"What happened in there?" I asked. "What's the matter?"

"Somebody's been in my room," she said.

"Who? The maid? Room service?"

"No, I mean somebody broke into my room. They've torn the place apart."

I stepped on the brake. "Are they still in there?"

Rhonda shook her head. "No. I don't think so."

"You don't *think* so? Jesus Christ, woman, you mean you don't know for sure?"

"As soon as I saw it, I didn't even go inside. I came straight back to the car."

I turned the wheel savagely and almost ran over a golf cart ferrying guests to their rooms.

"Where are you going?" Rhonda demanded.

"To the desk. We need to report this."

"No."

"No?" I echoed. "What the hell do you mean, 'No'?"

"Just what I said. Reporting it could take hours. I want to deliver those pictures first."

God keep me from stubborn women!

Exasperated, I started to argue and then thought better of it. After all, if she didn't feel an urgency to report it right away, why the hell should I?

"Which way do we go?" I asked.

"Right on Lincoln," she said. "Then south on Invergordon."

Following directions, I turned back onto Lincoln eastbound. I was only a block or so away when I saw a set of headlights come up fast behind us. He had his high beams on, so I noticed him right away. At first I didn't think that much about it. I could tell it was one of those big four-wheel-drive jobs driven by somebody with the typical four-by-four attitude—the-world-is-my-ashtray mentality. I expected him to race around us, and he almost did. But then suddenly, for no apparent reason, he dropped back behind us and stayed there.

That worried me. When yahoos like that don't pass, they've got to have a reason. I glanced in the rearview mirror, trying to get a better look at the vehicle, but the bright lights blinded me.

It was early evening on an October Saturday, and traffic was fairly light. I tried speeding up, so did he, maintaining the same distance between the two vehicles.

"What's wrong?" Rhonda asked anxiously.

"Don't look back, but I think we've got a tail. Where do we turn?"

"The next light."

It was just turning green as we approached. There was no chance of catching a red. Abruptly, I stepped on the brakes and almost stopped, forcing the vehicle behind us to come far closer than the driver of the pickup had intended. I could see enough detail then to know it was a dark-colored, late-model Toyota 4-X-4 with huge, outsized tires. In the glow of the headlights from the car behind him, I could see the silhouettes of four round driving lights, "asshole lights" we call them, studding the top of the cab.

Behind us a horn blared.

"What are you going to do?" Rhonda asked.

Without a weapon of any kind, there was no point in forcing a confrontation. "Lose him," I said.

It sounded good, but it didn't mean a goddamned thing. Back home in Seattle, where I know all the streets and their intersecting nooks and crannies, it would have been easy to do, but there in Arizona, in unfamiliar territory driving a car with no guts, it was a bad joke. My only hope was to drive erratically enough to attract the attention of some passing traffic cop. With luck I might manage to offend some poor bloke into reporting me on his cellular phone.

Jamming the accelerator to the floorboard, I fishtailed onto Invergordon with the 4-X-4 right behind me. Far ahead of us the orange light at the next intersection turned red.

"What's that street up there?"

"At the light? Chaparral," she answered. "The one after that is Camelback."

I recognized Camelback as one of the heavily traveled arterials.

"Make sure your shoulder strap's on tight," I warned grimly, snapping my own across my chest. "This could get rough."

Mentally I timed the light as I wound the Subaru up as tight as it would go. I sailed through the first one on green and made a mad dash for the second. I could see the passing headlights of cross traffic as vehicles moved sedately across Invergordon on Camelback. A pair of headlights approached the intersection from the other direction. Desperately I hoped that the light on Invergordon was a demand light set on a short cycle in our direction.

We were three blocks away and still accelerating when the light facing us turned green. It switched back to orange as soon as the oncoming car moved into the intersection.

I'm still not sure if Rhonda knew what I was planning, but she didn't say a word. The light was red as we started through the intersection. Naturally, there was one hotshot who jumped the light. He clipped our back fender and spun into the path of the 4-X-4, which dodged crazily from side to side. There was a chorus of honking horns in our wake, but I was too busy fighting to get the Subaru back under control to see exactly what happened in the intersection behind us.

For a moment or so, it looked like we had gotten clear. In the rearview mirror the pickup seemed to be trapped in a maelstrom of stalled vehicles, while before us Invergordon lay straight and flat and empty.

But before I could breathe a sigh of relief, I saw the DEAD END sign beside the street and knew we were still in trouble.

"Dead end!" I yelped. "What the hell do they mean, dead end?"

"The canal," Rhonda replied through clenched teeth. "The Arizona Canal. It's right up here."

"Shit! So how do we get out of here? Right or left?"

"I don't know."

I wanted to get off Invergordon and duck into a side street before the pickup got loose from Camelback. I figured there was a fifty-fifty chance of making the right choice. I swung left onto a small side street. For a moment I thought it was going to be all right, but then we ran into a T.

People on the run instinctively turn right, so I swung left again, hoping to outfox our pursuer. We came out on a street called Calle Redondo that seemed to run on a diagonal. Behind it was a tall chain link fence.

"What's beyond the fence?" I asked. "The canal?"

"Yes."

"Is there water in it?"

Rhonda craned her neck. "I can't tell. Probably."

"How deep?"

"Seven or eight feet."

"Great."

Beyond the canal was another street, one that appeared to cross the canal, if only we could find a way to get over onto it. The problem was, the guy in the pickup had come to the same conclusion. He must have seen me turn left off Invergordon and realized there was only one way out of the maze. As we came around a blind corner onto Lafayette, I saw him lying in wait, parked inside the fence on the access road that ran next to the canal. He was hanging back, hoping to pounce as soon as we surfaced.

"What are you going to do?" Rhonda asked.

"Something that son of a bitch doesn't expect," I told her. "Brace yourself."

Shoving the accelerator all the way to the floor, I aimed for the 4-X-4's looming front left tire and nailed that sucker head-on, doing a good thirty-five miles an hour.

From what I remember of Doc Ramsey's high school physics class at Ballard High School, when a moving object hits a stationary one, the stationary one shares the momentum of the moving one. During the intervening twenty-eight years, everything else may have changed, but the laws of physics hadn't.

The Subaru stopped dead in its tracks with its nose bent straight into the ground while the pickup started moving. As the shoulder belt cut painfully into my collarbone, I caught only a brief glimpse of the shocked driver's open-mouthed amazement as his behemoth truck went ass-backwards into the canal. With the oversized tires half floating and half bouncing off the bottom, the truck, still right side up, floated out of sight under the bridge.

In this updated, four-wheel-drive version of David and Goliath, the Subaru may have won hands down, but the folks at Alamo sure as hell weren't going to like it.

CHAPTER
16

Whoever said you can never find a cop when you need one was dead wrong. By the time I had helped a dazed but unhurt Rhonda Attwood out of the crippled Subaru, we found a whole wad of cops, or rather they found us, summoned to the scene by an irate jogger who insisted he had seen the whole thing and it was all my fault. The incident left me with a whole lot of explaining to do, although not nearly as much as I would have expected.

Once we gave him a description of the 4-X-4, the patrol officer in charge seemed to pay a lot closer attention to what I was saying. Within moments of hearing that Rhonda Attwood was Joey Rothman's mother, he was on the horn to his dispatcher, calling for a helicopter backup to search the canal for our assailant. His use of the word "assailant" struck me as important, especially in view of the fact that the jogger was still jumping up and down and telling anybody who would listen that I had attacked the pickup with my Subaru.

243

Subdued but uninjured, Rhonda seemed content to sit on the berm between the road and the canal with a blanket thrown around her shoulders while I worked my way through the tangle of paperwork. The last representative of officialdom was the tow-truck driver, a burly barrel-chested man in his late fifties who looked at the battered wreck of the Subaru and shook his head.

"I've picked up Alamo casualties for years," he said with a scowl. "But I've never heard that whole office so riled up as they are over this."

"They're pretty upset?" I asked innocuously. He nodded. "And you don't think it would be such a good idea for me to ride along out there with you tonight to get things straightened out?"

The tow-truck driver grinned. "It's up to you, buddy. Just how brave are you?"

"Not very," I said. "Maybe I'll send my attorney out to handle it in the morning."

"That's the ticket," he said.

I watched him load the crumpled remains onto a slanted rack on the back of his tow truck. The Subaru was neither driveable nor towable.

Boeing test pilots talk about flying the biggest piece home. They claim that you're all right as long as you keep the shiny side up and the greasy side down. The game little Subaru was still shiny side up, but her flying days were over.

"Detective Beaumont?" I turned to see who was calling. It was the Scottsdale patrol officer who had been first on the scene, although I didn't remember telling him or anyone else there my title as well as my name.

He motioned me over to his car. "We're about finished up here. Are you done with the car?"

I nodded. "He'll be gone in a few minutes."

"The Town of Paradise Valley has two detectives waiting for Mrs. Attwood at La Posada. We're sending one of ours as well. We'd like her to accompany the detectives when they go through her room. Another detective, one from Prescott, is on her way to pick you up."

"Delcia? How did she find out about it?"

"I wouldn't know about that, sir," the patrolman said, "but she should be here in a few minutes."

I went back over to where Rhonda was sitting. "Are you all right?" I asked.

"My collarbone hurts, where the shoulder strap cut into me, but I don't think anything's broken."

"Me too," I agreed, rubbing my finger along the painful bruise that cut diagonally across my own chest. "It could have been worse. That's why I aimed for the tire. The rubber took some of the shock."

"Have they found him yet?"

"No," I answered, "but I'm sure they will. A pickup stuck in the canal should be easy enough to spot."

Another car approached the scene, red lights flashing. "Come on," I said, gently helping Rhonda to her feet. "That's probably our ride."

It was. Delcia Reyes-Gonzales came around the

car to meet us. "Are you two all right?" she asked anxiously.

"So far," I told her. The tow truck was just pulling away, and she allowed her eyes to follow it. "I'm going to need some more help with Alamo," I said.

She nodded. "I can see that. Ready?"

Delcia held open the back door of her Reliant, and I handed Rhonda into the back seat. There wasn't enough leg room for me, so I went around and climbed in on the rider's side. Delcia's unquestioning acceptance of what had happened seemed odd to me. I expected her to ask who was in the 4-X-4 and why I had deliberately collided with him. Instead, she drove us back to La Posada in thoughtful silence.

We went by way of Camelback and Invergordon. An assortment of officers had cleared away the wrecked cars, but the intersection was still lit with flashing lights while someone armed with a massive broom finished sweeping broken glass out of the street.

"In the entire Phoenix metropolitan area, you couldn't have picked a worse place than this," Delcia said, as she eased her way through the still-stalled traffic.

"Why's that?"

"This is the borderline where Paradise Valley, Scottsdale, and Phoenix all meet. It's going to take weeks to sort out all the paperwork."

"Oh," I said.

Once back at the hotel, Delcia and I stayed with

the car while two Paradise Valley police detectives took charge of Rhonda.

No matter where I went, no matter what I touched, some other jurisdiction got dragged into the fray. If I thought about it very long, it would give me a complex.

"How are you feeling?" she asked.

"Fine. Better than fine, actually. Dumping that asshole in the drink did me a world of good. It beats sitting around doing nothing."

"Doing nothing sounds about right to me," she returned.

I glanced at my watch. It was only seven-thirty, a bare two hours after Rhonda and I had left Ames' house. "How did you get here so fast?" I asked. "It's a long drive down from Prescott."

"I never went home," she said. Closing her eyes, she leaned back and rested her head on the car seat.

"Why not?"

"Too busy," she replied.

"They were already looking for that truck, weren't they?" I ventured shrewdly.

Delcia straightened up and looked at me. "What makes you say that?"

"As soon as I described the truck, everything shifted into high gear. Despite all indications to the contrary, the officer immediately assumed we had been the ones under attack."

She shrugged, as though she was too tired to argue about it. "You're right," she said. "They were looking for a truck matching that description."

"Why?"

"Because I asked them to," she said quietly.

I could see that Delcia Reyes-Gonzales was bone weary, but her demeanor was far different from the way she'd been at lunch. Then she'd been alert and toying with me, sparring and taunting at the same time. Now the sparkle had been drained out of her as well as the subterfuge. She weighed her words carefully when she spoke, but she answered my questions without ducking them. For the first time, she was treating me like a fellow police officer, someone working the same side of the street. It made a new man of me.

"But how did you know they'd come here looking for Rhonda?"

"I didn't. I put out an alert on the pickup because of the kids in Wickenburg."

"Wait a minute. What kids?"

"Two junior high kids, a boy and a girl, out necking in the middle of the night without their parents knowing they were gone. They had slipped out of their respective houses and met down by the river the night Joey Rothman died. They saw a dark-colored 4-X-4 parked right beside your Grand AM."

"Jesus Christ! You mean you've got eyewitnesses?"

"One of them told the counselor at school the next morning. That's why I had to leave your interview, to go talk to those kids."

"Eyewitnesses," I repeated.

"Not exactly. They saw two people, a man and a woman. Three, counting Joey. The man did the dirty work, pulled the trigger, while the woman stayed in the truck. Afterward, the man drove the car away, and the woman drove the pickup. The kids saw the whole thing, but from a distance, and they were way too scared to report it that night."

"But can they identify them?"

"No." Delcia sighed. "No such luck."

We were quiet for a few moments.

I was amazed, not by *what* she was telling me so much as by the very fact that she *was* telling me. Those kinds of inside details aren't usually divulged to anyone outside the immediate scope of a homicide investigation, even people in the same department, yet here she was, unloading it on a complete outsider.

"Why are you telling me all this, Delcia? At lunch today, you wouldn't give me the time of day, and now, a few hours later, it's full-disclosure time. What's going on?"

"I've done some checking on you, Detective Beaumont," she said at last.

"Oh? What kind of checking?"

"I've talked with a number of people in Seattle—Captain Lawrence Powell, for one. Sergeant Watkins, and your partner, Allen Lindstrom."

"You have been busy," I observed. "What did they say?"

Irrepressible laughter bubbled up through her weariness. "They all said that you're a regular pain in the ass on occasion, but they all agreed unanimously that you're way too smart to shoot somebody with your own gun and then hide the weapon in your car."

"Some friends," I snorted.

Delcia grew serious again. "Convincing friends," she said. "Altogether, they made a pretty good case."

"So where do we stand?"

She didn't acknowledge my question. "Did Michelle Owens know where Rhonda was staying?"

I thought about it for a moment. "Michelle? I don't know. Why? I remember Rhonda saying that she had invited Michelle to the funeral. She may have mentioned then that she was staying at La Posada."

"Michelle Owens has turned up missing," Delcia answered grimly. "From her house, sometime during the night last night. I've been on the phone with her father off and on all afternoon."

"What does this mean? Did she take off on her own, or did somebody grab her?" I asked.

"My first guess, after I talked to him, was that she left of her own accord. Now, after this business here, I'm not so sure. Did anyone else know where Rhonda was staying?"

"I don't know. Ralph Ames, my attorney, and I both knew. And as far as that goes, Rhonda could have told any number of people."

Delcia nodded. "I guess you're right."

"You said you thought at first that Michelle left

on her own. Why? What did her father say?"

"That the two of them had had a big fight last night. He'd evidently made an appointment for Michelle to go to an abortion clinic in Tucson early next week, but she didn't want to go. He said he went to bed without worrying about it because he was sure he could get her to change her mind. This morning, though, when he got up, Michelle wasn't in her room. She's disappeared without a trace."

"Any sign of foul play?" I asked.

"None, and nothing seems to be missing. The officers on the scene are betting she has simply run away."

"So did she?"

"I don't know," Delcia replied. "If someone came looking for Rhonda, they might have come looking for Michelle as well."

"Exactly."

"And I don't like the score. Joey's dead. One attempt on Rhonda and two on you, so whoever's behind this isn't playing games."

"You've got that one right," I told her. "That bastard in the pickup wasn't out for a friendly game of chicken. He'd have nailed us good if I hadn't gotten to him first."

"There's a third possibility," Delcia said.

"What's that?"

"What if Michelle was the woman those kids saw in the truck?"

I didn't like it, but the theory carried with it a

certain ugly plausibility. Delcia didn't seem to like it much either.

"It's more likely that she just took off, that it all got to be too much for her. Think about it. The girl's pregnant, her boyfriend dies, her father wants her to have an abortion, the boy's mother wants her to keep the baby. That's a hell of a load for someone to carry around when they're only fifteen years old."

"It's a hell of a load at any age," I said, reminded once more of my own mother's struggles.

Again we fell silent. Although I appreciated the changed basis between us, I couldn't just let it go at that. I had to pick at the scab and know what lay under it.

"So how come I'm not a civilian anymore, Delcia? I don't mind, not at all, but I'd like to know why."

"Maybe I need the opinion of an outside observer," she replied. Her answer sounded coy, and I balked at the idea that she was putting me off again.

"Why?"

She sighed as though finally giving in to something she'd done her best to sidestep. "Today, after I talked to you at lunch, I did some checking into the prosecutor who arranged Joey Rothman's MIP. There seem to be some irregularities in the plea-bargain arrangement."

"Like what?"

"Like the charges should have been a whole lot stiffer than they were."

"You mean drugs?"

She nodded. "It wasn't a simple first offense, either. I'm still not sure how the prosecutor pulled it off. It could be nothing more than James Rothman's highly placed connections . . ." Her voice drifted away, leaving the sentence dangling.

"Or . . ." I prompted.

"You have to understand I've been curious about Ironwood Ranch for years. Not anything definite, not anything that ever made it as far as a conscious thought, but curious. There have been hints of trouble occasionally, but until the Rothman case, nothing ever got out of hand."

"That's because Louise Crenshaw always kept a lid on it," I put in.

"And Louise always had help," Delcia added.

"Who?"

"Sheriff Heagerty," she answered. "He's a former client of Ironwood Ranch, and so's the MIP prosecutor. Not only that, Calvin Crenshaw was a major contributor to Heagerty's reelection campaign during the last two elections."

"So what are you thinking?"

"That maybe they both got hung up in Louise Crenshaw's little sideshow."

"That would explain a lot, wouldn't it," I breathed, "but do you have any proof?"

"I'm working on it. In my spare time, but I'm on real thin ice, and I can't afford to go through regular channels on this. That's why I'm using you as a sounding board. I need someone I'm sure isn't tarred with Louise Crenshaw's brush. She never managed to get her claws into you."

I smiled at Delcia's comment. "I thought I was the only one who noticed Louise Crenshaw's talons. So what do you think? Are the Crenshaws involved in this business too? Are they part of Joey's supply system?"

"Maybe, and maybe not. I don't know what to think. I sure as hell can't afford to disregard them, but the problem is, I'm pretty much working alone, at least as far as Yavapai County is concerned. My guess is that Sheriff Heagerty wants me spread too thin to do anything constructive. If I hadn't been so tired, if I had been thinking straight, I would have asked for protection for Rhonda and Michelle both. Even then, it might not have helped, but still . . ."

She turned and looked me full in the face. "As far as Rhonda's concerned, you saved the day. I want you to know I'm grateful."

"You're welcome," I said, "for that and for saving my own ass too, but it would have been a helluva lot easier if I'd been armed. When that creep came after us, I felt like we were sitting ducks."

"Do you ever go to swap meets?" Delcia asked suddenly.

The abrupt detour in the conversation sounded as though Delcia Reyes-Gonzales had reverted to her earlier game-playing.

"Swap meets?" I asked stupidly. "You mean, like in garage sales?"

She nodded, but I shook my head. "Not me.

Buying somebody else's cast-off junk isn't my idea of a good deal."

"Maybe you should check into them," Delcia said seriously. "In fact, I believe there's one at Phoenix Greyhound Race Track on Saturdays and Sundays. I'd try it, if I were you. It's on Washington, east of the airport. Do you think you can find it?"

"I'm sure I can, but why would I want to?"

"The guy's name is Zeke. From what I've heard, he's there every weekend. He sells guns. Used, of course. From a private collection."

"Privately," I said, getting the picture. "So there's no three-day waiting period?"

"That's right."

"And you're suggesting I go get myself one."

"Who, me?" she asked innocently. "Certainly not. I never said anything of the kind."

Just then Ralph Ames walked up to the car and tapped on Delcia's window.

"Ralph Ames," he said, introducing himself to her. "Beau here is a client of mine. So's Mrs. Attwood. They told me inside that I'd find him out in the car with you. May I join you?"

He opened the door and climbed into the cramped back seat.

I completed the introductions. "This is Detective Delcia Reyes-Gonzales, Ralph. She's from Prescott. How did you get here?"

Ralph smiled at her. "We met on the phone." He turned to me. "When you two didn't show up at Vincent's I got worried and came here looking.

From what I've heard, Alamo is going to want to burn you at the stake. The next time you try to rent a car from them, alarms will probably go off on Alamo computers all over the country."

"At least I didn't take it to Mexico," I said. "That's the only thing I remember them telling me that I couldn't do. What's going on in there? It's taking a long time."

"They're about finished," Ralph said. "I suggested that considering the circumstances it might be wise for Rhonda to come stay with us. For tonight anyway. I'm sure I'll be far more at ease if I know she isn't staying by herself. We'll leave the Fiat parked here in the lot and make sure we aren't followed when we go."

I looked at Delcia. She was half dozing right there in the car. "What about you?" I asked. "Surely you're not going to drive all the way back home tonight."

"No. My sister lives across town in Peoria. I'll stay there tonight. If Ralph here can give you and Rhonda a ride home, I'll go ahead and take off if you don't mind. It's been a long day."

Ralph and I waited in La Posada's well-appointed lobby until the detectives finished with Rhonda's room. She arrived in the lobby carrying a suitcase and small overnight bag.

"I guess you're stuck with me for the night," she said apologetically. "They told me I shouldn't stay here alone. And what about the paintings?"

"Don't worry," Ames assured her. "I'll let Vincent know what happened."

We took her out to the car through the main entrance. Driving home, I made several quick maneuvers and doubled back once or twice, making sure we didn't have a tail. When we got to the house, Ralph insisted on parking the Lincoln in the garage.

Once inside the house, we settled down in the living room for a few minutes to recap what all had happened over the course of the evening. Ralph had heard bits and pieces from many sources. He was the one who gave Rhonda the bad news that Michelle was missing. She took that stoically enough, but when she heard that Guy Owens had been trying to coerce Michelle into having an abortion, she was outraged and wanted to get in the car right then and there to make the three-and-a-half-hour drive to tell Lieutenant Colonel Guy Owens what was what. We finally dissuaded her, but only barely.

Toward midnight, we ventured into the kitchen, where Ralph made us a late-night supper of cheese, cocoa, and toast. Munching away, we finished our play-by-play review of the evening at the kitchen counter, said our good-nights, and headed for our separate rooms. I was in bed with lights out when there came a light tapping on my door.

"Who is it?"

"Rhonda. May I come in?"

She came into the room and felt her way across to the bed. Once there, she sat down on the edge of it.

"What's the matter?" I asked. "Is something wrong?"

"What would have happened to me tonight if you hadn't been there at the hotel, waiting for me in the parking lot?"

"I don't know. That's hard to say."

"He must have been there, hiding in my room. Would he have killed me if he'd had the chance?"

"Maybe, and then again, maybe not. We still don't have any idea what he was after, but my guess is that they think you have something, maybe something damaging to the whole operation."

"But I haven't."

"That doesn't matter, as long as they think you do."

"So why am I scared now, hours after it's all over?"

"For one thing, it's not all over. If they still believe you have whatever they were looking for, you're still in danger. Stay alert, and don't fault yourself for being jittery after the worst of the action seems to be over. It happens that way sometimes. When you're in the thick of things, you're too busy to be afraid. Fear comes later."

She turned to face me. In the pale glow of moonlight shining through the window, her face was unnaturally white, eyes wide open. I reached out my hand and caught hold of her narrow wrist, feeling the pulse imprisoned within it.

"It's all right to be scared," I told her. "It's a normal reaction."

"Were you scared out there in the car when he was after us?"

"Shitless," I answered.

"What about now?"

"It's worse now," I said, suppressing a grin.

She snatched her hand away and leaned closer, peering at me closely in the hazy light. "Worse? Really? Or are you making fun of me?"

"I'm not making fun," I said. "Women scare me a whole lot more than 4-X-4s."

For a moment she looked hurt, then angry, then a tiny smile tickled the corners of her mouth. "You mean to tell me you're scared of me?"

"Absolutely. Out of my wits. Shouldn't I be?"

Within seconds, we were both laughing, giggling first then laughing uproariously, rolling on the bed, holding our stomachs, and gasping for air. When we finally quit laughing, we were still lying on the bed, facing each other. Neither one of us made a move to get up. Within moments I moved closer, folding her in my arms.

It was the most natural thing in the world.

CHAPTER
17

I slept, content in the knowledge that whatever incursions booze may have made against my liver, other pieces of essential equipment, unlike Calvin Crenshaw's, remained totally unaffected. I awoke to the sound of small scratchings, rodent sounds, only to discover that Rhonda Attwood, sitting curled up in the high wing-backed chair beside the window, was busily sketching away.

"Coffee or orange juice?" she asked, not looking up. "Ralph already brought us both. He's out cleaning the pool."

It was only to be expected that Ralph Ames was already up and on duty. He evidently also knew where Rhonda had spent the night. "Coffee," I said, a little sheepishly.

"Okay. Just a minute."

She finished what she was doing, examined it critically at arm's length with a slight frown pursing her brow, and then put the sketch pad on the table next to her. Pouring two cups of coffee from a stainless steel carafe, she padded barefoot across the room to the bed. She was wearing a knee-length blue nightshirt with Mickey and Minnie Mouse emblazoned on the front. Her hair was tousled, but from the strained lines and shadows around her eyes, I suspected she hadn't slept nearly as well as I had.

"What are you working on?" I asked, taking one cup of coffee off her hands.

"Nothing much." Careful not to spill her coffee, she lowered herself onto the bed beside me. "Just a sketch."

I reached over and let my hand fall on the smooth firm curve of her thigh. It rested there for some time, and she made no effort to move it away. Closing my eyes, I lost myself in the miracle of an instant replay until she jarred me out of it with a softly voiced question.

"Will you drive me down to Sierra Vista today?"

Surprised, I opened my eyes and looked at her. "To Sierra Vista? Why?"

"Because I've got to talk to Guy Owens."

I sat up in the bed. "I thought we already went over that. Your chances for persuading this guy are nil. He's one angry man."

Rhonda Attwood's blue eyes filled with tears. "I can try. I've got to try. Don't you understand? Joey was all I had, my only child. I was never able to have another one after he was born, even though I wanted one and tried for years. This baby, Michelle's baby, is part of me, too. I can't just turn my back and let it go. I can't." The last sentence was a strangled sob.

When God gave Eve the ability to cry, he stacked the deck against us. It hasn't been a fair fight since. I'm impervious to lots of things, but a weeping woman isn't one of them. Besides, Rhonda Attwood could easily have gone off on her mission alone, without telling me. My masculine pride was honored that she wanted to have me along.

"All right, all right," I said, knowing perfectly well that I'd been manipulated and sounding suitably crotchety. "I'll drive down there with you, but don't count on it doing much good."

Smiling through her tears, Rhonda Attwood leaned over and gave me a quick peck on the side of my neck. "Thank you," she said. "I'll go shower."

Gracefully she eased herself off the bed and disappeared into the bathroom. I drank my coffee, listening first to the rush of the shower and later to the hum of a blow-dryer. When I finished draining my first cup, I slipped on a pair of shorts and went over to the table to pour a second. The sketch pad was lying right there next to the carafe. I couldn't resist the temptation to pick it up and see what she'd been doing.

It was spooky—almost like looking in the mirror. The penciled sketch staring back at me was me. My eyes, my nose, my ever-increasing forehead. I was still standing there holding it when the bathroom door opened. I jumped as though I'd been caught doing something I shouldn't, afraid she'd be offended by my prying.

"You have good features," Rhonda said, stopping in the doorway. "Strong, masculine features."

Never at ease with compliments, I turned it aside with a question. "How do you do that?"

"Do what?" she returned. "Draw?" I nodded, and she shrugged. "I don't know. It's something I've always been able to do, from the time I was little. You don't, I take it?"

"Not me, not at all. I wouldn't have the foggiest idea how to go about it."

Rhonda smiled. "That's all right. I wouldn't have known how to drive the car into the pickup's tire, either, so we're even."

There was a knock on the door. "Are you two decent?" Ralph asked, in his unflappable manner. "There's a call for you, Beau."

I opened the door and took the cordless handset. "Hello."

"Beau, it's me, Delcia. They've got him, the guy from the truck. Phoenix P.D. picked him up a little after midnight, but I didn't find out about it until just a few minutes ago. Somebody neglected to call me."

"They caught him? Who is it?"

"I don't know yet, but according to the detective who called me, he's already got himself a very high-priced defense attorney, and he refused to say word one without his attorney present."

"So this is someone who knows the ropes."

"Sounds like."

"Do you need us to come down there with you?

I only got one look at him in the headlights as he was going ass-over-teakettle into the water. I'm not sure whether or not I could identify him."

"No," she said. "I'll be there. The City of Scottsdale's sending someone over. It'll be enough of a crowd without having you there as well. Just keep me posted as to where I can reach you if I need to."

"I thought I'd check into the swap meets around here. I understand the one at Greyhound Race Track is pretty good."

Delcia laughed. "That's what they say."

"And then Rhonda and I may take a ride down to Sierra Vista."

The laughter stopped. "Why?"

"Rhonda wants to talk to Guy Owens. She's hoping to get him to change his mind about Michelle having an abortion."

There was a pause. "Well," she said at last, "as long as you're there to keep an eye on her, I suppose it'll be all right."

"Any word on Michelle?"

"No. Nothing so far. When will you get back?"

I glanced at Rhonda. She had picked up the sketch pad and was standing next to the window, adding a few deft lines here and there with her pencil. Her blonde hair caught the sunlight from outside and glinted like a burnished golden halo. Rhonda Attwood was a beautiful, desirable woman.

"I don't know," I said to Delcia. "Probably sometime late this afternoon or evening. We'll leave a telephone trail with Ralph Ames."

When I hung up, Rhonda was looking at me. "How soon do we leave?" she asked.

"Look, are you sure you want to do this? The funeral is tomorrow. Shouldn't you stay here? Aren't there people who'll want to see you?"

"Just because Joey's dead doesn't mean I have to make a public spectacle out of myself. The only person I want to see is Michelle."

"She knew you were staying at La Posada?" I asked.

"Yes."

"Did anyone else?"

"Not really. I didn't take out an ad in the *Arizona Republic*, if that's what you mean. What are you getting at?"

"I'm trying to figure out who else besides Michelle, Detective Reyes-Gonzales, Ralph Ames, and me knew where you were staying."

"That's all," she said. "I didn't even tell Vincent, and not the people at Renthrow Gallery either. I didn't want people being able to find me, people and reporters."

I was gratified to hear that she differentiated between the two. It gave us something in common.

"But somebody else must have known."

She shook her head. "I can't think of anybody."

At that juncture, Ralph Ames, who had obviously never heard of cholesterol counting, summoned us to breakfast—an Eggs Benedict extravaganza served poolside. He wasn't terribly enthusiastic about our proposed drive to Sierra Vista, but he nonetheless offered us the use of his Lincoln, saying that for safety's sake the Fiat should probably remain parked where it was for the time being.

"I agree about the Fiat, Ralph," I said, "and thanks for the offer, but I think I hear Alamo calling me. After all, the insurance will cover the damage. Besides, none of it was my fault. They owe me a car."

Ralph Ames grinned. "You are one stubborn man, Beau. They may not agree with you, but I'll see what I can do."

In the end, Ralph prevailed. Rhonda and I left the Alamo office driving a low-slung Chevrolet Beretta, having taken the extra collision insurance at an additional ten dollars a day and with the rental agent's final prohibition once more ringing in our ears that we were not, under any circumstances, to take the car to Mexico.

By ten-fifteen we were in the parking lot at Phoenix Greyhound Race Track. The people who frequent the swap meet, vendors and customers alike, struck me as a new lost generation, one that had started out in the late sixties making love not war. Almost twenty years later, these folks still hadn't gotten their act together.

There were plenty of wear-dated peace symbols in evidence, and the people displaying them were middle-aged earth-mother types with ample bosoms and long-haired men whose ponytails and beards were flecked with gray. It struck me as ironic that Zeke, Delcia's illegal-arms merchant, should be hiding out in the open, peddling his lethal wares among all the militant peacenik anti-nukers. I would have expected them to run him off as well since, statistically speaking, the attendees are far more likely to be shot than they are to be nuked.

For a while Rhonda and I wandered through the milling aisles. Finally, though, impatient to get out of there, I asked one of the vendors if he knew where I could find Zeke.

"Sure," he said, eying me suspiciously. I didn't fit the typical customer profile. "Next aisle over. Far end on the right."

We found Zeke's stall without any trouble, but the first thing I saw when we got there wasn't Zeke or his guns—it was the rattlesnake.

The snake, so similar to Ringo that they might have been full brothers, sat waist-high on a wobbly card table. Unlike Ringo, however, this one was dead, thoroughly dead, forever frozen by some taxidermist's art into a ferocious striking position. The curved fangs were bared, and the charcoal-colored body coiled back on itself, while the glassy eyes stared straight ahead—directly at me. Just looking at it was enough to prickle the hairs on the back of my neck. Instinctively, I dodged back.

"Purty, ain't he," growled a yellow-toothed man with a fat chew of tobacco stuffed in one cheek. His weighty peace symbol, three inches tall and made from hand-pounded silver, dangled on a frayed leather thong in front of a worn red flannel shirt that was stretched taut over a bulging midsection. "Bagged him myself last year up near Bumble Bee. I'll sell him to you cheap—a hun'red fifty. You won't do no better 'an that."

"No thanks," I said, still maintaining a wary distance.

Rhonda stepped closer and examined the snake curiously. "It does look like Ringo," she said before turning to the vendor. "Are you Zeke?" I had told her who we were looking for and why.

Zeke nodded slowly, giving her a lecherous up-and-down appraisal as he did so. "Sure am, ma'am. What can I do for you today? If'n you don't like snakes, how 'bout a Gila monster then?"

He paused long enough to spit an arc of brown tobacco juice over his shoulder where it landed unerringly in a two-pound Folgers coffee can several feet behind him. "Got me one of them, too. That'll run you 'bout two hun'red even. Or somethin' a little smaller maybe—scorpions and centipedes. These here are s'posed to be plastic paperweights. Real classy if'n you work in an office."

The guy took off his hat and wiped a shiny bald pate with his red bandanna. When he put the Stetson back on, I noticed it was decorated with a rattlesnake skin hatband and several multicolored feathers. Considering his alligator boots and hand-tooled leather belt, this dusty overweight specimen was someone the Earth First folks should have picketed right along with all those fur-wearing, opera-going society matrons.

"We're more interested in guns," I said casually. He blinked. "I've got me some of them, too," he said tentatively. "What kind you lookin' for?"

He pointed me toward a second rickety table, this one covered with guns. The weapons, mostly aged specimens, were a collection of ten or so rifles and shotguns of various makes and models. Some were undoubtedly antique quality with ornate handmade inlay work on the stocks. Others were just plain old.

"Not any of these," I said, dismissing the entire table with a wave. "These are all too big. I was thinking of something smaller."

He looked at me closely.

"A friend told me about you," I added as a further reference, "a nameless, mutual friend. She said you had quite a collection, but if this is all you've got . . ."

Zeke, watching me closely, made up his mind. "I can't afford to put 'em all out," he said quickly. "Somebody might rip 'em off. Exactly what kind of gun might you be lookin' for, mister?"

"A handgun," I said. "Thirty-eight caliber."

"A .38," he repeated thoughtfully. "I just might have one of them. It's small, though. Only a two-inch barrel."

"Small's fine," I said.

He nodded then called over his shoulder, "Hey, Carl. Would you keep an eye on my stuff for a while? I gotta go out to the parking lot for a minute."

Carl, a permanently sunburned blond, occupied a booth that advertised genuine Zuni hand-tooled silver jewelry, although Carl didn't look like any American Indian I'd ever seen. He waved a careless hand in response. "No prob, Zeke. Take your time."

Zeke led us through the parking lot to where a beat-out Volkswagen was parked. Someone with more patience than brains had carefully painted it so that it bore an uncommon resemblance to a mini-Greyhound bus. The inside, however, had been specially fitted with a set of custom mini-blinds which shut off the interior of the vehicle from any outside snooping.

Turning off an elaborate auto alarm system, Zeke unlocked the side door, heaved himself up into the van, and returned to the doorway carrying a heavy tool chest. With a grunt he set the chest down on the floorboard in front of us, opened one compartment, and extracted a cloth-wrapped package.

"This here one's a beaut," he said, lovingly untying the string and unwrapping the cloth to reveal a blued-steel Smith and Wesson Chief. "Five shots not six, and it comes complete with its own clip-on holster."

He handed me the gun with its stubby barrel, and I hefted the weapon in my hand. It was lighter than my old standard-frame .38, but, depending on the kind of ammunition used, I knew it could be every bit as deadly. I snapped it apart and looked it over. It was clean and had been well cared for, either by Zeke or by its previous owner.

"Looks like you've handled one of them before," Zeke observed approvingly. " 'Course, that thing ain't no good for shootin' rabbits."

"We both know what these are good for," I answered shortly. "I won't be hunting rabbits."

Zeke ducked his head and, with feigned interest, examined the scuffed toe of his cowboy boot. "Make you a good deal on it," he said at length, still looking down. "It's a steal at one and a quarter."

"Is it a steal?" I asked.

Zeke looked up quickly, an offended frown on his face. "You mean is it hot? Hell no, man, it ain't hot. I don't fence shit for nobody. This is my very own private collection. I wouldn't be sellin' none of it, but the wife's been sick and had a lot of doctor's bills and all."

"Sure she has," I responded, "but this gun's not worth a dime over sixty bucks, so stop jacking me around."

Zeke yelped like he'd been stuck with a hot poker. After several rounds of negotiating back and forth, we finally settled on eighty-five dollars, cash-and-carry. Ten minutes later, without benefit of anybody's three-day waiting period, we were on our way.

Once we were beyond Zeke's earshot, Rhonda Attwood burst out laughing. "What's so funny?" I asked.

"Remind me to take you along if I ever decide

to sell my Fiat. Now that I've seen you in action with Zeke, I'll bet you can handle car salesmen, too."

It's nice to be appreciated.

CHAPTER
13

On Zeke's advice we stopped by an army-surplus/ammo shop on Thomas Road and purchased a box of Remington 125-grain semi-jacket hollow-point shells. Hollow points aren't armor piercing, not much good for shooting through cars or doors, but when they land in a human body, they stay there. It's the kind of ammunition that keeps medical examiners in business.

Rhonda, walking with me through the shop, didn't question my purchase of the shells, but she raised an eyebrow when I asked for earplugs.

"Target practice," I explained as the clerk went to get them. "Guns are like women, you know. They all come with the same basic equipment, but you need to field-test each one individually to know exactly how it works."

"Right," she said, responding in a lighthearted, bantering tone. "And not all field-testers are created equal."

I was still worrying about that one when we left the store. As we drove south on Interstate 10, the extra ammunition was stowed in the trunk, but

my new used .38, loaded but still untried, rested
in its leather holster, clipped securely inside the
waistband of my pants and concealed under the
folds of my sport jacket.

I hadn't bothered to ask anyone in authority if
my Washington license to carry a concealed
weapon worked in Arizona because I didn't want
to know the answer. Instead, I welcomed the presence of the gun, the slight pressure of its shape
molded against the flesh of my gut. I was armed
once more, carrying a Smith and Wesson. For the
first time in weeks, I felt completely dressed.

Above us the sky changed from metropolitan
smoggy, hazy blue to brilliant azure as we cruised
past a rocky citadel Rhonda told me was called
Picacho Peak. She kept up a running commentary
as we drove, pointing out the names of Indian reservations, mountain ranges, and small towns with
the glib geographical ease of a native. As I listened
to Rhonda's engaging patter, I wondered if she
herself was aware of the defense mechanism at
work, if she realized that the constant barrage of
small talk kept other, more intimate or hurtful
subjects at bay.

South of Tucson she insisted we stop at a truck
stop, The Triple T, for coffee and hot apple pie.
Forty miles south of there, we turned off I-10 near
a place called Benson and headed down Highway
90, a secondary road leading to Sierra Vista and
Fort Huachuca.

The farther south we had driven, the more distance I had put between myself and Ironwood

Ranch, the better I felt. The same didn't hold true for Rhonda. Once we turned off the interstate, her travelogue faltered and she fell strangely silent.

"How will we find out where they live?" she asked at last.

"I'm a detective, remember?" I countered with a grin, but Rhonda was beyond the reach of humor, so I answered more seriously.

"With any kind of luck, Guy Owens will be listed in the phone book. That's what they teach us at the police academy, you know. Check the phone book first. Let your fingers do the walking."

I glanced at Rhonda again, but she didn't crack a smile. Her face was pale, lips compressed, brows knit in a frown.

"What's the matter?" I asked. "Where did you go?"

"What if I convince the father to change his mind and then Michelle decides she doesn't want the baby?" Rhonda asked.

"You'll have to cross that bridge when you come to it," I told her. "But remember, you shouldn't be able to force her to have the baby any more than her father can force her not to. It's Michelle's decision, not yours, not his."

She didn't answer for a long time while miles of blacktop spun away under the moving tires.

"Yes," she said finally, sounding at last resigned to the idea that ultimate control for the decision was beyond her. "I suppose you're right," she added reluctantly.

We drove the rest of the way into Sierra Vista in virtual silence.

At first glance Sierra Vista, all fast-food franchises and gas stations, seemed like a blotch of urban blight spilling out across the desert from the main gate of Fort Huachuca. I turned left down Fry Boulevard and stopped at the first gas station I saw, a self-serve Circle K. The phone book had long since disappeared from the booth outside, but inside I found a frayed, dog-eared edition. The book contained listings for all of Cochise County, and Sierra Vista was close to the back. Sure enough, Lieutenant Colonel Guy Owens had both a listed number and a listed address—141 Quail Run Drive.

"You want to call him and tell him we're coming?" I asked, when I returned to the car.

Rhonda shook her head. "Let's just show up," she said.

It turned out that Quail Run Drive was actually outside the Sierra Vista city limits. It was part of a development called Desert View Estates and set back from Highway 91, which ran south along a range of mountains Rhonda informed me were called the Huachucas. The roads in Desert View Estates were gravel rather than paved, and the houses, on seemingly huge lots, were set far back from the street.

We found 141 with no difficulty. It was a low red-brick structure with thick arches across the front. The arches and the recessed windows beyond them gave the house a sleepy Spanish look.

Inside I caught a glimmer of somebody moving through the shadowy interior.

"At least somebody's home," Rhonda said, noting the Isuzu Trooper parked in front of the house as well as a sporty blue CRX sharing space in the carport with a decade-old maroon Cutlass.

"He may have company," I said. "By my count that's two more cars than drivers."

I pulled to a stop behind the Isuzu. The windows had been tinted so dark they were practically black. That's something that makes sense in the Arizona desert but not in sun-starved Seattle. The plates said Sonora, Mexico, so presumably Guy Owens did have company.

Without waiting for me, Rhonda got out and hurried to the door. She rang the bell, but by the time I joined her, no one had answered.

"Try again," I said. "I'm almost positive I saw someone moving around in there as we drove up."

She rang the bell again. Eventually, after what seemed like a long wait, the dead bolt clicked and the door handle turned. A haggard Guy Owens stood in the doorway.

"Sorry, Sue," he said, looking directly at Rhonda. "I won't be able to go to lunch with you and John. I'm not feeling well."

Sue??? Rhonda had opened her mouth to speak, but she stopped, stunned by what he had said. I could understand her confusion. Was this a genuine case of mistaken identity, or was something else going on?

"Wait a minute," she said, moving toward the door. "You don't understand. I've got to . . ."

Guy Owens caught my eye. There was no mistaking the warning shake of his head, but I didn't know what to do about it. Following Guy's lead, I quickly took hold of Rhonda's arm.

"Come on, Sue," I said, trying to pull her away. "We'll talk to him tomorrow when he's feeling better."

She looked up at me questioningly, but was allowing me to lead her back toward the car when a man emerged from the shadows behind Guy Owens holding an AK-47 assault rifle. He motioned for us to come inside. Just then a second man came loping around to the front of the house from the carport. The second one was wearing military fatigues.

At first I thought he might be there to help us, but I was wrong. He was carrying a 9-mm semi-automatic which he trained on me all the while shielding it with his body from the view of people on the roadway. The handgun may have been more subtle and more readily concealed than the AK-47, but it was sure as hell as lethal. Now we were trapped between the two.

"Looks like you and the lady better go on inside," the man with the 9-mm said, prodding me forward with the barrel of the gun.

He had Hispanic features and a decided accent. He was slight and scrawny. Hand to hand, he wouldn't have lasted a minute with me, but with the gun . . . Without argument, I went inside.

"They're friends of mine," Owens was explaining to the man with the rifle. "We were supposed to go out to brunch."

The importation of AK-47 assault rifles had been banned by the Bush Administration. Unfortunately, the old adage is proving true—if arms are outlawed, only outlaws will have arms. The crooks carried AK-47s long before the ban and they carry them now that the ban is in effect. Up against them, my puny little five-shot .38 was nothing more than a glorified peashooter.

"These friends of his sure as hell ain't going to brunch now, are they, Paco." The second man grinned an evil, gold-toothed grin and strutted his way into the house, shutting the door behind him. "Brunch? No. A little ride? Sí. And maybe after that, a long siesta."

Rhonda looked anxiously from face to face, trying to make sense of what had happened. "I don't understand. What's going on here?"

"They've got Michelle," Owens answered, his voice thick with defeat. "They brought me back here to get the money."

"What money?" I asked.

"Money Joey Rothman evidently stole from these people. Or maybe it was plain old-fashioned extortion. I can't tell which. However he got it, Joey left the money with Michelle for safekeeping."

"Is Michelle all right?" Rhonda asked.

Owens nodded. "I guess so. For now."

"Shut up," the man with the semiautomatic snapped.

Paco looked at his partner questioningly. "Did you find it, Tony?"

Tony nodded. "I think so. Right behind the dryer, just like she said. I was about to pick it up when the doorbell rang. Maybe the lady here would like to go get it for me while the rest of us wait."

He waved his weapon in Rhonda's direction, and she shrank away from it and him.

Guy Owens nodded reassuringly toward an open doorway. "The laundry room is just beyond the kitchen," he said. "Michelle said she hid the briefcase behind the clothes dryer."

Rhonda nodded mutely then disappeared through the doorway, while Tony stationed himself and the semiautomatic near enough to the opening that he could keep an eye on her as well as on us. He seemed to be in charge, but I still wasn't quite sure.

Cop or crook, in this business overconfidence can be a deadly mistake. So far, it hadn't occurred to either one of these gun-toting clowns that the people coming to take Guy Owens to a Sunday brunch might possibly be armed and dangerous themselves. Owens had faked them into believing his story, that we were nothing more than casual, harmless friends, and they hadn't bothered to search us. Considering the difference in firepower, it was a small mistake, but a mistake nonetheless, enough to give me an inkling of hope.

I tried to catch Owens' eye to see if he had any ideas, but he too was watching the doorway, waiting for Rhonda to reappear. She did, carrying a man's thick briefcase. Her face had gone deathly white, and I was afraid for a moment that she was going to faint. Instead, she stopped in the doorway and dropped the briefcase from knee level. It flopped onto the carpeting and fell over, but it didn't pop open.

"Come over here and open it, Paco," Tony said. "Let's make sure his little girl isn't jerking us around. There's supposed to be money in there, and some kind of paper as well."

It was issued like an order, and Paco obeyed without question. Putting his AK-47 on the floor beside him, he knelt and fumbled with the lock.

"Shit, man," he said after several futile attempts. "I can't. It's one of those damn combination locks. Want me to shoot it open?"

"Don't," Rhonda said. "I can open it. At least I think I can."

Surprised, we all looked at her.

"It's JoJo's," she explained. "I gave it to him for Christmas years ago when they were first coming out with the combination locks. Of course, if he's changed the combination . . ."

"Wait a minute," Tony said. "Whose did you say?"

Without bothering to answer him, Rhonda knelt on the floor and began tinkering with the lock, biting her bottom lip in concentration, oblivious to the two men watching her every move. Noticing their momentary lack of attention, I caught Guy Owens' eye.

Paco, kneeling beside Rhonda, was closest to Guy, and the deadly AK-47 still lay where he had left it, on the floor near his feet. Guy Owens rolled his eyes toward Paco in silent acknowledgement, while I calculated the seemingly immense distance between me and the death-dealing semiautomatic.

I knew only too well that we were taking a terrible risk. Withering fire from the semiautomatic would cut us to pieces if I was even a moment too late, but it was now or never. We wouldn't ever get another chance.

I edged closer to Tony, willing Rhonda to keep his attention focused on her slender, nimble fingers, praying that the creeps wouldn't sense the sudden surge of almost electric tension in the room.

The lid of the briefcase popped open revealing a briefcase full of money—tens, twenties, and hundreds, bound in careful stacks. That much money has a magnetic effect on some people, crooks in particular. Fortunately for us, both Paco and Tony were highly susceptible. While their eyes remained riveted to the spilling contents of the briefcase, Guy Owens and I launched our attack.

I didn't see Guy's well-placed kick. Instead, as I threw myself toward Tony, I heard the thud of a shod foot connecting with flesh followed by an agonized groan as Paco fell face down on the floor.

There was no time for me to draw the .38. I threw myself toward Tony, aiming low, hoping to catch him in the abdomen before he could raise the gun to a firing position. He grunted in surprise as I crashed into him. The force of the blow knocked the pistol from his hand and sent it spinning onto the hard tiled surface of the dining room floor. Tony fell backward, carrying me with him through the dining room door where he sprawled face up on a glass-topped table.

We struggled there for a moment, both trying to gain an advantage. The table swayed crazily beneath our combined weight until the over-stressed wrought-iron supports gave way and bent double. The glass itself crashed to the floor, splintering into huge shards four and five feet long.

When we landed, I was still on top and hanging onto Tony's legs, preventing the damaging kicks that were sure to follow if I let him loose. I saw Rhonda scramble desperately out of the way, kicking the assault rifle in front of her. For a moment Tony seemed stunned, breathless, then he began to clutch at my face. His sinewy thumbs were probing for my eyes, trying to blind me. I shook my head from side to side, trying to elude his grasp without letting go of his legs.

Just as his hands closed over my face, I heard Rhonda's voice say, "Freeze!"

There was unmistakable authority in the menacing word. Tony's fingers went suddenly limp, and he winced with pain.

"Get off him, Beau," Rhonda said urgently. "Be careful."

I glanced around, unable at first to see where her voice was coming from although she seemed to be somewhere behind me. When I tried to get up, I had to ease myself up over the assault rifle, which Rhonda Attwood held firmly, pressed deep in Tony's crotch. He tried to wiggle away.

"Don't you move," she ordered.

I wasn't sure at the time if she was bluffing or not. In fact, I'm not sure to this day whether or not she would have shot his balls off, but she sure as hell sounded serious, and Tony wasn't willing to call her on it.

I reached out to take the gun, but she shook her head and held onto it. "Check on Guy," she said. "He may need help."

Actually, Guy Owens didn't need any help at all. With the semiautomatic in his hand, he was prodding the writhing Paco to his knees and forcing him over against the wall. As he moved, Paco clutched his gut and blathered that he needed a doctor.

Guy handed me the 9-mm. "Watch these guys," he said. "I'll be back in a minute."

"Are you going to call for help?"

"No," he said. "I'm going after super glue and duct tape."

"You're crazy," I yelled after him. "If you don't call the cops, I will."

"Don't bother," he said. "They already cut the phone lines."

"I'll go to one of the neighbors then," I said, as he came back into the room carrying a gigantic roll of duct tape and a vial of super glue. Taking the lid off the super glue, he went straight to Paco.

"Open your mouth," Owens ordered.

Paco looked at me, rolling his eyes in fright. "Open your mouth, damn you," Owens repeated.

Reluctantly, Paco opened his mouth and Owens spread a thin line of glue like a welder's bead across the terrified man's lower lip. "Hold 'em together, now," Owens said. "And don't move."

Paco did as he was told. I was afraid Guy Owens had gone totally round the bend.

"Look, Guy, this has all been too much for you. You've got to settle down and start thinking calmly. I'll go next door and call the sheriff."

"The hell you will," he said to me, and then to Rhonda, "Bring that other one over here. We'll glue his mouth shut, too."

Tony came across the room at Rhonda's urging and submitted to the super-glue treatment. As soon as he had administered the glue, Guy began the process of stripping off their clothes and taping their hands and feet together. He worked quickly, purposefully, with no lost motions.

"Are you listening to me?" I demanded. "What in the hell do you think you're doing, Owens? Why are you messing around with glue and duct tape? This has gone just about far enough, don't you think?"

Owens didn't stop as he answered. "Their boss-man, some asshole named Monty, gave us two hours to come down here to the house, collect the money, and get back. If we're not back by the deadline, he'll kill Michelle."

"So what's the matter with calling the sheriff? It's a kidnapping, for Chrissake. Call in the fucking F.B.I."

Guy Owens turned to Rhonda. "What's your name?"

"Rhonda," she answered. "Rhonda Attwood." He did a momentary double take as her name registered, then he caught himself.

"Get the truck then load all that money back in the briefcase, Rhonda. We'll need to take that along. And you," he said to me. "Help me get these creeps loaded into their Isuzu. They made me drive. I left the keys in the ignition. We'll bring it right up to the door so the neighbors don't get an eyeful."

Without a word, Rhonda jumped to do his bidding. She left the money where it was and went to get the Trooper. I lingered for a moment, and Guy Owens rose to his feet, leaving Paco and Tony on the floor with their feet duct-taped together and their forearms taped to their thighs. Almost the same size, we stood there glaring at one another across the two bound men.

Unlike me, Lieutenant Colonel Guy Owens was used to having his orders followed without question. When I didn't move, he finally lost patience.

"Get with it," he bellowed into my face. "You want me to call the sheriff, do you? Well, I called the goddamn sheriff yesterday and they wouldn't even take a goddamn report. Said Michelle was probably a runaway. Said to call them tomorrow if I didn't hear from her today."

Dismissing me, Owens turned away and started toward Paço as Rhonda came back in through the door. Obeying his orders to the letter, she had left the Trooper right outside with its motor running.

Owens picked up Paco and began muscling him toward the door.

"These two jokers picked me up this morning while I was out jogging and dragged me up the mountain to meet their boss. He wanted me to see for myself that they were holding Michelle. As soon as she saw me, Misha told them where to find the missing briefcase. Monty sent us back here to get it and said that if I tried anything funny, if any cops showed up when we came back, he'd kill her. Now do you understand?"

I was beginning to. "Where is she?"

"Up in the mountains at a place called Montezuma Pass. It's near the southern end of the Huachucas in the Coronado National Monument. From the rest area up there, Monty can see for miles in any direction. He'd know well in advance if I was bringing help with me. If we throw some clothes over these two clowns and fasten them in the car with the empty AK-47 next to Tony's shoulder so it looks like he's still got me covered, we may be able to trick him."

"What about us?" Rhonda called from behind us as she snapped the briefcase shut on the last of the money. "What can we do to help?"

"I thought about that while I was out getting the tape," Owens answered. "Monty doesn't know you, and he doesn't know that little blue car of yours. It's Sunday. Lots of people go up into the Huachucas for picnics on Sundays.

"You two go on ahead," Guy Owens continued. "Monty won't expect help to get there before I do. Michelle is in a blue Blazer parked near the restroom. When I get up there, I'll create a diversion somehow, draw Monty away from his truck, while you go in and try to get Michelle out."

I don't know if Guy Owens' job called for him to be a military strategist, but he sure as hell was one. In minutes he had evaluated the forces available and come up with a plan that was gutsy enough that it just might work.

"Gotcha," I said, and started moving Tony toward the door. Rhonda, holding the AK-47, hurried ahead to open the door for all of us.

"Help Guy with our passengers," she said briskly. "I'll go back and get the money."

CHAPTER
19

We loaded the bound and muzzled Paco and Tony into the Trooper and taped them into place with more duct tape, fastening them securely to seat belts and seat supports. Guy taped the stripped-down AK-47 to Tony's shoulder. That way, it would be invisible through the blacked-out side and rear windows, but for someone up on a mountain watching with binoculars, the silhouette of the weapon would be clearly visible through the windshield. Meanwhile, Rhonda had the presence of mind to put together a packet that contained a blanket, thermos, and enough food to make us look like a pair of legitimate picnickers.

Rhonda took my .38, checked it in a very businesslike manner, and put it inside her jacket pocket. I took possession of the 9-mm. Owens disappeared into his bedroom and returned carrying his military dress-uniform side arm, a formidable Colt .45 that looked more like a cannon than a handgun.

Years before, Rhonda told us, she had been to Montezuma Pass on a weekend camp-out with a

Girl Scout troop that had hiked the Huachuca Mountains' Crest Trail. Since she knew the way, Rhonda drove. Like a bat out of hell.

The Beretta had shown a mere twelve hundred miles on its odometer when we had picked it up at Sky Harbor International earlier that morning. None of those miles could have been nearly as tough as the ones Rhonda put on it that afternoon. By comparison, our jaunt up Yarnell Hill in her Spider several days earlier could have been a tame carousel ride.

Once we were off Highway 92, the road was paved for only a mile or two. As soon as it changed to chuck-holed gravel, we started climbing. The road was steep and full of switchbacks and one-lane turns, but Rhonda drove with fierce concentration, heeling the Beretta around corners and gunning the engine on the straightaways.

"How'd you know it was JoJo's briefcase?" I asked. Making asinine conversation helped take my mind off her driving.

"I told you. I recognized it, initials and all. He hasn't used it in years, I'm sure, but he's physically incapable of letting loose of old briefcases. He must have a dozen or so lined up out in his garage. He had half that many when I moved out, and obviously, if he still has this one, he hasn't thrown away any of them."

"And the combination? How did you know that after all these years?"

"His birthday. Not very original, is it?"

The car sawed dangerously as she wheeled it

around a washboarded curve faster than she should have. I swallowed the lump in my throat as she fought the bucking Beretta back under control.

"What are we going to do when we get there?" she asked.

"Find a place discreetly close to the blue Blazer, throw down our blanket, and neck up a storm."

"Are you kidding?" she demanded.

"No. I'm not kidding. There's nothing so boring as watching somebody else neck. If we make it embarrassing enough, maybe Monty will forget about us entirely."

"It'll be dangerous, won't it?"

"No more dangerous than being shoved around by that creep in the 4-X-4 last night. Besides, if Guy's got his information straight, there'll be three of us and only one of him. But we'll have to move fast, before he figures out how come his friends aren't getting out of the Trooper."

She nodded her understanding, and I reached over to pat her leg. "Are you scared?"

"Not yet. Later, I guess, right?"

"Right," I answered. "Later."

By then we were nearing the top of the pass, but the idiot light in the dashboard was beginning to glow dully. The engine was overheating. The Beretta was built for sedate freeway driving. Rhonda Attwood was treating it like a damn mountain goat.

With the temperature light glowing bright red and a cloud of steam rolling out from under the hood, we pulled into the rest area parking lot near the top of the mountain. There were only three other cars parked in the lot, two of them sedans side by side near the restroom building. One was a robin's-egg-blue Dodge Dart with South Dakota plates, while the other, a four-door Dodge Aries from Arizona, wore a bumper sticker that said, "We're spending our children's inheritance."

The blue Chevy Blazer occupied the parking spot nearest the road and as far away from both the restroom and the other vehicles as possible. Like the 4-X-4 that had pursued us in Phoenix the night before, the Blazer was another window-blackened behemoth.

I attempted to glance inside the Blazer as we pulled into the lot. No one was visible, but I didn't want to attract attention by appearing too interested.

Rhonda parked three spaces away, halfway between the other vehicles and the Blazer. As soon as she stopped the car, Rhonda got out and stretched, looking as though she'd been driving for hours. When I got out of the car and came around to stand beside her, she flung her arms around my neck and kissed me passionately on the lips.

"You want necking, fella?" she whispered in my ear. "I'll show you necking."

I pushed her away. "Let's go use the restroom," I said. "We'll try to get the lay of the land."

We stopped long enough to open the hood of the car and let billows of steam roll skyward.

"Should we add water?" Rhonda asked.

"No," I said. "Don't worry about it. It'll cool off of its own accord."

Guy Owens had told us that he'd give us a ten-minute head start, so there wasn't much time for reconnoitering. The restroom, built from rough-hewn stones, would have made every environmentalist's conservationist heart go pitter-pat. A brass plaque affixed to an inside wall announced that the chemically treated composting toilets were a totally nonpolluting system and had been manufactured by some little one-horse company in Newport, Washington—wherever that is.

Unfortunately, I was far more concerned with finding adequate cover than I was with nonpolluting toilets. I tried looking out the eye-level window in the men's room, but that was no good. It faced in the wrong direction.

Back outside, I mingled with the occupants of the other two cars, touring retirees holding an informal coffee klatsch, as they drank coffee and munched sweet rolls. They were all totally oblivious to the drama unfolding around them.

One of them, a white-haired little woman leaning on a four-pronged cane, looked up at me and smiled. "Nice weather after all that rain, isn't it?"

I nodded and said nothing. What I wanted to do was tell them to get the hell out of there. To run for cover while spending their kids' inheritance was still an option, but I couldn't. Any sudden change in behavior would have alerted our quarry that we were onto him.

Rhonda still hadn't emerged from the ladies' room when off to the left, just above the parking lot, I spied a slightly raised ledge with a small bench on it. When she finally did appear, I seized her by the hand and dragged her in that direction.

"Let's go sit up there," I urged.

She nodded happily and trotted along, looking for all the world as though she was having the time of her life. People seeing her from a distance would have thought she didn't have a care in the world. They couldn't see the troubled look in her vivid blue eyes.

"What's going to happen?" she whispered anxiously, leaning close to my shoulder.

As if I knew, but I took a stab at it anyway. "We'll sit up there to begin with. Then, when we see Guy pulling into the lot, we can split up and go in opposite directions. At least that way he won't be able to get all of us at once. If it looks like he's getting away, shoot for the tires or the radiator, not the interior. We might hit Michelle."

She nodded. "Okay," she said, but she punctuated the word with a quick hoot of laughter that made it sound as though I had just cracked some incredibly funny joke.

Still laughing, she scampered over to the Beretta to fetch the thermos and bag of food. She came back toward me, smiling and swaying her hips—showing off. It made me wish we were all wearing flak jackets. Whatever was about to go down, I didn't want any harm to come to Rhonda Attwood's sleek little frame. Or my much larger one either, for that matter.

According to Ralph Ames, Rhonda was a talented artist. Now I learned firsthand that she was also a consummate actress. She was vibrant. She was happy. She was brimming over with infectious laughter. She was on. We made our way up to the bench, but she set the thermos down without pouring coffee. Instead, she wrapped her arms around my neck, ran her fingers through my hair, and pulled my face close to hers. The ardor in her probing kisses set fires in my system that almost made me forget why we were there.

Eventually, laughing again, she drew away. "Can you see anything?" she whispered.

"Can I what?"

"See anything. Through the windshield."

"No," I said, chuckling too in spite of myself. "I had my eyes closed."

She punched me in the arm, playfully and seriously at the same time. "Look this time, dammit." And then she kissed me again.

Below, I heard the sound of a vehicle laboring up the hill. Almost ten minutes had passed, so I was sure it was Guy Owens. It had to be. I pushed Rhonda away so I could peer over her shoulder and get a clear view of what was happening. Across the parking lot, the group of retirees chose that exact moment to begin dividing up into separate cars.

Guy and I had spoken briefly about what he would do. Spilling the money was an old trick, trite and clichéd, but it had already worked once that afternoon, and it might work again. He planned to get out of the Isuzu, walk close enough for Monty to see it, and then let the money go tumbling all over the parking lot. We figured the diversion would give Rhonda or me or both of us time to get close to the Blazer.

But we hadn't counted on a crowd scene right there in the parking lot.

"Get moving," I urged fervently, willing the old folks to leave.

Rhonda pulled away from me. "Not you," I whispered. "Them! We can't do any shooting at all while they're still in the line of fire, understand?"

She nodded, her body tense and shaking with anticipation, but it never came to that. The crooks must have had some kind of fail-safe system, some prearranged warning code, that told the driver of the waiting Blazer that something was wrong. Long before the Isuzu crested the final ridge, and just as the Dodge Dart started for the rest area's exit, the engine of the Blazer roared to life. It lurched out of its parking place and shot off down the western side of the pass in a cloud of dust, leaving two carloads of shaken tourists staring in its wake.

There was never any question of us firing a weapon after him. It would have endangered a good half-dozen innocent bystanders.

Rhonda and I had leaped off the bench and were racing back to the Beretta as the Trooper came into sight. Frantically we waved at Owens, motioning for him to follow the fleeing Blazer. Fortunately, our desperate message got through. Without slowing down, the Trooper lunged past us and down the other side of the mountain while we were still clambering into the car and groping for seat belts.

We didn't take time to discuss strategy. It wasn't necessary. Rhonda dove for the driver's seat, and I climbed in the other side, rolling down the window as I went, preparing to fire from the vehicle if that proved necessary. The 9-mm was a far better weapon for that purpose than the .38 would have been, and I had no doubt that I was the better shot.

After all, Rhonda Attwood's business was painting pictures. Mine was catching killers.

We knew both vehicles were ahead of us, but not because we could see them. The steep grades and blind curves limited the sight line. Occasionally we caught sight of the glint of sun on metal, but mostly what we saw were the two distinct clouds of dust that roiled up over the horizon, muddying the clear mountain air behind the fleeing vehicles.

Now, instead of the idiot light glowing, we could smell the odor of overheated brakes. The downgrade was incredibly steep, rocky and wash-boarded in spots, and crisscrossed by boulder-laden streams still swollen from recent rains.

Rhonda deftly picked her way through them, side-stepping the biggest rocks, avoiding the worst of the ruts. Once or twice the low under-carriage of the Beretta dragged on something, and I worried about what Alamo would have to say this time. But at least we weren't in Mexico. According to my calculations, the international border was at least a good half mile away.

We came down out of the mountains into a rolling rangeland that seemed like a mistake. It was as though we had left the red Arizona desert on the other side of the Huachucas and landed in the middle of the Great Plains. For miles before us spread a vast valley of lush green rolling hills, dissected by the narrow, rutted road meandering through it like a willful stream.

A herd of curious white-faced cattle hurried toward the road to watch us pass and see what all the excitement was about. Meanwhile, ahead of us, the two separate clouds of dust still pointed the way.

"Where the hell are we?" I demanded. "This doesn't even look like Arizona."

"It's the San Raphael Valley," Rhonda answered. "It's usually one of my favorite places, but not right now. How will we ever catch them?"

Her question was answered with terrifying immediacy. Like anxious flight controllers watching the separate blips of planes on a radar screen, our hearts sank as the blips suddenly merged, as the two clouds of dust became one that billowed skyward in an explosive eruption.

"Jesus!" I exclaimed.

"What happened?"

I knew instinctively what had happened although I couldn't have explained how. Thinking the Trooper was his only pursuer, the driver of the Blazer must have rounded a blind corner and then stopped, lying in wait until the Trooper rounded the same corner and then ramming it as it came by.

"Hurry," I commanded. "But don't get too close. Try to stop while we're still out of sight."

Following directions, Rhonda slowed and stopped in the middle of the narrow, rutted road just before the crest of a small hill. We left the Beretta where it was and scurried up the bank, using a small stand of scrub oak for cover. In the basin ahead of us, the smashed Trooper lay on its side with the two upper wheels still spinning, but the attacking Blazer hadn't escaped unscathed.

It stood drunkenly on two flattened tires, steam spilling from a ruined radiator. I wondered hopefully if maybe the driver had been injured, but just then the door swung open and a giant of a man emerged. He opened the back door and reached inside, dragging out something that could have been a helpless kitten for all the ease with which he picked it up and tossed it over his shoulder.

And then he was walking in my direction, striding toward the lifeless Trooper. As he came closer, I realized with a clutch of despair that the limp form slung across his shoulder was the inert body of Michelle Owens. Behind me, I heard Rhonda's quick intake of breath, but I turned and motioned her to silence, because in the crook of his other elbow he carried another death-dealing AK-47.

"Shit!" I whispered.

"What are we going to do?" Rhonda returned.

"He's got another rifle," I told her. "Guy must be injured or unconscious. I'll have to try to get closer, to get within range."

With that I started running through the trees. They were situated beside a small streambed that ran parallel to the road for about a quarter of a mile. I half expected Rhonda to follow, but when she didn't, I could hardly blame her. Why should she put her life on the line?

Monty—that had to be the giant's name—dropped Michelle on the ground and went to the disabled Trooper. He tried the back door, but it was apparently jammed. Next he looked inside. Setting his gun down so it leaned against the roof of the crippled vehicle, he clambered up onto the side. With nothing but his bare hands, he wrenched the door from its hinges. He plunged his arm down into the interior, but whatever he wanted was farther away than his outstretched arm could reach. Shaking his head in disgust, he dropped into the Trooper and momentarily disappeared.

Maybe he went to get the money, I thought, all the while dreading the bark of a gunshot that would tell me he had also had some other, more murderous purpose.

I ran then, straight out, breaking across the open field. The sheltering trees had allowed me to get even with the Trooper and go a little beyond it, so now as I cut back toward the road, I was coming from the south and slightly toward the west, the place from which he was least likely to expect an attack.

Monty and I must have heard the sound of the approaching vehicle at exactly the same time. His head popped out of the top of the Trooper like a gopher peeking out of its hole. He looked back up the road the way he had come. Just as quickly, he disappeared back inside without even glancing in my direction.

I looked to see what was coming and was astonished to see the Beretta hurtling down the rutted road toward the Isuzu. I still wasn't quite within range when he reappeared in the door of the wrecked car. As soon as I saw him the second time, I knew what was in his hand—Guy Owens' cannon-sized Colt .45.

Cringing, I thought about how a powerful slug from the Colt would slice through the thin metal shell of the Beretta and through the soft flesh of Rhonda Attwood as well.

Monty was leaning on the frame of the Trooper, using it to steady his hand and arm. There's a moral decision to make the first time you fire a weapon at another human being. You make that decision once. That's the hardest. It's never as tough the second time.

He fired and I fired. With a yelp of pain, he jerked back into the Trooper while the .45 spun away into the dirt.

Mine was a bad shot. A terrible shot. I'd aimed

for his heart and hit him in the goddamned arm.

Beyond the Isuzu, the wounded Beretta clanked and clattered as the timing belt broke and the pistons pounded into the valves. Mortally injured, it kept on coming, making no attempt to brake, no attempt to stop even when the seizing motor quit with an explosive bang.

She's dead, I thought wildly. Rhonda's dead! The son of a bitch killed her!

The Beretta, caught in the ruts of the road, waddled on past me like a faltering drunk, then scraped to a stop against an uphill bank ten yards away.

I ran like a man on fire, ran to the car and ripped open the door, but the car was empty. No one was there. A flat river rock the size of my shoe was duct-taped to the gas pedal.

I'll be damned! I said to myself.

Turning, I looked back up the road. Rhonda Attwood was running toward me, waving my .38 over her head in triumph. In the other hand she carried Guy Owens' much-used roll of duct tape.

"We got him," she crowed as she came down the hill. "We flat out got him!"

CHAPTER
20

As suddenly as it had come, the triumphant grin on Rhonda's face vanished, displaced by an expression of stunned fear. She stopped, frozen in place like a headlight-blinded deer. I turned and looked in the same direction just in time to catch sight of the briefcase erupting straight up from the hatch-like opening in the side of the disabled Trooper.

The case landed flat in the dirt several feet away, kicking up a small flurry of dust. And behind the briefcase came Monty himself. His one arm hung broken and useless. Still, he dragged himself up and was getting ready to vault out of the vehicle.

"Stop right there," I shouted, raising the semi-automatic. "Freeze!"

He did.

"Hands over your head," I continued.

He turned and regarded me with calculated insolence as if gauging whether or not I'd be tough enough to pull the trigger a second time. I was, but he didn't know that. He had no way of knowing I was a police officer. I had underestimated him, made an almost fatal mistake. It chilled me to think how close he'd come to retrieving his own AK-47. He wouldn't get another opportunity like that, not if I could help it.

"I can't raise my arm," he called back. "I think my arm's broken."

"Get the other one up, then," I said. "Behind your head and keep it there."

While holding the semiautomatic on Monty, I directed Rhonda to bring back both the AK-47 and Guy Owens' Colt. Once she did so, I motioned Monty out of the Isuzu. One-handed and wounded, he still made it out in only one try. That son of a bitch was tougher than nails.

Hurrying over to where Michelle lay motionless on the ground, Rhonda shook the girl and spoke her name, but there was no response. Anxiously, Rhonda looked to me for advice.

"Is she still alive?" I asked.

Rhonda took Michelle's wrist and checked for a pulse. "Passed out, I think. Maybe drugged. What should I do?"

"Leave her for now," I replied.

"Hey, man," Monty interrupted. "How about helping me with my arm before I bleed to death? At least let me sit down."

He had dropped the insolent attitude in favor of an affronted whine. His injured arm was still spurting blood and he swayed like a falling tree, but the sudden change in attitude made me wary. Compared to me, Monty was a mountain, six-seven at least with a girth to match. I knew if it ever came down to hand-to-hand combat, I wouldn't stand a chance. Not only was he huge, he was also cagey and determined. Despite his injuries, he had still tried to make off with the briefcase full of money. That kind of single-minded tenacity doesn't evaporate within a minute's time.

"Strip off your clothes," I ordered. "All of them. Throw them on the ground."

"Hey, man, wait a minute," he objected. "You can't do this. I know my rights."

"The hell with your rights," I growled back. "The only right you've got at the moment is the right to a bullet between your eyes if you don't. Strip, and strip now! Do it!"

Slowly, one at a time, keeping a watchful eye on the gun, he began to peel the clothes off his massive frame. The arm continued to bleed, but he seemed oblivious to it. He was focused on me and the semi-automatic in my hand. I could sense him wondering how good a shot I was and whether or not he should make a break for it. Finally, when he stood there naked except for his shorts, I had him step away from the pile of discarded clothing. He shrugged as if I had gone crazy, but he complied.

"Check them, Rhonda," I ordered, "and stay out of my line of fire."

"Check them?" she asked with a frown. "What do you mean?"

"For weapons," I said. "He may have another gun or a knife."

Frowning doubtfully, she hurried over to the wadded pile and brought it back to me, pawing through it as she came. The switchblade had been hidden inside a sock. So I had called the shot. I nodded in satisfaction.

Wonderingly, Rhonda held up the knife. "How did you know it was there?" she asked.

"An educated guess."

She glanced at Monty, whose impassive face suppressed all indication of the fury he must have felt.

"Remember Ringo?" I asked.

Rhonda nodded.

"This character needs to be handled with about the same amount of care."

"What about my arm?" Monty asked again, still whining.

Rhonda had dropped the roll of duct tape at my feet, but I didn't take my eyes off Monty long enough to reach down and get it. I wasn't taking any chances.

"Toss him the tape," I said to Rhonda, and to him, "Put a tourniquet on it. Use that."

Just then, Guy Owens' crew-cut head slowly emerged from the top of the Trooper. He seemed dazed, and there was a long jagged cut along one side of his jaw. His face screwed up with pain as he made the effort to hold himself erect.

"Are you all right?" I asked.

"My leg," he said. "I think it's broken. What about Michelle?"

"She's all right, I think." I turned to Rhonda.

"Can you keep our friend here covered while I go help Guy?"

"With pleasure."

Guy moaned low in his throat as I lifted him out of the Isuzu and eased him onto the ground near his unconscious daughter, then I went back to the Trooper, crawled up on top, and checked on the other occupants. In the back seat, the duct tape and seat belts had held. Paco, leaning against the far window, was out cold. Tony, his lips bleeding profusely where he had torn away the super glue, dangled crazily to one side.

When my face appeared above him, he yelled at me in incomprehensible Spanish then switched to enraged English. "That sumbitch left without me!" he screamed. "He took the money and went without me!"

"He didn't get far," I told him, leaving him there, still dangling in midair, still ranting and raving at the injustice of it all, learning once and for all that there is no honor among thieves.

As I turned back to the disaster on the road, I realized I was dealing with a case study in triage—who was hurt worst and needed the most attention? The problem was, I didn't dare do anything about injuries while mountainous Monty was still on the loose. Rhonda was holding the gun on him, but even with him covered, I didn't dare get too close. I longed for a pair of handcuffs, but the only thing available was still that old reliable handyman's helper—duct tape.

It seemed to be working fine as a tourniquet—

the bleeding on Monty's arm slowed to a trickle. The prisoner stood staring at us defiantly, one arm raised over his head and the other hanging uselessly at his side. The swaying, an unsuccessful ruse, had stopped.

"Sit down," I told him, still aiming the semi-automatic squarely at his chest. "Wrap the tape around both ankles. Tight."

The wonderful thing about duct tape is that it is designed to bond best to itself, although it did all right on Monty's hairy ankles. Once his ankles were wrapped, I handed Rhonda the gun.

"If he makes any sudden moves, if he does anything at all that you don't like—shoot him."

She nodded grimly. "You bet," she said. "With pleasure." She sounded as though she meant every word.

While Rhonda kept Monty covered, I directed him to lie down flat on the ground where I bound his wrists to his thighs and his elbows to his ribs, mummy-style. As I stepped back to survey my work, he gave a tentative, testing pull against his restraints, followed by a howl of pain at the self-inflicted punishment to his wounded arm.

The result was precisely what I wanted—a clear case of cause and effect, a variation on a theme of that old parental prerogative. Any attempt to escape would hurt him far more than it would hurt me.

Reasonably assured that Monty would now stay where we left him, I returned to where Guy Owens sat on the ground, close to the Trooper. He was holding Monty's fully loaded AK-47 and keeping a watchful eye on the two remaining occupants of the disabled Isuzu.

"They still haven't gotten loose," he said.

"You're right. We'll leave them there for now. That duct tape works like a charm. What are we going to do about your leg?"

"Is there any tape left?"

"Some. Why?"

"Get the other assault rifle from the Isuzu. Maybe we can use the tape to turn the rifle into a splint."

Which is exactly what we did. The splint was only a make-do measure, but at least it stabilized the bone so Guy could be moved without damaging the leg any worse than it already was. That done, I carried Michelle over close enough to him so he could hold her head in his lap. We all tried to waken her, but she was either seriously injured or in a drug-induced stupor. We had no way of knowing which it was or whether or not she'd ever come out of it.

"What now?" Rhonda asked, standing up with her hands on her hips and surveying the damage around us. By now we'd been in that same spot for nearly forty-five minutes without another vehicle passing.

Of the three of us, Guy Owens lived nearest to this deserted stretch of potholes that doubled as a pretend road.

"How far to civilization?" I asked him.

Owens shook his head. "I don't know. There's

probably a ranch or two on up the road, but I have no idea how far."

I retrieved my most recent freebie Alamo map from the dead Beretta and read the bad news for myself. Nogales, a town which looked as though it might be big enough to have its own hospital, was a good twenty miles away, but the faint gray lines leading to it were the same ones we were already on. In my estimation, that indicated dirt tracks, not roads. Sierra Vista appeared to be much closer, but only as the crow flies, and to get there we would have to cross back over Monte-zuma Pass.

In that case, the vehicle situation was downright hopeless. Only one of the three wrecked cars—the Trooper—seemed potentially driveable, and that was only if we could somehow manage to tip it over and get it back on its feet.

Even then, I couldn't see how we'd make do since our current tour group included seven passengers, four of whom were wounded and three of whom were prisoners. Nice bunch.

After a brief consultation with Guy, we decided to try to right the Trooper. That wasn't such a crazy idea once we discovered that the Blazer came complete with a winch. With Rhonda and me doing the moving and with Guy Owens sitting guard with the remaining assault rifle, we removed Paco and Tony from the Trooper and fastened them to the Beretta. Paco was still dead to the world, and Tony didn't offer any resistance. He was still so pissed at Monty leaving him that he seemed to have abandoned all thought of getting away in favor of getting even.

Rhonda managed to start the Blazer and maneuver the limping hulk into position. We were just beginning to hook up the winch cable when Guy Owens alerted us to look up the road, where a swirl of dust announced the swift approach of an oncoming vehicle.

I looked at the carnage around us, broken cars and bound and battered people, and wondered if anyone would believe our story. If some local rancher happened on the scene, would he take time to listen, or would he shoot first and ask questions later?

The vehicle turned out to be an ugly yellow Forest Service Suburban driven by an earnest young man in a brown uniform. I've never been so happy to see an untried, beardless youth in my life.

He stopped the van next to the wrecked Beretta and got out, moving forward uncertainly. As soon as he saw the weapon in Guy Owens' hands, he stopped short and began to scuttle back toward his truck.

"Wait," I called. "Please. We need your help. People are injured."

He checked his headlong flight, but only barely. He ducked his head and cleared his throat before he spoke as if he was having trouble swallowing.

"Looks like you're having a little difficulty here," he croaked.

"As a matter of fact, we are," I said. "I'm a police officer. You wouldn't happen to have a radio in that thing, would you?"

"Yes. What's the problem? Are these guys wet-backs or what? Do you need me to call the border patrol?" Now that he had found his voice he spat out the questions one after another without waiting to hear any answers.

"Actually, there's a whole catalog of calls to be made," I said. "Start with the nearest hospital, the local sheriff's department, and the F.B.I. And when you finish with them, you should probably call a tow truck."

"The hospital in Sierra Vista?" our rescuer faltered.

"No, not that one," Lieutenant Colonel Guy Owens interrupted from his seat on the ground several feet away. "Call Colonel Miller at the base hospital on post. Tell Joe, if one's available, to send a chopper for a dust-off."

"A what?" the beardless youth stammered.

All I can say is he must have been a babe in arms during the Vietnam War. The term mystified him.

"A Med-evac helicopter," Guy grumbled in explanation. "My name's Lieutenant Colonel Guy Owens. Give him our location. Tell him it's for me and Michelle. Joe'll handle the rest."

What followed could easily have passed for a mini-convention of local law enforcement personnel. Guy and Michelle Owens were already loaded into the helicopter and on their way to Raymond W. Bliss Army Community Hospital at

Fort Huachuca before the first patrol car arrived, bringing a Santa Cruz County deputy who had come across the valley from some place called Patagonia.

Next a Border Patrol van showed up, not because they were summoned, but because they had been on their way. One of their informants had notified them that something unusual might be going on up in the pass. They had been coming to check that rumor out when they heard the series of emergency radio communications from the Forest Service Suburban.

Two ambulances, an enthusiastic D.E.A. officer, and a tow truck arrived from Nogales almost simultaneously, followed closely by two F.B.I. agents summoned from Tucson who disembarked from another helicopter and immediately took charge.

Time and again Rhonda and I explained what had happened as far as we knew. All three of the prisoners seemed to be a more-or-less known quantity to the D.E.A. guy, who was beside himself with joy at the idea of having all three of them in custody.

According to him, Paco and Tony each had long rap sheets. Monty, presumably a much bigger fish, had never before been nailed, although both his existence and his name had long been rumored in drug-dealing circles.

What seemed to puzzle everyone concerned was why guys who were basically successful drug runners would suddenly involve themselves in the much less lucrative and potentially far riskier crime of kidnapping. It wasn't logical. I certainly couldn't shed any light on that topic, and the prisoners didn't either.

With everyone else deciding who should go where and how it should all be accomplished, there was little or nothing for Rhonda and me to do but sit in the background, huddle under ambulance blankets, try to keep warm, and watch the three-ring circus unfold around us.

"You know that .38 I gave you earlier?" I asked her in a careful undertone when we were alone.

"Yes. What about it?"

"So far it hasn't been fired, right?"

"Right."

"So how about if I make you a gift of it? I don't want any of these hotshots getting me on a concealed weapons charge."

"What about me?" Rhonda asked.

"You're an artist, not a cop. People expect artists to do crazy things."

She nodded and laughed. "Thanks for the present," she added. "Remind me to return the favor."

The sun had gone down and it was becoming increasingly chilly when one of the tow-truck drivers—there were now three separate tow trucks on the scene—came looking for us.

"You J. P. Beaumont?" he asked.

I nodded.

"I called Alamo," he said, almost apologetically, "you know, to see where they wanted me to tow the Beretta. Someone from there is on the radio. They want to talk to you."

I'll just bet they do, I thought, as he led me to his truck and handed me the microphone. I pushed down the switch. "This is J. P. Beaumont. Over," I said.

"Mr. Beaumont?"

"Yes. Over."

It was a woman's voice, controlled but furious. "My name is Lucille Radonovich, District Manager for Alamo Rent A Car."

"What can I do for you, Ms. Radonovich? Over." I tried to sound reassuring, engaging, casual. It didn't work.

"You are a dangerous man, Mr. Beaumont," she declared.

"Look," I said, reasonably, "I took the extra collision insurance you sold me. Ten dollars a day. Everything's fine, right? Over."

Lucille Radonovich was not to be dissuaded. "Mr. Beaumont, everything is not fine. You may have taken the additional insurance, but it may or may not be valid depending on the exact geographical location of the accident."

"It wasn't an accident," I interrupted helpfully. "That guy shot it with a Colt .45. On purpose. Over."

She continued, as though I hadn't spoken. "Mr. Beaumont, I have been directed to tell you to turn your keys over to our representative, the tow-truck driver. Immediately. Is that clear?"

"Yes, ma'am."

"Later on, someone from this office will be in touch with either you or your attorney to settle your account."

"Does this mean I don't get another car? Over."

I already knew the answer to my question, but I had to ask, had to hear it from her own lips.

And Ms. Lucille Radonovich's reaction was exactly what I expected—no more, no less. A pause. A long pregnant pause, and then a slowly released breath like a dangerously stressed valve letting off excess pressure.

"Some things go without saying, Mr. Beaumont. Over and out!"

Without a word, I handed the keys to the Beretta over to the tow-truck driver. He looked at them for a moment, then walked away, shaking his head.

I watched him go and realized that it would be a hell of a long walk back to Ralph Ames' home in Paradise Valley some two hundred miles away.

I went back to where Rhonda sat waiting. She was chilled. Her teeth were chattering. I put my arm around her shoulder and she snuggled close to me.

"Are these the people who killed Joey?" she asked. "Or was it somebody else?"

I squeezed her shoulder and held her tight. "No way to tell," I answered, "at least not right now."

We sat there for another half hour and watched while the tow trucks began to haul away wrecked cars.

"How are we going to get home?" she asked,

lifting her head off my shoulder to look at me as though the thought hadn't occurred to her before.

"I don't know. It could be a very long walk."

Rhonda Attwood must have been starting to feel better.

"You mean that nice Ralph Ames won't come get us the way he did for you up in Prescott?" she asked.

"We'll see," I said. "He may have run out of patience with me the same way Alamo has."

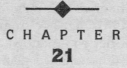

C H A P T E R
21

Fortunately, Ralph Ames is a forgiving man—a most forgiving man with an inexhaustible supply of good connections. Once alerted to our plight, he hired another helicopter and came to Tucson to get us.

By three the next morning he had successfully extricated Rhonda Attwood and me from the clutches of the F.B.I. By four he had dragged us home to Paradise Valley. When it was time to go to bed, Rhonda made not the slightest pretense of going to her own designated room. She undressed in mine, crawled into bed, snuggled contentedly against my chest, and instantly fell asleep.

There was no seduction, no game-playing. We were both far too tired. I drifted off within minutes as well and slept the heavy, dreamless sleep born of exhaustion. My body's resources had been driven far beyond the reaches of endurance.

My own noisy snoring woke me up the next morning. The sun was already well up behind the looming hump of Camelback Mountain, and I was in bed alone.

Guiltily, I wondered if my snoring had awakened Rhonda and driven her from the room, but a quick check of her room showed it was empty as well, the bed untouched. I glanced at the bedside clock. It was already almost ten—high time to be up and about, especially considering the fact that Joey's funeral was scheduled for three that afternoon.

I hurried into the bathroom, took a quick shower, dressed, and then went prowling Ames' house in search of intelligent life. There wasn't any. Rhonda Attwood was nowhere to be found, and neither was Ames, but the coffee carafe was full of hot, aromatic coffee. I was just pouring myself a cup when the phone rang.

"Detective Beaumont?"

I recognized Guy Owens' brisk voice at once. "Hello, Guy. How's Michelle?"

"Much better, thank you. They pumped her stomach. She's up and around."

"What about you? How's the leg?"

"In a cast, but it'll mend." He paused, sounding somewhat uncertain. "I need to ask you a question, Detective Beaumont. I never had a chance yesterday, but today I need to know the answer."

"Shoot."

"Why did you and Rhonda Attwood come to Sierra Vista?"

I could feel myself being painted into a corner. I sensed the hidden traps inherent in any answer

I might give, so I waffled. "You should ask Rhonda that question, Guy, not me."

"Put her on the phone, then, and I will," he returned.

"Sorry. She's not here right now."

"But now is when I need the answer," Guy insisted stubbornly.

I heard a hard edge come into his voice, a tone that I recalled hearing once before during our long, fruitless wait in my cabin, that night seemingly eons ago. Then we had been linked by the mutual bond of outraged fatherhood. A lot of painful water had gone under the bridge since then. Now, five long days later, my connection with Rhonda Attwood had somehow, inexplicably, forced me into a separate camp. Guy Owens and I were no longer on the same team. I could hear it in his voice.

"I'm sure Rhonda will be back soon," I countered. "She may just have gone out to have her hair done or do some shopping."

Truthfully, neither of those two options sounded much like the Rhonda Attwood I knew, but they were the best I could come up with at a moment's notice, and Guy Owens didn't question them.

"There are decisions to make," Guy Owens replied stiffly. "Important decisions, and they need to be made now. This morning. So you tell me, Detective Beaumont. Why did she come to the house? What did she want?"

And suddenly all the responsibility for the future of Rhonda Attwood's single potential grand-child was thrust solely onto my shoulders. With Michelle Owens already a patient in a hospital where the lieutenant colonel's best buddy ran the show, I knew there wouldn't be any problem scheduling her for a bit of minor surgery. The innocuous diagnosis would say that some unspecified female difficulty had prompted a routine D & C. In the process, the embryo of Joey Rothman's posthumous progeny would be summarily scraped out of existence.

"Rhonda wanted to talk to you," I said lamely.

"What about?"

Guy Owens wasn't making it easy for me. "To try to talk you out of the abortion," I replied. "She's willing to help with the baby, financially, I mean, and with raising it too. Joey was her only son, you see, and—"

Guy Owens cut me off before I could say any more. "That's all I wanted to know," he said bluntly, hanging up the phone without bothering to say good-bye.

I stood there holding the handset, looking at it gloomily, listening to the empty buzz of dial tone, and knowing I'd blown it. Completely blown it! Maybe Rhonda herself could have convinced him, but I sure as hell hadn't. Feeling both powerless and inept, I flung the phone back into its cradle. Where the hell was she anyway? Why wasn't she here to handle her own damn problems?

Far away, in some other part of the house, I heard a shower turn on. It was a welcome diversion. It meant someone besides me was still hanging around. I settled down to drink a cup of coffee and to wait and see who would appear.

Ames, still bleary-eyed, stumbled into the kitchen a few minutes later. He headed straight for the coffee. "Rhonda's still asleep?" he asked.

I shook my head. "Up and gone already," I told him. "I thought you and she had taken off somewhere together."

"Are you kidding? Not me. I just woke up a few minutes ago. Where'd she go, and how?" he asked.

"Beats me." I shrugged, but I was beginning to feel uneasy about her absence. Walking over to the door that led out to the garage, I opened it and looked inside. Ames' enormous white Lincoln wasn't parked where we had left it.

"Did you give her permission to use your car?" I asked.

Frowning, Ames came over to where I was standing and looked out at the empty garage for himself. "No," he said, shaking his head. "Not that I remember."

He turned back into the room and checked in the cupboard drawer where he usually deposited the fistful of car keys whenever he entered the house.

"The keys are gone," he announced.

"Stealing car keys must run in the family," I commented humorlessly.

Ralph ignored me. "She must have taken it, then. Are you sure she didn't leave a note somewhere telling you where she was going?"

"No. Not that I found."

"Great," Ralph muttered. "That's just great. Here we are, stuck without a car, and she's off God knows where doing God knows what. We'll just have to wait for her to turn up, that's all."

Maybe Ralph is constitutionally capable of sitting patiently and waiting for someone to "turn up," but I'm not. I'm terrible at waiting.

"You could always call and report the Lincoln stolen," I suggested.

"Are you kidding? Have Rhonda Attwood arrested for car theft?" Ralph asked incredulously. "Not on your life. She'll come back. You'll see. I'm going to go out and sit by the pool. Care to join me?"

"No thanks."

Instead, I paced the floor for a while, trundling back and forth through the house, looking out the windows and peering up and down the street hoping to catch sight of the Lincoln as it turned in at the end of the driveway. No such luck.

Time passed. I don't know how much, but finally, when Ralph came in to pour himself another cup of coffee, I couldn't wait any longer. I picked up the phone and dialed Detective Delcia Reyes-Gonzales' direct number at the Yavapai County Sheriff's Department. It was Monday morning, and she was at her desk.

"I see you're splashed all over the front page of the *Republic* again this morning, Beau," Delcia said with a musical laugh when I identified myself.

"There are only fourteen counties in this state, and so far you've raised hell in five of them. How much longer do you plan on staying around?"

"This is serious, Delcia," I cut in. "Rhonda's missing."

"No!" Delcia sounded alarmed.

"I woke up around ten, and she was gone. So is Ralph Ames' car."

"No note?"

"Nothing."

"Any sign of a struggle?"

"No."

"These bastards don't give up easy, do they," Delcia breathed. She was leaping to the same uncomfortable conclusion that was beginning to dawn on me.

"Not very. What do you suggest?"

"Have you reported her missing?"

"No. Ralph didn't think it was necessary. He won't even report the car being gone. He's convinced she's just out running errands and that she'll be back."

"He could be right," Delcia said dubiously, "but I'm not so sure, especially considering what all's happened in this case during the last few days. But since it *is* his car . . ."

She let the end of the sentence linger in the air. After a momentary pause she asked, "What did those guys want, anyway? Why did they snatch Michelle? The newspaper story didn't shed much light on the whys."

"Money, for one thing, I guess. Money Joey had

lifted from somebody and turned over to Michelle for safekeeping."

"How much money?"

"A hundred grand."

Delcia whistled through her teeth. "Sounds like big-time drug money to me. So maybe he wasn't lying about that after all."

"No," I said. "Maybe not. And since he seems to have been grabbing at money anywhere he could find it, my guess is that he got in a tight spot with his suppliers and was trying to make good on what he owed them. Either that, or to skip out altogether."

"Literally robbing Peter to pay Paul," Delcia put in.

"That's right. The creeps also said something about a paper as well as the money, but all I saw in the briefcase was green stuff, so I don't have any idea what the paper could have been."

"Maybe Michelle knows something about it," Delcia suggested. "The F.B.I. may have learned something from her about that. Do you know? Did they ask her?"

"They never got a chance to talk to Michelle, at least not while I was there. The chopper from Fort Huachuca had lifted off before the F.B.I. guys arrived on the scene. As far as I know, they still haven't interviewed either Guy or Michelle."

"Is it possible that the feds learned something from the prisoners?"

"Possible," I agreed, "but you know the F.B.I. They didn't breathe a word to anybody else."

"At least not to you," Delcia interjected good-humoredly.

My temper flared. "You're right. Not to me. You might have better luck on that score. You're a helluva lot prettier than I am, for one thing, and you're an official detective with an official connection to the case for another. Who am I? Just the poor stupid schmuck who happened to get caught in the cross fire with live bullets flying in every goddamn direction. Why the hell would I need to know anything?"

"Don't get all bent out of shape," Delcia cautioned. "I'm scheduled to call the F.B.I. this morning. If I find out something you should know, I'll tell you. As soon as I finish with them, I'm on my way to Phoenix for the funeral. Maybe Ralph Ames is right and Rhonda's out getting ready for the funeral. If she shows up in the next hour or so, have the dispatcher put you through to me in the car. Otherwise, when I get there, we'll see what other courses of action to follow."

"All right," I said grudgingly, knowing full well it was the only sensible thing to do.

I understand how missing-persons reports work. Police jurisdictions don't much like receiving them when the person in question has been missing less than twenty-four hours. It generates too much wasted paperwork.

"One more thing," Delcia added. "I did have a call for her. It came in to the department last night. The guys on duty thought it might be important and called me at home."

"A call for Rhonda?" I asked. "What kind of call? Who from?"

"A man. Gave his name as Denny Blake. Said he was a neighbor of Rhonda's up in Sedona. He said he was worried because he hadn't heard from her in several days."

"Why'd he call you?"

"He read about the Joey Rothman case in the Sedona paper and knew I was working on it. He left a message with me to have Rhonda call him."

"You didn't tell him where she was staying or give him this number, did you?"

"I'm a cop, Beau," Delcia answered, a sudden chill creeping into her previously cordial voice. "And I'm not stupid."

"Sorry," I said hurriedly. "I didn't mean for it to sound that way. It's just that I'm worried, that's all. I'll see you when you get here."

"Hopefully she'll be there by the time I am," Delcia added, but she didn't sound totally convinced, and neither was I.

"So we wait?" Ames asked, peering at me over his raised coffee cup as I put down the phone.

"We wait," I told him.

But as I said before, I'm terrible at waiting. It goes against the grain. I have a compulsion to *do* something even if what I do may not always be right. Ten minutes later, I picked up the phone, dialed Arizona information, and asked for Denny Blake's number in Sedona. There was no problem. The phone number was there, unlisted. When I dialed it, a man's voice answered on the second ring.

"Blake's residence," he said.

I'm used to phone calls being much more difficult to make, people being harder to track down. Denny Blake answered before I had a chance to figure out what I was going to say.

"My name is Beaumont," I stammered. "J. P. Beaumont."

"Oh yes," he answered. "Rhonda mentioned you. From the sound of it, you must be some kind of he-man."

Denny Blake's sibilant s's allowed me to assume that he wasn't. His words had a vaguely English cast to them that could have been real or could have been affected, I couldn't tell which, but what he said about Rhonda gave me cause for hope.

"You're talking about what happened yesterday?" I ventured.

"She told me *all* about it," Denny Blake declared enthusiastically. "Everything! From what she said, it must have been exciting. Too exciting for words!"

"It was exciting, all right," I muttered, but I was beginning to feel better. Obviously Rhonda had been in touch with Denny Blake sometime during the course of the morning.

"Rhonda doesn't happen to be there right now, does she?" I asked cautiously.

"She didn't come all the way *here*," he answered archly. "I wouldn't let her do *that*. Not with the funeral this afternoon. I met her at a little place in

Camp Verde, J J's. They make the most marvelous biscuits and gravy."

For a moment I was speechless. "So you met her there?" I finally asked. "Why?"

"To give her the package, of course. I assumed it was important, since Joey had obviously gone to some trouble to send it. I was sure she'd want to have it. ASAP, if you know what I mean."

"Package?" I asked stupidly. "What package?"

"I didn't *know* it was from Joey, not for sure, but I assumed. It had the initials J. R. penciled on it up in the left-hand corner where the return address is supposed to go, although it was postmarked Sierra Vista. I don't know *how* he could have gotten all the way down there to mail it, but he must have, poor thing."

"The package. How did you get it?"

"The mailman left it with me. Saturday morning, I believe it was. He does that, you know. Leaves things for Rhonda with me if she's not home and stuff for me with her if I'm not. Yes, I'm sure it was Saturday morning, but Rhonda wasn't here. That's not like her, not at all. She usually tells me well in advance if she's going to be away or calls if her plans change. We're pretty much on our own out here—the last of the Mohicans, as it were. The two of us simply *have* to stick together."

"But how did you find her, to let her know about the package?"

"I didn't. She called me. Around seven this morning. Said she'd just realized that when she came to pick up her things, she'd forgotten to stop by and tell me she was heading back to Phoenix. She must have been *positively* wild, or she would have remembered. She called as soon as she remembered so I wouldn't worry. That's when I told her, and we agreed to meet."

"And did you?"

"I already told you. We had biscuits and gravy, at least I did, and I gave her the package."

"What was in it?"

"It wasn't a package so much as an envelope. You know, one of those big zipper-type envelopes—the kind bookstores and libraries mail books in when you order them."

"What was in this envelope?" I persisted.

"Why, books of course. Several of them, actually. What did you expect?"

"What did they look like?"

"Oh, you know. The blank ones."

"Blank?" I asked.

"Haven't you seen them? They sell them everywhere in all the stores. Nothing but glorified notebooks really. People use them for diaries, I guess, or to scribble reams and reams of poetry. These had a frightfully ugly paisley design on the covers. A matched set, I'm sure."

"Notebooks. Did she read them?"

"Don't be absurd. Not while I was there, of course not. Rhonda would never be so rude as to read them in front of me, and it would have been incredibly gauche of me to expect her to. As soon as I finished my coffee, I left her alone so she could read them in private. Words from beyond the grave, as it were."

"Did you notice what kind of car she was driving?" I asked.

"I don't notice cars particularly. I suppose she was driving her little green car, whatever that ugly thing is. I could never see how an artist could own such an unsightly automobile."

"So she was driving the Fiat? Did you see it?"

"Who are you?" Denny Blake asked, as though he'd suddenly lost track of the beginning of our conversation and couldn't remember who I was or what I wanted. "Why are you asking me all these questions?"

"I'm trying to locate Rhonda, that's all," I said placatingly. "She left here driving a Lincoln Town Car, and now you say she's in the Fiat."

"I didn't say anything of the kind," he returned haughtily. "I didn't *notice* what kind of car she was driving. Why would anyone pay attention to cars in Camp Verde? What an *absurd* notion!"

I heard some kind of racket in the background, a loud insistent buzzing.

"I've got to go now," Denny Blake said energetically. "That's the timer on my oven. I'm baking bread. The biscuits inspired me."

He hung up. I didn't. I redialed the Yavapai County Sheriff's Department and asked to be patched through to Detective Delcia Reyes-Gonzales.

ASAP.

CHAPTER
22

"The diary," Delcia murmured immediately, as soon as I told her about my conversation with Denny Blake. "That has to be what else those guys were after."

"Right," I said. "That's what I figured, too, the moment he mentioned it. Only Michelle didn't have it. By then it was already sitting in Sedona waiting for Rhonda to show up and take possession."

"Whatever's in it must be hot stuff for them to run the kind of risks they did to get it back."

"There was the money," I suggested. "Don't forget that."

"I'm not," Delcia replied, "but the diary may have been their primary target and the money almost an afterthought."

Delcia was driving between Prescott and Phoenix. Radio transmissions were somewhat spotty. At times I had difficulty hearing her.

"You said you saw Joey writing in his notebook while you were roommates?" she asked.

"Yes. One that matched that description, anyway."

"So given what we know about the Crenshaws..."

She paused. For a moment I thought she had
gone out of range, but instead, she was thinking.
"Maybe I'd better take a run over to Wickenburg
to check on the Crenshaws before I come on into
Phoenix. What kind of car is she driving?"

"I don't know, not for sure. There's some confusion about that. She left here driving Ralph
Ames' white Lincoln Town Car, but she may have
gone over to La Posada and picked up the Fiat."

"I need to know for sure, Beau," Delcia said.

"Right. I'll find out and let you know. What
about the F.B.I.? Did you find out anything from
them?"

"You were right. They never got close to either
Michelle or her father last night. They plan to interview both of them this morning."

Again the transmission faded. "I'm losing you,
Delcia. You're breaking up."

Delcia came back in, her words intermittently
fading in and out. "... try to find ... about car ...
let me know."

"I will," I answered, unsure whether she heard
me or not. I turned around to Ralph. "Where's the
phone book?"

He took one from the cupboard and handed it
to me. "Who are you going to call?"

"A taxi," I told him. "We've got to find out for
sure about the car."

I called for a cab and was promised one within

the occupational standard delay time of twenty minutes. Not wanting to waste those precious minutes in empty waiting, I tried reaching Raymond W. Bliss Hospital on base at Fort Huachuca.

I expected to be told that Michelle was either in surgery or in the recovery room, but I gambled that Guy Owens would feel enough obligation to Rhonda and me for saving his ass that he'd tell me what he knew, if anything.

Calling the hospital was an endlessly complicated process because the base telephone exchange was in the process of transferring from one set of prefixes to another. It was another sad case of the right hand not knowing what the left hand was doing. The phone company information operators kept sending me on wild-goose chases to numbers that were no longer valid or to phones that rang forever without anyone hearing or answering.

I'm a stubborn man, though, and I kept dialing away, one number after the other, all the while cursing the dimwits who broke up the Bell system. Those screwballs obviously never heard that old tried-and-true maxim: If it ain't broke, don't fix it.

At last I was connected to the base hospital. I asked to speak to either Lieutenant Colonel Guy Owens or his daughter Michelle. "They're both patients there," I said.

"I'm sorry," the operator returned smoothly. "We have no one listed by that name."

She was lying, stonewalling me, that was certain. On a fainthearted whim, I tried another tack and asked to speak to Colonel Miller, commander of the hospital, but occasionally even the most unlikely wagers pay off. The hospital operator didn't hesitate.

"I'll put you through," she purred, and did.

"Colonel Miller here," a gruff voice said into the phone a moment later.

"My name is Beaumont," I said. "J. P. Beaumont. I'm looking for a patient of yours, a Lieutenant Colonel Guy Owens."

"He's gone," Miller replied shortly. "Dismissed."

"Dismissed," I echoed. "What about his daughter? What about Michelle?"

"Mr. Beaumont," Colonel Miller said, "Guy mentioned you to me. In fact, he spoke very highly of your efforts on his behalf as well as his daughter's, but when he left here, he gave me very clear instructions that I wasn't to give any information to anyone other than to say they had both left the hospital. No exceptions. He seemed to think he and his daughter might still be in some danger."

"That's a distinct possibility," I agreed.

"When I talked to them, that's what the F.B.I. said as well, but I told them the same thing. Guy and Michelle are gone, and I don't know where. I can't tell what I don't know."

I could almost hear Colonel Miller smiling into the phone. He had gotten a charge out of telling the F.B.I. to go piss up a rope. Rank notwithstanding, stonewalling notwithstanding, he sounded like my kind of guy.

"I don't suppose that sat too well with the F.B.I., did it?" I observed dryly.

"Not particularly," he answered with a brief laugh. "As a matter of fact, I don't think they liked it at all. One thing I would like to say, though, Mr. Beaumont . . ."

"Yes? What's that?" I asked hopefully, thinking maybe he'd relent after all and tell me something useful.

"I personally would like to thank you for what you did for Guy and Michelle yesterday. Guy Owens and I have been friends, good friends, ever since 'Nam. As far as I'm concerned, I owe you one."

The cab arrived outside and honked twice.

"You're welcome," I said. "I've got to go. If you hear from Guy, tell him to get in touch with me right away. I need to talk to him. It's urgent."

"I certainly will," Colonel Miller replied. "You can count on it."

Instinctively, I knew I could. Miller hadn't given me any more information than he had given the F.B.I., but now at least I had some confidence that it was because he really didn't know anything more. And having somebody like him owe you one isn't all bad. You never can tell when that kind of obligation might come in handy.

Ralph had gone to the door to tell the cab driver

I was coming. "Hurry," he urged. "The guy says the meter's running."

"Give me an extra set of keys for the Lincoln," I said.

"Why?" he asked. "If you're taking a cab, why do you need keys?"

"Because if the Lincoln's there in the lot at La Posada, I'll come back in that. If it's not, I'll hotwire the Fiat. Or would you rather I hot-wired the Lincoln?"

"I'll get the other keys," Ames said.

He fished around in the drawer for an extra set, and I was out the door in a flash. At La Posada, the Lincoln was nowhere in sight. The Fiat remained parked exactly where we'd left it. I paid off the cabbie, hot-wired the Spider, folded myself inside, and drove home.

Back at Ralph's house, I got myself patched back through to Delcia, who had turned off Black Canyon Highway and was headed for Wickenburg.

"She's in the Lincoln," I said. "As far as we know."

"That still doesn't sound very definite," Delcia returned.

"All I can tell you is the make of the car she left here driving this morning. That's the best I can do."

"It'll have to do. I'll alert people to be on the lookout for it. Give me the DMV number."

With Ames' help I gave Delcia the license number as well as a complete description of the missing Lincoln, then I went on to tell her that Michelle and Guy had left the hospital at Fort Huachuca bound for an undisclosed destination.

"Is there a chance they went home?" Delcia asked. "We need to talk to her, to find out if she can help us shed any light on this diary thing. Have you tried calling their house?"

"I thought of it, but there's no point," I said.

"Why not?"

"Because the assholes who snatched Michelle also cut the phone lines. I doubt anyone has gotten around to fixing them. It's the weekend, you know."

"You're probably right," she said. "So what are you going to do?"

In the background, Ralph was hustling around the kitchen, juicing oranges, frying eggs, toasting bread.

"It looks like I'm going to eat breakfast before I do anything else," I said. "And then, if Rhonda doesn't show up here by two or so, we'll go over to the church and hang around. The funeral's scheduled for three. I can't imagine her missing that. What are you going to do?"

"I'll see the Crenshaws first, at least try to, and then . . ."

"Not without a backup, I hope."

"No," Delcia reassured me. "Not without backup. I've radioed for Mike Hanson to meet me there. You remember, the deputy from Yarnell."

"I hope he moves faster than he did the day I called him," I said glumly, still packing a grudge about my shabby treatment the day I had called for help.

"Don't worry. Mike'll be there in plenty of time. Whatever happens, I still plan on being at the funeral."

"Me, too," I said miserably, suddenly feeling left out of the action. "Whatever happens."

While Ames and I had breakfast, I finally had the opportunity to tell him what we had learned about Calvin and Louise Crenshaw's extracurricular sexual activities. Ralph was thunderstruck.

"I had no idea. They have such a good reputation in the recovery community, and they get such good press."

"We have an idea why, now, don't we? They have strings, secure puppet strings, on any number of people who go through that program, and my guess is they're not above pulling them."

"Choke chains is more like it," Ralph declared forcefully, "and I intend to see that something is done about it. Is everyone in on it? All the counselors, for instance?"

I thought about what Scott had told me about Burton Joe, and I thought about Dolores and Shorty Rojas. "No," I replied, "I think in this case the rot is localized pretty much with the Crenshaws themselves."

Ralph nodded and ate in thoughtful silence. God knows I should have been hungry, but the food landed in my stomach and formed into an indigestible lump. I toyed with it, pushing congealing egg yolk around on my plate with a piece of cold toast.

"You're not eating," Ralph observed. "I don't ever remember seeing you when you couldn't stow away a fullback's breakfast. Something's wrong. What is it?"

"I'm missing something in all this mess, something important," I said. "It's as though I'm trying to see what's happened through a thick, smoky haze. The pieces are all there, but I can't quite make them out. It's driving me crazy."

"Well," Ames said, getting up and beginning to clear away the dishes, "sitting here stewing isn't going to help. It's almost one now. How about if we get dressed and go on over to the church to wait. Rhonda's bound to show up there eventually. Surely she won't miss her own son's funeral."

And that's what we did. I didn't have many appropriate choices of dress available—one lightweight navy sport jacket, a pair of haphazardly dryer-creased trousers, a clean white shirt, and a clean pair of socks that matched. Ames appeared in a disgustingly proper gray three-piece suit with a maroon tie and matching silk scarf, precisely folded, in his lapel pocket. "Ready?" he asked.

And so, with Ralph Ames riding shotgun in his sober suit, and with my knees touching the bottom of the steering wheel, we drove in Rhonda Attwood's hot-wired Fiat to Joey Rothman's funeral at elegant St. John's Episcopal Church on

Lincoln Drive. It all seemed suitably inappropriate.

The church, a thick reddish adobe affair set into a rocky hillside, was surrounded by mature natural vegetation—trees I recognized now as full-grown ironwood and palo verde. It looked as though the church had sprouted there, sprung up out of the ground like a man-made miniature of Camelback Mountain itself. St. John's Episcopal was backed by a high-walled patio. Ralph explained to me that the patio was lined with high-priced niches where, for a sizeable donation to the church coffers, family members could have their loved ones' ashes sealed away forever.

"A mini-condo cemetery," I said.

Ames nodded. "A high-priced mini-cemetery," he agreed, "and no doubt very lucrative to the ongoing building fund."

We were the first guests to arrive, turning up in the midst of a flurry of delivery vehicles. Van after van pulled up and dropped off flower arrangements. Near the fellowship hall, a caterer's crew was busily unloading tables, chairs, and massive amounts of food.

JoJo and Marsha Rothman maintained a certain position in the community, and that position was not to be taken lightly. Honor was to be paid, proper decorum observed, even over the death of an admittedly ne'er-do-well son. Joey Rothman's funeral was going to be done right whatever the cost.

An anxious white-haired and white-collared

minister arrived about one-fifteen. He gazed at the massed flower delivery vans with a frown of disapproval. I caught up with him as he turned back toward the church preparing to go inside.

"Excuse me," I said. "You wouldn't happen to be officiating at the Rothman funeral this afternoon, would you?"

He rounded on me. "What do you want?"

I backed away, put off by his surly attitude. "My name is Beaumont, J. P. Beaumont. I'm a friend of Rhonda Attwood's. You haven't happened to hear from her, have you?"

"The last I heard, Mrs. Attwood was staying at La Posada, but all the arrangements have been made through Mr. and Mrs. Rothman. The *present* Mrs. Rothman," he added meaningfully.

He turned and started away from me before I quite realized what had been said. "You said Mrs. Attwood was staying at La Posada? How did you know that?"

His voice hardened. So did his eyes. "My good man, the Rothmans are good parishioners of mine. If you have any questions, I suggest you address those questions to them."

With that he turned on his heel and stalked away. The message was clear. JoJo and Marsha Rothman's churchly contributions were paying his wages and keeping the building fund afloat. Rhonda Attwood's weren't. So much for Christian charity. And beyond that, if the minister had known where Rhonda Attwood was staying, any number of other people could have found out that information as well.

It was another bit of the puzzle to chew on.

By two o'clock the vans were gone. The altar area inside the dimly lit church was banked with flowers. Only in the kitchen and adjoining fellowship hall did the feverish activity of preparation still continue. A party, I thought, a party after the funeral. I've never understood those, and probably never will.

I was looking at my watch and still worrying over Rhonda's whereabouts when Delcia Reyes-Gonzales came striding across the gravel parking lot. I hadn't seen her pull in and park. She waved at the occupants of a Buick Regal that was just parking in a handicapped area near the main door of the church.

Delcia hurried over to the driver's side, opened the back door, and brought out a pair of crutches, which she handed to the driver as he opened his own door.

Puzzled, I watched, wondering who it could be. Delcia was talking animatedly, so it was obviously someone she knew. Then she went around to the rider's side of the car and opened the rider's door to help someone out. I could see it was a female, but that was about all. Meanwhile, the driver got out of the car, head bent as he slowly maneuvered on the crutches.

Only when the three of them started moving toward the church did I finally realize who the new arrivals were—Lieutenant Colonel Guy Owens and his daughter Michelle.

"I'll be damned," I said aloud to Ralph Ames. "I will be damned!"

CHAPTER
23

The three of them moved toward the church slowly, keeping pace with Guy's still-awkward use of the crutches. The cast on his leg went from his hip to his toe.

Suddenly, Michelle, walking with her head ducked, looked up and saw me. There was a momentary hesitation, then her face came alive with recognition and something else, a kind of light I had never seen in Michelle Owens before. She abandoned Delcia and her father and came rushing toward me, throwing herself at me from three feet away, locking her arms around my neck.

"Thank you," she said over and over, her lips muffled against my chest. "Thank you, thank you, thank you."

I've saved people's lives before, on occasion, but I don't quite know how to handle that kind of effusive gratitude.

"You're welcome," I said, prying her arms away and holding her at arm's length so I could look at her. When I did, I was shocked. Michelle had come to Joey Rothman's funeral, her lover's

349

funeral. Tears brimmed in her eyes. Her skin was still pale from her ordeal, yet there was a glow of happiness in her eyes that was unmistakable. I saw more joy in her face, more animation, than I had seen during the entire month we had spent together at Ironwood Ranch. What the hell was going on?

Suddenly, her face darkened as though a shadow had fallen across it. "I'm sorry about Ringo," she said.

"Ringo?"

"I was keeping him in my room until Friday. That's when Joey was supposed to leave, and I didn't have a roommate right then. I fed Ringo that morning. I mean, I gave him the mouse. I didn't like it, but Joey asked me to.

"But then later, when I found out what had happened to Joey and my dad told me we were leaving, I didn't know what to do. I knew Dad would never let me take him home, and I couldn't just turn him loose, so before we left, I took him to your room and left him along with the extra mice. I didn't know what else to do. If Ringo got out, I must not have tied the knot in the pillowcase tightly enough."

Michelle stopped talking abruptly while the brimming tears in her eyes threatened to become a full-fledged deluge.

"It's all right," I said easily. "It wasn't a problem. He didn't hurt me."

Much, I thought to myself, but I felt a sudden rush of relief as part of the burden I had been carrying around was lifted from my shoulders. Ringo's presence in my darkened cabin had been an accident, not some kind of deliberate plot. Joey Rothman hadn't tried to kill me after all.

Delcia Reyes-Gonzales and Guy Owens stopped behind Michelle.

"Is she here?" Delcia asked.

I shook my head. "No."

Owens let go of the crossbar of one crutch and held out his hand. "Good to see you," he said gruffly.

"Yes," I said awkwardly, "same here."

"Where's Rhonda?" he asked, looking around.

So Delcia hadn't told them that Rhonda Attwood was among the missing. She was leaving me to do the dirty work.

"She's not here yet, but we're expecting her any minute."

Owens glanced down at Michelle and the absolute tenderness of it, the stupid hang-dog devotion in his gaze, put a huge lump in my throat.

"Do you have any idea where she's going to sit inside?" Guy Owens asked. "Misha thought we ought to sit with her. Under the circumstances, that's probably the right thing to do. With these damn crutches, though, I'd like to go on in and get settled."

I'm a slow learner, but I do catch on—eventually. Guy Owens had changed his mind. Michelle was there glowing with happiness because she *hadn't* had a D & C. She was going to have Joey

Rothman's baby after all, and she was going to keep it.

From the sound of things, she wouldn't be doing it alone, either. Michelle would have not one but two doting grandparents to help her.

For a moment I was almost overwhelmed by the immensity of the job my own mother had done, raising me alone. When I was born, my mother had been only a few months older than Michelle Owens was now. No one had lifted a finger to help her.

I found my voice eventually and gave Michelle a gentle shove on the shoulder and pushed her toward her father.

"You two go on inside. Sit somewhere close to the front. I'll wait out here for Rhonda and tell her to look for you when she gets here."

Guy Owens nodded and started away, taking Michelle with him. "I'll go too," Delcia said.

The three of them disappeared into the church. The door had no more than closed behind them when a shiny gray stretch limo pulled up and stopped. The driver hurried around to open the door and the Rothmans clambered out—JoJo, Marsha, and Jennifer. Jennifer waved a downcast, halfhearted wave to me as she went past. JoJo Rothman nodded stiffly, but Marsha walked past with her eyes lowered and her shoulders hunched.

The change in her was alarming. Grief had aged her. In the few days since I had seen her last, she seemed to have closed the more-than-ten-year gap between Rhonda Attwood and herself.

Strange, I thought, seeing how badly she was taking it. Ironic for a stepmother to be so much more affected than Joey's biological mother. And yet, as she walked by I wondered if, for all its apparent ravages, Marsha's grief wasn't like the post-funeral food being prepared in the kitchen—appropriate but just for show, because it was expected.

Without pausing to chat with anyone, the three Rothmans disappeared into the church.

By two-thirty, other guests began to filter into the parking lot and mill around the doorway. I noticed a news camera or two, but it wasn't as blatant as I've seen at times. At least I didn't see anybody shoving a microphone in one of the mourners' faces.

But there was still no sign of Rhonda. Not by two forty-five, not by two-fifty. Even Ralph Ames was beginning to show impatience as he paced back and forth. "Something's wrong," he said ominously. "Something's terribly wrong."

I felt it too, but I didn't know what to do about it.

At five to three the black-robed minister once more appeared in the doorway. "Aren't you a friend of the mother's?" he asked.

I nodded.

"Where is she?" he demanded.

"I don't now."

"If she isn't here in five minutes, I'm starting without her."

"That's fine," I said. "Go ahead."

He glared at me for a moment and went back inside, closing the door on the melancholy organ music that had followed him outside.

"What are we going to do?" Ralph asked.

I shrugged. "Wait inside, I guess."

At three o'clock we went to stand inside the vestibule where, although the ushers had closed the doors into the sanctuary, we could still hear the electronically amplified voice of the minister.

I can remember my mother telling me once that she did some of her best thinking in church. As the service droned on, the haze before my eyes started to clear.

In my mind's eye I saw Rhonda Attwood and Marsha Rothman, so alike and yet so dissimilar, standing side by side. Marsha wore her grief outwardly for all to see. Rhonda pretended hers didn't exist, but it did. I knew it was there, but it had become such an integral part of her life that she carried it like a forgotten piece of jewelry, a wedding ring, for instance, that becomes a permanent part of the hand that wears it.

Flashes of Rhonda Attwood spun through my head like so many still photographs. Rhonda driving the Fiat up the mountainside. Rhonda in bed. Rhonda sitting in the chair sketching my portrait. Rhonda holding a gun. Rhonda kneeling over the briefcase twirling the lock. Rhonda telling me about JoJo's attachment to his discarded briefcases . . .

There's no rational way to explain insight, but

the two things came together in my head with the impact of colliding continents—the secondhand image of a shelf of much-used briefcases lining JoJo Rothman's garage and Jennifer Rothman telling me innocently enough that the best place to hide something was in plain sight.

I jumped like someone waking from a nap and headed for the door.

"What's the matter?" Ames whispered harshly, following me toward the door. "Where are you going?"

"Take everyone back to the house right after the funeral," I returned. "Delcia, Michelle, Guy Owens. Everybody, understand?"

Ralph nodded, but he looked puzzled. "Why?"

"Don't ask questions. No time," I said over my shoulder as I fought open the heavy door. On my way to the car, I fumbled in my pocket for the much-used Alamo map which I had stuck there more out of habit than necessity. I glanced down at the map as I went, getting a fix on Carefree and what looked like the quickest way there.

The Fiat didn't much like being hot-wired, but it started and ran again. I sped north along Scottsdale Road, not daring to go too fast because I couldn't stand any official scrutiny. At what looked like one of the last outposts of 7-Eleven civilization, I whipped into the parking lot and stopped beside a phone booth long enough to locate the Rothmans' address. Then I went on.

Alamo's map didn't include any kind of detail of Carefree, and the first road I saw leading off to a residential area had a guard shack. It was time to try bluffing.

I swung in to the shack and whipped out my Seattle P.D. badge. "The Rothmans'," I barked at the youthful security guard in my most officially intimidating fashion. "How do I get there?"

Police badges work wonders. I don't think he even looked closely enough to see that it was from out of state. He pointed up the hill behind him. "Up there. Take the first right and then the second left. Third house on the right. You can't miss it, but they're all at the funeral right now, sir."

"I know. I'll wait."

I drove away from the guard shack, feeling the clammy sweat under my armpits, still not knowing whether I was right or wrong. Until I turned right as directed. Until I saw Ralph Ames' Lincoln Town Car pulled off to the side of the road and parked beside someone else's mailbox. I parked there too. I glanced in the window of the Lincoln as I walked by. Rhonda's purse was there, lying on the front seat. So was a large brown envelope.

As I approached the Rothmans' sprawling house, I was surprised to see that one of the doors to the three-car garage had been left open. If what I suspected was true, JoJo and Marsha were putting far too much faith in their puny security guard, since both Rhonda and I had managed to breach that perimeter without any difficulty.

But then another thought crossed my mind. Maybe JoJo and Marsha hadn't left the garage open. Maybe somebody else had. As a warning.

I walked directly up the driveway, my feet crunching noisily in the gravel, afraid that any skulking around on my part would alert one of the other residents. I knew that as soon as I stepped out of the bright sunlight into the shadowy garage I would be temporarily blinded, but I had to do it. It was the only way.

"Rhonda?" I said. "Rhonda, don't shoot. It's me. Beau."

Behind me, the garage door silently began to go shut. I turned toward where I supposed the control panel would be, and there stood Rhonda Attwood. Just as the door went shut, darkening the garage completely, I caught sight of the .38 in her hand.

"What are you doing here?" she demanded. The icy control in her voice chilled me despite the warmth of the interior of the garage.

"I came looking for you. You're making a mistake."

"There's no mistake," she said firmly. "I found what I was looking for."

"What? Money?"

"See for yourself."

The overhead light came on and again I saw what I expected. There were ten briefcases in all, lined up and sitting open on the floor between a silver Jag and a white BMW. Each case was full of tightly banded bills. No wonder JoJo Rothman had been such a successful developer. He must have always had a ready supply of cash when some kind of bargain showed up in the real estate market. He was a dealer and a money launderer at the same time. That cut out several expensive middlemen.

"You're making a terrible mistake, Rhonda. Listen to me."

She shook her head stubbornly and kept the gun trained on me. It didn't help to know that I myself had loaded the .38 with its lethal cargo of bullets. I could see one other thing as well. She was wearing gloves, sheer latex gloves, so whatever prints they found on the gun would be mine—and Zeke's, too, the poor guy.

"You've read the diary?" I asked.

"Enough of it to know what went on," she returned coldly.

"And you think killing them will make it better?"

"It will make *me* feel better," she whispered fiercely. "I know now how she did it, how she got Joey under her thumb and kept him there."

"How?" I asked, lifting one foot and putting it down a few inches closer to her. "How did she do it?"

A ragged sob escaped her lips, but the gun didn't waver. "It's all there, in the book."

"Rhonda," I said. "Tell me. How did she do it?"

"She seduced him, that's how!" Rhonda spat out the words with such ferocity that a small drop of spittle landed on my face. I didn't brush it away. I couldn't risk any sudden movement that might distract her. I couldn't risk doing anything that might break her concentration. Instead, I slowly shifted my other foot a few inches closer.

"When?" I asked.

"He was just a baby," she sobbed. "It was molestation at first, just touching. That started when he was nine and she was seventeen. The other came later. Why didn't he tell me? I would have had her arrested, I would have done something..."

"And then she threatened him if he told."

Rhonda's startled blue eyes met mine. "How did you know?"

"Because that's the way it works. That's what abusers do. They terrify kids into keeping quiet, into not telling their ugly secrets."

"She turned him into her slave. Wrecked his life. Made him do her dirty work."

"Joey's probably not the only one," I said, inching another half step closer. Rhonda was only about four feet away now. If she pulled the trigger, I was a dead man.

"Not the only one?" she asked, her voice faltering.

"What about that kid she sent after us the other night? Probably him, too. Believe me, Joey wasn't the only one. It never works that way."

"She's a monster. I swear, I'm going to kill her. And JoJo, too."

"No," I said.

Suddenly she noticed where I was. "Stop," she commanded. "Don't come any closer. I'll shoot."

"Let the law take care of them, Rhonda."

She laughed, almost hysterically, and I was

afraid I was losing her. "They think they're above the law and they probably are."

"No," I insisted. "Not this time. How did you get in here, Rhonda?"

"Why do you want to know?"

"Did you leave any fingerprints on the brief-cases when you opened them?"

"I wore gloves," she answered coldly.

"Good," I said. "Then close them and put them back, just the way you found them."

"Why? Why should I?"

"Because as soon as you turn Joey's notebooks over to Delcia, she'll be out here with a search warrant within forty-five minutes. They don't know you've found the diary, but if they're going to run—with all this money here, I'll bet that's the plan—they'll do it as soon as they finish with the funeral. We don't have much time."

"I don't need a search warrant. All I have to do is wait here and shoot them when they show up."

"But you'll go to prison. Premeditated murder."

"It doesn't matter," she spat back.

"That's where you're wrong, Rhonda. It matters. Guy Owens has changed his mind. He and Michelle are waiting for you at the church. You're going to be a grandmother."

It was silent in the garage. Deathly silent for five seconds, ten, I don't know how long. Then Rhonda Attwood dropped the gun, gave a pained whimper, and fell weeping into my arms.

And as the snub-nosed .38 went skidding off under JoJo Rothman's polished silver Jaguar, I thanked God and Zeke both that it didn't go off and shoot one of us in the foot.

CHAPTER
24

The rest was easy.

While I retrieved the gun, Rhonda closed the briefcases and put them back up in the rafters the way she had found them. Then, with all evidence of breaking and entering carefully concealed, we hurried out to the cars. We drove back out to the guard shack in the same cars we'd used to drive in, with me pausing long enough to tell the security guard that the Rothmans wanted me at the church after all.

Once out of sight of the guard shack, I stopped and waited for Rhonda, then we switched vehicles so I could use Ralph's mobile phone to begin pulling the rope tight around JoJo and Marsha Rothman's necks.

Ames had followed my instructions to the letter and had herded everyone, including a protesting Delcia, back to his house as soon as the service was over. Delcia sounded angry when I first began to explain the situation, but as soon as she grasped what was going on, she was ready to leap into the fray and assemble search warrants and whatever local law enforcement personnel might be necessary.

"And you? What are you going to do?" she demanded, as soon as I had finished briefing her.

"I'm coming back to Ralph's house to put my feet up," I told her. "This is Arizona, not Washington, remember?"

"I'm glad you do," she returned.

When we reached Ralph's house, Delcia's car was long gone, but the Owenses' borrowed Buick Regal—which actually belonged to Colonel Miller—was parked out front. Driving the Fiat, Rhonda followed me into the driveway. She had driven with the windows open, so her cheeks were flushed and her hair disheveled.

She got out of the car patting her hair self-consciously. "Do I look all right?" she asked nervously.

"You look fine," I said, taking her arm and propelling her toward the house.

No wonder she felt awkward. She had seen Michelle Owens once—Michelle, the girl who would never exactly be her daughter-in-law but who would forever be the mother of Rhonda's only grandchild.

At the time of that first encounter, the younger woman had been unconscious, lying in a drugged heap on the ground where the fleeing Monty had dropped her. So the two of them—women who had nothing in common except an inexplicable love for Joey Rothman—were about to meet for the first time.

I rang the bell, and Ames opened the door.

"Anybody home?" I asked.

He nodded. "They're in the other room," he said.

I led Rhonda Attwood into the expansive living room. Guy Owens, sitting on the low leather couch, began to struggle with his crutches in order to rise to his feet. Michelle, sitting beside him, seemed glued to her seat. She opened her mouth as if to speak but changed her mind. Her braces caught the sunlight, reminding me once more of how very young she was and how unsure of herself.

Rhonda looked around the room and sized up the situation instantly. She motioned for Guy to sit back down. As he sank gratefully back onto the couch, she smiled warmly at Michelle.

"I'm Rhonda Attwood," she said to the girl. "But I believe you can call me Grandma."

Epilogue

Delcia handled the arrests like the pro I knew she was. JoJo and Marsha Rothman were arrested without incident. Jennifer, poor little Jennifer, was made a ward of the court.

Late in November Ralph Ames sent me a typed copy of Joey Rothman's diary. Ralph has been busily making arrangements with a major New York publishing house for the journals to be published in book form under the title *Better Off Dead*, which was evidently taken from the lyrics of some rock song or other.

It almost made me sick to read the details, and I'm sure it will have the same effect on others, but Ralph tells me that there was another similar book published years ago, an adolescent true-life cautionary tale called *Go Ask Alice*. The publisher believes Joey's book will have much the same impact on the current crop of teenagers.

After reading it, I've had to reassess my opinion of Joey Rothman. I know now that years of abuse at the hands of his stepmother made him the way he was. There's the widespread belief that only girl children are sexually abused. Certainly it is more common with girls, but when it happens to boys, it's every bit as devastating.

Until he met Michelle, I don't believe Joey was conscious that it was possible to love another human being openly, without selfishness, without demanding something in return. Until Michelle, sex for him was nothing but a bartering chip, a weapon to be used to manipulate other people. And even after he knew Michelle, old habits died hard, hence his abortive attempt to blackmail Louise Crenshaw and to glean information about me from Kelly.

From reading the last month's entries, I could tell that knowing Michelle had a profound effect on him. Had he lived, maybe he would have grown away from her and the magic would have gone out of their relationship, but that didn't happen. There wasn't enough time. Joey Rothman died still believing that his newfound love would save him, and Michelle is left with the same kind of loss and mixed emotions that I feel about Anne Corley. What Anne and I had together, what Joey and Michelle had, was wonderful, but it was not enough. It will never be enough.

Being with Michelle did change Joey Rothman. The scales fell away from his eyes and he was finally able to see Marsha and JoJo Rothman for the scum they really were. And he was able to see his mother as well. What Rhonda had wished for all those years, the chance of getting him back, almost came true. But of course it didn't. There wasn't enough time for that, either.

The place in the diary that really choked me up was the next-to-last entry, the one he wrote after he had gone to Carefree to collect Ringo and the diaries. In that one, he worried about what would happen to Jennifer after he was gone. And in that, he wasn't alone.

I worried about her too. I knew it was her innocent revelations to me that had led to the collapse of the Rothman drug-dealing/money-laundering empire. Knowing she was languishing in a foster home someplace, hearing echoes of news reports on her parents' progress through the criminal justice system, sickened me.

The last entry was written the morning of the day Joey Rothman died. He told how he had filched a briefcase full of money from his parents' stash thinking it wouldn't be noticed, but he worried that it might be. He hoped that the threat of exposing the drug empire would be enough to ensure his safety. Taking precautions, though, he gave the snake, the money, and the diaries to Michelle for safekeeping, telling her to send the diaries to Rhonda if anything ever happened to him.

He was scheduled to graduate from the program on Friday of that week, and when he left Ironwood Ranch for good, he planned to take the snake, the diaries, and the money and disappear, expecting to send for Michelle later when he found a place to live. He had hoped to go back to school and study writing.

But something must have alerted Marsha. I have no idea what, and I don't know how she managed to lure her stepson to the flood-swollen banks of the Hassayampa River, but she did. She met him there with one of her henchmen—the same punk who followed Rhonda and me from La Posada—and the two of them murdered Joey Rothman in cold blood.

Ringo, that poor old ancient snake, now a permanent resident at the Arizona-Sonora Desert Museum in Tucson, is a nice guy compared to Marsha Rothman.

When killing Joey failed to turn up either the diaries or the money, Marsha called for reinforcements, using Monty and some of her other Cocaine Alley drug connections from southern Arizona. She sent them after Michelle, and the outcome of that would have been entirely different if on a sunny October Sunday morning Rhonda Attwood hadn't insisted on going to Sierra Vista to talk to Guy Owens.

It's lucky for all concerned that Rhonda Attwood is an uncommonly stubborn woman.

Reading *Better Off Dead* is no picnic. I found myself close to tears at times as I read the last few entries and realized that Joey had not been able to live to see the fruition of some of the potential he was showing, both as a writer and as a human being.

No matter how the book is received by the public, though, Ralph Ames has managed to come up with a financial arrangement that will probably pay for Michelle Owens' education and maybe more besides.

Ralph also tells me that the Crenshaws have sold out their interest in Ironwood Ranch. I don't know where Louise and Calvin have gone, but the ranch itself has been purchased by a consortium that includes Burton Joe as the temporary executive director.

I've been in touch with Delcia. Criminal charges have been filed against the prosecutor in Maricopa County on the MIP plea-bargaining case. So far, though, Sheriff Heagerty seems to have escaped unscathed. He used his influence to keep Ironwood Ranch from getting any adverse publicity, but so far Delcia hasn't uncovered anything illegal. One can only hope, however, that the next time there's an election, the voters will speak and this cloud will come back to haunt him.

So the Crenshaws have gone to ground. They may be truly screwy people, but the program at Ironwood Ranch isn't all bad. Flawed people can still do good work. As I sit here tonight, drinking coffee instead of my former drink of choice, I know that wouldn't be happening without my having gone there. I know too that if I'm going to stay sober, it's up to me and nobody else.

Ralph asked me if I wanted to invest in the consortium, but I told him I thought I'd pass. Ironwood Ranch is fine, but I don't want to have anything more to do with it. Ever.

So it would seem as though everything was coming up roses, but as I've walked around here in Seattle this past month, working again and trying to stitch my life back together one day at a time, there's been a lingering hurt, one continuing fly in my ointment, and that is Jennifer Rothman.

I've had some late-night arguments with God about her, demanding to know how come the innocent have to suffer right along with the guilty.

This morning I got my answer.

A package was delivered to me down at the department. Inside I found two things, one a matted painting—a handsome watercolor portrait of me painted from that rough sketch Rhonda did and signed by the artist herself. Ralph tells me it'll probably be valuable someday, so I'd better frame it and take care of it.

The other was a note:

Dear Beau,

Just thought I'd let you know that JoJo's attorney has been in touch asking if I would be willing to take care of Jennifer. If you've read Joey's book, and Ralph tells me you have, then you know my answer. I figure the more the merrier.

Come visit us soon.

                                                    R

Nationally Bestselling Author

J·A·JANCE

The J.P. Beaumont Mysteries